Sunset Over Napa Valley

Other Books by Monica Garner

Summer on Cape May

Sunset Over Napa Valley

Monica Garner

kensingtonbooks.com

DAFINA BOOKS are published by

Kensington Publishing Corp.
900 Third Avenue
New York, NY 10022

Content warnings: terminal illness, miscarriage, parental death, rape, sexual assault

All Kensington titles, imprints, and distributed lines are available at special quantity discounts for bulk purchases for sales promotion, premiums, fund-raising, and educational or institutional use. Special book excerpts or customized printings can also be created to fit specific needs. For details, write or phone the office of the Kensington Sales Manager: Kensington Publishing Corp., 900 Third Avenue, New York, NY 10022. Attn. Sales Department. Phone: 1-800-221-2647.

DAFINA and the Dafina logo Reg US Pat. & TM Off.

ISBN: 978-1-4967-5042-6
First Kensington Trade Paperback Edition: May 2026

ISBN: 978-1-4967-5043-3 (e-book)

10 9 8 7 6 5 4 3 2 1

Printed in the United States of America

The authorized representative in the EU for product safety and compliance
is eucomply OU, Parnu mnt 139b-14, Apt 123
Tallinn, Berlin 11317, hello@eucompliancepartner.com

Sunset Over Napa Valley

Chapter One

Remi

"I called your phone like ten times. No answer!" Gerard's usually composed voice was filled with frustration. His tone wasn't loud, but it was sharp—cutting, stern, and unfamiliar. Remi shuddered; tears almost filled her eyes, but she willed them away. Her gaze dropped to the hardwood floors—the ones they'd discovered under aging carpet and spent three days sanding and staining together. She had never heard him speak to her like this. Not Gerard. Her sweetheart, her husband of many years had always been her peace. Her voice of reason. A man with a rare gift of easing the tension in any room with a steady gaze and the right words. He was always deliberate but gentle. But today was different.

"What is this really about?" she asked him softly. Her shoulders relaxed a bit. "Because I missed dinner?"

She had completely lost track of time. Her meeting with Selena Townes had run long. Selena was in town briefly on other business, and when she offered to meet that same day, Remi jumped at the chance. As it turned out, they knew some of the same people, belonged to the same sorority, and by the time the business pitch ended, they were knee-deep in personal stories and laughter.

"You didn't just miss dinner, Remi. You blew it off." His jaw tightened, his arms crossed, his muscles tensed beneath his dress shirt. "You knew how important this was to me, for both of us to meet with this client and his wife. I was left sitting there looking like a damn fool."

Gerard frowned, his eyes narrowed. He was disappointed. Standing there at six foot three, broad-shouldered, caramel-skinned, with flecks of gray in his hair and beard—he was every bit of the man she'd fallen in love with at LSU. He was her college sweetheart. Over the years he'd become her champion. The one who had urged her time and again to pursue her dream of buying the winery. He'd told her to take the leap after Zoe left for college. He had been there through every draft of the business plan. She couldn't count the times they'd sat in their kitchen hashing things out, setting a budget, making solid plans for this business.

Had he forgotten all of that? All they had dreamed up—together?

"I didn't just blow it off, Gerard," she said, her voice heightening. "I lost track of time. And I've apologized profusely. I don't know what else to say." Remi Landry knew in her heart of hearts that she was fighting a losing battle.

"I get it now," he said, shaking his head, eyes narrowing as if he had it all figured out. "This dream of yours, this winery, it matters more than the ones we already built. The ones that put food on our table."

She flinched. The words landed hard. She was taken aback. Had he really reduced *Joie* to just *her* dream? Had he forgotten the endless conversations on the porch of their Napa summer home, sipping red wine and scribbling names for their future label on the backs of napkins, receipts, or anything they could get their hands on? It had been her vision, yes—but it became *their* project.

They had agreed that Remi would lay the initial groundwork, flying back and forth, partnering with their friend Paloma Ortiz and her family's vineyard. For years, the Ortiz land had housed a dormant winery that had once been owned by the Ortiz family. Though it hadn't been in use for some time, the old winery had good bones. They would renovate it, revive it, breathe life into it, and chart their own path and build a new brand. The vineyard would grow the grapes, while the winery would produce and sell the wine. It was the plan they'd developed.

Gerard had agreed to gradually shift his business from New Orleans to California, because it was going to take them relocating to Napa for this to work, as so much needed to be done. It was never just about her. After spending long summers in Napa, they had built this plan together. Dreamed it together. Even gave it the name—*Joie*. And now, standing in the kitchen they had remodeled together by hand, Gerard looked at her like she was a stranger.

"Don't be like that." Her voice dropped. She was becoming more deflated by the minute; exhausted even. She wanted nothing more than to kick off her heels, peel her clothes from her body, and hop into a hot shower. Why was he behaving this way? "Your career is important, yes, but so is *Joie*. And let's not forget, I've spent years taking a back seat to your career. Supporting you and cheering you on. But now that I'm stepping up, trying to secure capital, taking the lead on this venture, suddenly you can't handle it?"

"I was fine with you taking a lead," Gerard said, tugging at his tie. "As long as it didn't interfere with Zoe or my work. We agreed to take our time with this."

"Interfere?" Her eyes bulged; her brows raised; her jaw tightened. "That's what this is to you—interference?"

"Yes, interfere," he snapped. He yanked off the tie and unbuttoned the top of his dress shirt. "Let's just be real, Remi. I'm the breadwinner here."

Remi looked into Gerard's eyes, a wrinkle in her forehead, fury in her heart. *Did he really just say those words to her?* He looked away, having realized that his words may have been too harsh. He didn't apologize, though, and she was silent for a moment. What she wanted to say involved profanity and that would've intensified things. No doubt she was wounded, but she chose her words carefully.

"You of all people know what *Joie* means to me. I've spent years pouring myself into this family. Years of homemaking. Homeschooling. Supporting your business. And now that I want something for me, suddenly it's inconvenient."

He knew that starting the winery wasn't just a business venture; it was her reclamation. A return to herself. Journalism had once been her passion—it was what she'd studied at LSU and even thought she might want to do it as a profession. But journalism had taken a back seat when Zoe was born. She'd chosen to stay home, to raise their daughter, to build their life around his growing business. Now, with Zoe gone to college, *Joie* was her next chapter. It lit her up in ways she hadn't felt in years. And the pieces were finally falling into place.

"I get it," Gerard said. "You have dreams. But relocating is a major move, and being an entrepreneur isn't a hobby. It's not glamorous. You saw how long it took me to get my business off the ground. Years, Remi. Years of scraping, building, barely breaking even before I finally turned a profit."

"What are you saying, Gerard? You don't think I can handle it?"

"I'm saying that you shouldn't move too fast. We need major capital for a business like that, and especially in Napa."

"Hence my meeting tonight, which went very well, by the way. I think I've found our investor, Gerard." Her voice smiled, excitement oozing from her. She still felt the joy in her chest.

The satisfaction of accomplishment made her just feel good inside.

He didn't hear her, though. Or didn't want to. His face wrinkled in frustration. "You're still missing the point."

No, *he* was missing the point. Did he not hear what she said? The capital that they needed for *Joie*; she got it.

His voice held frustration. "You weren't here, and you didn't call. And you know what, I was humiliated, Remi. I needed you to show up for me tonight of all nights, and you didn't."

Her heart was thudding in her chest now, fast and loud. His dismissal of her win was a slap in the face, and it infuriated her. Instead of them savoring her own moment, he expected her to respond to his hurt, as she'd always done.

"I got the capital for *Joie*." She blurted it out instead, unable to contain her excitement. "No, it's not everything that we need, but what we don't have, we could supplement from our own investments. Gerard, we have an investor." The last part she said with joy, with pride. She wanted him to be happy for her—*for them*. She smiled a radiant smile, a hopeful one. She wanted him to celebrate the news with her. But he didn't say a word.

She'd waited so long for his validation. Even in this moment, she was still reaching for it.

One of Remi's friends from LSU knew she was looking for an investor and had made the call on her behalf. She had set up the meeting on a whim—the woman was only in town for a day, leaving Remi with no time to prep, no time to overthink it, no time to worry about her hair or to second-guess her pitch. In her rush to get there, she had forgotten to run the details past Gerard. Instead, she had gone in and sealed the deal on her own. Thinking he would be proud that she'd taken the initiative to catapult their business to the next level. But now, what was supposed to be a shared victory suddenly didn't feel like it at all. Gerard was unmoved by her revelation.

For years she had placed her dreams on the back burner, completely immersed herself into Zoe's world and Gerard's ambitions. But today, this was hers. A day that belonged entirely to her, and it felt damn good.

Still, guilt crept in. The aroma from Gerard's dinner with his colleagues still lingered in the air. He'd prepared something Creole and spicy. Gerald was one of the best cooks she knew, and she was sure that he had impressed his client. She stood in the center of the great room of their home—a home they'd purchased twenty years ago, with its perfectly buffed hardwood flooring, floor-to-ceiling windows, the dazzling antique crystal chandelier that hung just above the wingback chair. They'd been so excited to move into their new home—a step up from the Seventh Ward neighborhood she'd grown up in, with its tree-lined streets and its vibrant, Caribbean-inspired colors. No, their 1920s renovated East Carrollton home was a far cry from her upbringing.

They'd fallen in love with the architecture, the charm, the screened-in wraparound front porch, the French doors that opened to the pool area and the chef's kitchen, which Gerard used often. A chef in the making, he could prepare just about everything—all their New Orleans favorites: red beans and rice, étouffée, jambalaya, and his dishes were much better than the ones in any of the fancy restaurants in the French Quarter. He did most of the cooking for their family, and whenever they entertained or threw one of their elaborate parties, their guests expected a Gerard-inspired meal. They'd started their family in this house. Their daughter, Zoe, had taken her first steps on that front porch.

"I can't believe you didn't tell me that you were meeting with an investor." Gerard shook his head, a frown on his face. He paced the length of the great room. "An investor, Remi?"

She followed him with her eyes but didn't move from her place by the chair. It wasn't the response she was looking for, *at all*. "Anytime I brought it up—setting up meetings, finding investors—you either discouraged me or told me to wait. Someone had to take the bull by the horns, Gerard."

"Listen, don't get me wrong." He must've realized that he was being too harsh. His tone softened just a bit. "I'm not against opening the winery, but . . ."

"But what? Zoe's grown. She's in college. I have more free time than I know what to do with. This is the perfect time." She sank into the chair, removed the dressy pumps from her aching feet. Her whole body ached. She reached up, pulled the colorful wrap from her hair, and set her coils free. She closed her eyes for a moment and exhaled. "I can't tell if you're more upset that I missed your dinner or that I'm doing this . . . finally doing something for myself."

Gerard stopped pacing and turned to face her. "I can't believe you didn't talk to me about it first. You went behind my back and made a major decision about our lives without even consulting me." His voice rose, not loud but firm. It was accusatory. His jaw clenched and his lip curled, his eyes searching hers as if begging for an explanation.

Remi rose slowly. "This was a decision about *my life*."

Gerard's eyes narrowed. "What exactly are you saying, Remi? That you're in this marriage alone?"

The question floated between them. The room felt like it was closing in around her, and she wanted to change the conversation—didn't want to open old wounds about his absence from home during times when she *had* felt alone in their marriage. Times when he'd left for work early and arrived home late. It would be so easy to lash out; to talk about all the days it had been just her and Zoe, and all the evenings she'd eaten dinner without him. To remind him of all the conversations started and never finished because his work couldn't wait. But she didn't go there. Not now. Not tonight.

Instead, she forced herself to breathe.

"Of course not!" Her tone was quieter, more measured now. "I'm not saying I've been alone in our marriage. I'm saying, I need this. *For me.* I want this for us—but mostly I want it for *myself.*"

Gerard was unusually silent. Had he conceded? Finally seen her side? Remi watched him carefully, her pulse still quick from the heat of their exchange.

"Hello, earth to Gerard," she teased half-heartedly, trying to get a response. "Don't grow quiet on me now."

Still nothing.

He stood motionless by the fireplace, shoulders square but tense. A strange stillness settled onto his tall frame. Beads of sweat formed on his forehead, although the fireplace was off. It wasn't the heat.

"Gerard?" Her voice lost its edge, softened.

His hand reached out, trembling slightly as he moved toward the wingback chair. He gripped the arm of it tightly, like he needed it to hold him up. The rhythm of his breathing seemed off, shallow and unsteady. Then short. Tears filled his eyes. Gerard stumbled toward the mahogany antique coffee table. The piece had been his great-grandmother's. Many of the pieces of furniture in their house were antiques—the nineteenth-century Victorian coffee table with beautiful art in the center, the antique lamps, the vintage settee, and the chair that had been reupholstered. All the furniture had been in the Landry family for years.

"Sweetheart, what's wrong?" She stood and rushed across the room to him. She wrapped her arms around his waist and tried to steady him, although he was much taller, more stout, and his body was much too heavy for her to stabilize. His legs buckled under him, and he collapsed next to the antique table.

What was happening?

Remi dropped to her knees.

"Gerard," she cried, shaking him. "Stay with me, baby, please. . . ."

His lips moved, but barely a whisper came out.

She grabbed her phone from the chair and dialed. Her fingers shook so hard she almost dropped it. Remi cleared her throat. "Yes, I need an ambulance . . . please . . . my husband just collapsed. He's not responding."

The room spun. All the furniture, the antiques, the life they'd built, even the argument—none of it was important now. All that mattered was the man on the floor.

"Ma'am, where is your husband right now?"

"He's on the floor, holding onto his chest." Her heart raced and her muscles tensed. Her breath was so short, she felt as if she was having a panic attack.

She heard the operator say, "If you have an aspirin somewhere in a medicine cabinet, please give it to him right away, if he's not allergic . . ."

Remi struggled to tear herself away from Gerard, afraid to leave him even for a second. But she rushed to the bathroom, searched the medicine cabinet, sorted through the bottles of NyQuil, allergy medication, and vitamins in search of aspirin. There was none.

"We don't have any!" she shouted into the phone.

"It's okay," the operator said.

Remi rushed back to the great room where Gerard lay stretched on the floor, his hands fallen to the side. Her voice shook as she managed to give the operator her location.

Earlier, she'd been in the mood for Ella Fitzgerald when she came home and listened as her voice belted from the old record player in the great room. "Summertime." As she crouched on the floor next to Gerard, "Summertime" repeated over and over, and she wished she could make the record stop, but she didn't dare leave Gerard's side again or stop trying to save him.

"The paramedics will be there shortly." The operator's voice was calm and soothing, a direct contrast to the panic attack Remi felt coming on. "Is he responsive?"

"He's not moving."

"I know it's scary but try to keep calm."

The operator's voice dissipated as the phone slipped from her shoulder, fell to the floor. Tears fell from her eyes and stained his shirt. She trembled with fear, felt cold and then a tightening in her chest.

When the paramedics finally rushed into their home, a pool of tears had already flooded Remi's face. She watched closely as they moved her out of the way and went to work to revive Gerard. Tears filled her eyes as she looked upward. Remi tried to ease herself into the chair that she'd sat in earlier but missed it. Her body collapsed to the floor instead. The world stood still. Her life had changed in an instant.

Her Gerard was gone.

Chapter Two

Remi

Three Weeks Later

Remi lay curled into a fetal position in the center of her bed, the curtains drawn, her mind racing, trying to make sense of her life now. It had been two days since she'd moved from that spot except to empty her bladder, and three weeks since she'd lost Gerard.

"Remi!" A familiar voice echoed through the house. "Remi, are you here?"

She heard the voice but didn't respond—couldn't. Her entire body felt numb. She didn't move when she heard the footsteps on the wooden stairs. Remi didn't even flinch when she finally saw Bianca appear in the doorway.

"Oh no, Remi." Bianca moved toward the curtains and pulled them open.

Remi frowned as daylight swept against her face.

"How long have you been like this? Have you been downstairs? When was the last time you had something to eat?"

Remi shrugged. There were too many questions she didn't feel like answering coming her way.

Bianca sat on the edge of the bed. "Oh honey, you have to get up. You cannot stop living."

Tears burned Remi's eyes. *Why couldn't she stop living?*

"You have to get up, honey." Bianca pulled her up and into her bosom. "You seriously need a shower."

Remi was wearing the same green sweatpants and a pink and green T-shirt with the letters AKA embroidered on it that she'd worn two days before. Her light brown, curly tresses a beautiful mess on her head.

"I don't know if I can go on." She said it softly, her voice trembling. Her head hurt from all the crying.

"Yes, you can, sweetheart. And you will. You're strong, and capable. And you have to be strong, for Zoe. She will need you now more than ever."

Remi breathed in deeply, thinking of her daughter. "I know."

"She'll be home for the summer soon, right?" Bianca asked.

"Yes," Remi whispered. Having to face Zoe and have those hard conversations about Gerard's death caused Remi's chest to tighten. She was dealing with her own grief; she didn't know if she was capable of dealing with her daughter's too.

Bianca lifted Remi's chin and looked into her eyes. "I will be here with you every step of the way. It will take time, but you will get through this."

"Are you sure?"

"I'm positive, Rem."

Bianca escorted Remi into the bathroom and started the shower. Remi sat on the toilet with the lid down, her face in her hands.

"You have to try to organize some things. Have you been taking care of things—the house, utilities?" Bianca asked.

Remi looked up. "I just haven't been able to do anything, B. Gerard handled everything. The house, the cars. He took care of everything . . ."

It was true. Over the years she had sort of checked out and let him handle things. She had drifted from the parts of herself that once felt ambitious, driven, even though it wasn't really who she was at the core. In fact, it was she who had helped Gerard launch his business in the first place. It had been her business plan that had gotten him into doors, her footwork, her late nights with him to brainstorm. But she'd become too comfortable since then, focusing solely on keeping house, raising Zoe, and being a wife. Little by little those things had snatched her identity. She didn't even remember when the shift happened; it just did.

"I know he took care of everything. It's okay. We'll figure it out." Bianca gently wiped the tears from Remi's face with her fingertips. "While you shower, I'm going to make you something to eat."

"I'm not hungry."

"I know, but you have to eat. At least try."

Remi nodded in agreement, and Bianca left. She removed her clothes and dropped them into a pile in the center of the bathroom floor. She stepped into the shower; allowed the water to cascade over her face and mix with her tears. She closed her eyes tightly and wrapped her arms around herself. She didn't know how she was going to make it. She rested her back against the cold wall of the shower. Her body slid down the wall until her bottom rested against the coldness of the shower floor. She was stuck there; paralyzed, lost in her thoughts and her what-ifs. What if she had just made it to Gerard's dinner with his clients that night? They wouldn't have argued. Things had escalated so quickly. It was her fault that he'd gotten so worked up. The realization of it caused a loud, painful howl to leave her lips—a sound that she didn't even recognize as her own voice. The pain caused her chest to hurt.

Soon the smell of garlic and onions danced across her nose. As she heard Sade's voice flowing from the stereo downstairs, she stood, still numb, and wiped the tears from her face with her hands. She stepped out of the shower and wrapped a plush towel around her body. She moved into the bedroom and slipped on a pair of khaki shorts and a T-shirt. A pair of Victoria's Secret slippers on her feet, she headed downstairs to the kitchen.

Bianca Fuentes Perez was no stranger to the kitchen. Her friend of thirty years was a jack-of-all-trades, and cooking had been one of her specialties, much like Gerard. In fact, there had been plenty of times Bianca and Gerard had challenged each other to cook-offs. While Gerard had mastered his New Orleans–style cooking, Bianca's traditional Cuban dishes, which were passed down from the generations of women in her family, were second to none. And Remi was obliged to be their judge.

Bianca was dressed in a pair of denim jeans that hugged her shapely figure—a figure that looked more twenty-seven than forty-seven. The tangerine-colored blouse was undoubtedly her own design, a piece from the rack of her boutique in the French Quarter. Her long, dark, curly hair pulled back into a ponytail, she smiled at Remi with deep dimples; poured her friend a cup of coffee.

"Two sugars, no cream. Just like you like it." Bianca smiled and slid the mug in front of Remi. "And I made your favorite, a veggie omelet."

Remi took a seat at the large island with white granite and watched as Bianca moved around the kitchen with ease. It was the same seat she'd sat in so many times, watching Gerard work his magic in their kitchen, dancing to the sounds of Earth, Wind & Fire, while singing some of the verses—off-key. He always wanted her to taste something.

What does it need? he'd ask, placing a spoon against her lips.

A little less spice, she would always say with a laugh.

He loved things a bit too spicy in her opinion.

"That means it's perfect," he would tease, then roar with laughter. "You're such a lightweight."

"Because I don't want my mouth on fire?"

"Because you can't take the heat, girl!" he would say.

They would talk for hours about everything that came to their mind and laugh heartily. He would tell her how beautiful she was. And she'd blush. Even after twenty-five years of marriage, he still had the power to make her blush.

"Thank you," Remi said to Bianca while sipping her coffee and staring out the kitchen window. She watched as the leaves on the huge live oak tree blew in the wind. She could hear the loud roar of the trash truck moving through their upscale neighborhood and realized she had missed placing the trash on the curb. She thought of Gerard and of all the things he'd done for their family—removed the trash to the curb, handled the repairs, took care of the lawn, paid the bills. Fear suddenly consumed her. *What would she do without him?*

Tears streamed down her cheeks again.

Bianca, seeing her tears, grabbed Remi's hand and squeezed it tightly. "Oh honey."

Remi closed her eyes, tried to get through the moment. It was why she'd stayed in bed so long, for days. It was just easier that way—to numb from the pain. Bianca held her hand until the moment had passed, and then she pulled a plate from the shelf and placed the omelet on it. Then she placed it in front of Remi and handed her a fork.

"Here, Rem. Try to eat something."

"We were headed to Napa Valley next week," Remi blurted out.

"I know. For your summer thing."

"Yes, and to get the winery up and running. There's so much

that needs to be done. Hiring contractors, getting licenses, and such. Zoe was going to meet us there after her finals." Remi sighed long and hard. The tears were brimming, about to return. "But now . . ."

Bianca cut her off. "You and Zoe should still go. Get away for a while. I think it would do you good. And I think Gerard would want you to continue with your plans of getting *Joie* off the ground."

"I don't even know if I have it in me to open the winery anymore. The desire is gone."

"You have to muster the energy. And I don't believe the desire is gone. That's all you've talked about for the past year. I mean, you've taken all these freaking courses in . . . God knows what."

A faint smile flickered across her face. "Viticulture, enology, and winemaking."

"Yeah that." Bianca grinned.

It was true. In every spare moment she'd had over the past year, Remi had buried herself in the study of wine—taking classes at the local university, visiting local vineyards, obsessing over soil types and fermentation methods.

"It was the thing we argued about right before . . ."

"He would want you to move forward with the winery, honey."

Remi sighed heavily. She was unsure about how Gerard would feel about *Joie* at this point. She knew that he loved Napa Valley as much as she did and cherished their summers at the beach, but after hearing the thunder in his voice that night, she wasn't sure of his wishes about the winery.

"*Joie* was *my* thing."

"And you've secured the capital for it. Therefore, you should move forward with it. Besides, it would be a great distraction for you."

"It would certainly be a distraction. Take my mind off things."

"I can help make some calls for you, or do some research. Whatever you need. I close the boutique at seven. I can come back by and we can hash things out. We'll make a to-do list. It'll be like when I opened Chic Threads—how you helped me," Bianca said. "And you know Mila is a wonderful artist. Let her play around with a logo design for you. Even if you don't use it . . ."

Bianca's daughter, Mila—the girl who she'd known since birth—was studying graphic design at UCLA.

"You think she would?"

"Graphic design is her major. I think she'd be honored."

Remi contemplated Bianca's suggestion that she open the winery as planned. Honestly, it was the one thing that made her heart feel better.

"Gerard always said that if anything ever happened to him, to spread his ashes along the Sonoma Coast." Remi covered her face with her hands. "I always just laughed when he said it—like *that* would ever happen. He was supposed to be here forever. He was not supposed to leave before me."

Bianca walked over to the outside of the island and held her friend. She rocked Remi until she was consoled.

"I'm so glad you're here," Remi whispered.

"I would not be anywhere else." Bianca reached into the pocket of her jeans. "And plus, I got a key." She held the bronze-colored key into the air.

"Yes, you have a key for emergencies."

"Good thing too! Because today was an emergency. You weren't answering your phone or calling me back. I didn't know what was going on."

"I felt numb."

"It's called grief, honey. I mean, it's only been a few weeks. It's all so new, but time will heal. You'll get through it."

"I know. Just like I did when Daddy died," Remi said.

"Exactly." Bianca made her way back to the stove. She tossed garlic and onion into a pan.

Remi cut a small piece of her omelet with her fork, tasted it. "I'll go to Napa if you come with me." She glanced at the television mounted on the kitchen wall. The weatherman was reporting that temperatures would be in the high eighties, which wasn't unusual for May in New Orleans. Then she looked back at Bianca.

"What?" Bianca asked.

"Yeah. You, me, the girls. We can spend the whole summer, and I can get the winery up and running."

"I can't go to California, Rem. Definitely not for the whole summer. I have the boutique to run, and Mila is spending the summer with Harry. They usually go to that cabin together for a few weeks." Bianca moved to the pantry, grabbed a plastic cup, filled it with water from the faucet, then poured it into the plant resting on the windowsill. A few of the leaves had begun to turn brown and she picked them out. Remi had completely forgotten about the plants that she usually cared so deeply for. Bianca lifted the window to allow a breeze to flow into the kitchen.

"Of course. I know that you can't just drop everything. And I forgot that Mila spends the summer with Harry. I'm sorry for even suggesting it."

Bianca sighed, glanced at Remi with her head cocked to the side. "I don't know. Maybe Amelia could mind the shop for me . . . probably not the whole summer, but at least for a week or two. And maybe Mila could miss the first few weeks with Harry—go to the cabin later in the summer."

"It's too much to ask." Remi regretted suggesting it.

"It's not an outrageous request. Maybe . . ."

"It would mean so much to me." Remi clasped her hands together before Bianca finished her sentence. "The winery would be a major undertaking. Gerard and I were going to do it together. . . ."

She needed to get through this thing that had suddenly become her life. Over the years she'd been so involved in being a wife and mother, she'd somehow forgotten herself. Gerard and Zoe were her purpose, her reason. Without them, she felt lost.

"Let me see what I can work out," Bianca said.

Remi managed a smile. It was the first time in three weeks that her heart felt happy.

Chapter Three

Bianca

Bianca tapped on the dressing room door, handed the woman a larger size of her outrageously popular blue jeans with the pearls down the sides and fringe at the bottom.

"Ooh girl, these are perfect, Bianca!" the woman yelled over the dressing room door.

"The fourteen works, then?" Bianca asked.

"Yes. So cute. I want both styles."

Chic Threads was Bianca's baby, a place where she proudly sold a blend of her own designs as well as her unique finds and vintage treasures—clothing, jewelry, and shoes. She'd built a very loyal clientele. Situated right in the French Quarter, Chic Threads had started as a small consignment shop and quickly grown into an insanely popular boutique in just a few years.

A vase filled with fresh, white southern magnolias rested on the countertop. The gentle smoky, spicy fragrance from candles burned in each corner of the room, and the romantic sounds from Phillip Lester's Spanish guitar oozed from the speakers, serenading customers in a spalike vibe. Spanish colonial furniture and vintage hand-painted cabinets gave the place its rustic charm. The sun shone brightly through the front picture window.

Bianca's phone rang and she pulled it out of the back pocket of her jeans. She glanced at her daughter's face on the screen. It was almost as if she was staring at her own reflection in the mirror, except Mila's hair was a much lighter brown, with a purple streak in the front—the part she could see anyway; the top of her head was covered in a tan knit winter toboggan, as if it weren't summertime already. Her lashes were much longer than Bianca would ever dare, though her own style had always been bold and unique. Bianca was still young at heart. She still tiptoed on the edge.

"Can you wrap those up for her when she's ready?" Bianca asked, lightly touching Amelia's arm. "I need to take this call."

"Of course." Amelia gave Bianca a smile.

Bianca made her way to her back office and shut the door. Her office was beautifully decorated in orange and yellow hues. The desk she used was situated in a feng shui position at the center of the room, diagonally opposite the door. She was just as concerned about how energy moved through her space as about what she put into her body. Eating and living clean had become a way of life for her.

She slid her finger across her phone's screen. "Hi sweetheart."

"Mom, what's this about Napa? And a winery?"

"You finally got around to reading my text." Bianca chuckled. "I'm going to Napa Valley with Remi to help get her winery up and running. Zoe's going, too, and I thought you might want to come along with us. I know you'd love to catch up with Zoe. You two haven't spent much time together since Thanksgiving, and with Gerard gone, I'm sure she could use a friend."

"I feel terrible about Uncle Gerard. That whole thing is so messed up. But Napa . . ."

"Maybe you could delay your summer at the cabin with your dad by a couple of weeks."

"Mom, that's not really fair to him. And besides, we're not going to the cabin this year; we're going to Maine for a few days right after my finals."

"What's in Maine?" Bianca asked.

"Mom." Mila said her name as if warning her not to ask too much.

"What? What's in Maine?" she asked again.

"Dad wants me to meet Jen's family—her parents and siblings. Not that it matters to you, but he's going to propose to her."

Bianca was silent for a moment. She felt as if her heart had dropped into the pit of her stomach. She'd always held on to a small glimmer of hope that she and Harry might someday reconcile—as silly as it was. Her heart ached as she repeated Mila's words in her head: *he's going to propose to her*. She eased down into the leather chair. Her head began to spin. It was as if the breath had left her body.

"Mom, are you there? What is going on with you?" She was becoming increasingly impatient with Bianca. She always had been. Most of the time their conversations were strained.

"Yes, I'm here." Bianca wanted to change the subject—quickly. She tried to recover from the blow she'd been dealt. "How are things going? Classes? Did you pass your first final?"

"I won't know until later."

"That's good. I'm sure you did well." Bianca twirled around in her chair, reclined as she glanced out the window and watched as a street musician blew his saxophone for a group of tourists who had gathered in the French Quarter.

"Dad bought me a ticket to Maine, so as soon as I'm done with my last exam this week, I'm headed there."

"Okay, I see."

"Maybe after the proposal and everything he has planned; I can ask him if he minds if I fly out there for a few days . . . to Napa. I'd really love to spend some time with Aunt Remi and Zoe."

No mention of spending time with *her*. She tried not to let it bother her, but it did.

"That sounds like a wonderful idea. I'll send you a ticket."

Mila sighed heavily. "Mom, let me talk to Dad first, make sure he's cool with it, and I'll let you know."

"So, you're going to get permission from your dad to spend time with your mother?" She felt fury at the thought of it. She blinked her eyes rapidly and clenched her jaw.

"Mom, you know I spend my summers with Dad. We go through this every year," Mila said softly.

"Well, maybe you shouldn't spend your whole summer with him. I mean, you're old enough to make your own choices, but I haven't seen you since spring break. And even then, we didn't really spend any time together—you were gone with your friends . . ." Bianca sighed, trying to recover from the thought of Harry proposing to his much younger girlfriend. She composed herself. "I don't want to fight."

"Mom, you always want to fight when it comes to Dad. And I just really . . . I have to go. I have to get to class."

"Call me later," Bianca said.

"I'll try to call you tonight." Mila ended the call much sooner than Bianca was ready for.

She sat there for a moment, clutching her phone, contemplating making a phone call to Harry. *What would she even say?* She had no right to quiz him about his marriage proposal, though jealousy raged through her veins. He wasn't hers anymore, and soon he'd be someone else's.

Her mind drifted back to the day he asked for the divorce. He said it with no emotion and without any hesitation whatsoever.

"I've had the papers drawn up, and I would really like for you to sign them. You can keep the house. I don't want to uproot Mila. And you can keep your Mercedes truck. I've made provisions for Mila's tuition and I'm leaving you with a nice settlement."

She'd felt a physical ache in the pit of her stomach when he said it. She hadn't expected that. She thought they would talk, that maybe counseling could help. They'd discussed trying it and making one last attempt at saving what was left. But instead, he handed her a manila envelope.

"I'll leave these with you. If you'll just sign them, it will save us both a lot of time and energy . . . *and money*."

The coldness in his voice cut through her like ice. This man, who had once adored her, who used to hang on her every word, was now distant—detached. He treated her like she was a stranger.

"We'll work out the details of custody."

"Custody?" she asked. "Of *my* daughter?"

"You don't want to fight me on this." Harry gave her a pointed look that told her he was up for a fight over Mila.

He was right. She didn't want to fight anymore. It seemed they had been fighting relentlessly, and it was exhausting, not to mention unhealthy for their daughter, who was sixteen and completely heartbroken that her parents were falling apart. He had already moved out of their uptown New Orleans home and into the Roosevelt Hotel.

He had given Bianca a life she'd never dreamed of having. The daughter of Cuban immigrants, she'd grown up in chaos. Her father had fled back to Cuba when she was twelve to avoid arrest, and her mother soon followed—leaving Bianca and her younger brother, Antonio, to be raised by their grandmother. Her tumultuous childhood was the reason she moved through life so cautiously and guardedly. It taught her to keep secrets close and trust no one. She'd grown up feeling disposable and unwanted. She acted out in school and landed herself in trouble more times than she could count—the juvenile detention center had felt like home because she was there so much.

But then she met Harry.

It was at Xavier University that their paths had crossed. He was an ambitious investment broker with a quick wit and a dazzling smile. He didn't quite take her breath away, but he was solid, and he grounded her. They married in secret at the justice of the peace barely a month later, much to the dismay of her grandmother, who had begged her to finish school first. And if she had to marry, she should have a proper Latin wedding, not some rushed courthouse affair. Still, her *abuelita* came around. Eventually, she grew to love Harry and began to see that he was good for her granddaughter.

Bianca had loved him. A part of her still did. If Harry showed up on her doorstep tomorrow and asked for a second chance, she'd say yes without blinking. She had held on to hope for so long that one day he'd forgive her—that they'd rebuild their family.

The news that he had a girlfriend totally blindsided her. But hearing that he planned to propose? That had shattered her.

Chapter Four

Remi

Remi wheeled the pewter-colored SUV through downtown San Francisco, past the skyscrapers and through the busy traffic and neighborhoods of hotels and happy-hour hot spots. She made her way to the Bay, with its turquoise waters and to the entrance of the Golden Gate Bridge. It was this picturesque route across the Pacific Ocean that she loved so much; reveled in it. She usually took pictures when she'd driven across it with Gerard. She glanced over at Bianca, who sat straight up in the passenger's seat, her eyes bulged with amazement, her smartphone in video mode. She was grateful that her friend was able to join her on this trip.

"This is the most beautiful thing I've ever seen." Bianca looked over at Remi.

"I was floored the first time Gerard and I drove this route." Remi bit her bottom lip, her thoughts a chaotic jumble of emotions. She gazed out the window to rid her mind of it; a pair of Ray-Bans on her face, she fought back tears as she breathed in deeply and then exhaled.

"You okay?"

"Fine." Remi gave her friend a light smile. "Nostalgia."

Bianca grabbed Remi's hand and squeezed it. "I know."

The two of them had been close for as far back as Remi could remember—best friends, but more like sisters. Though Remi had a sister, Sophia, and they were as close as any two sisters could be, she was much closer to Bianca. The pair grew up in the same diverse Louisiana community, with a rich history, in a neighborhood that blended many ethnicities. Remi and her sister were from a stable, two-parent family of African Creole descent, while Bianca was raised by her Cuban grandmother. They were as different as night and day: Remi, the more levelheaded one who'd chosen a journalistic path in college, while Bianca changed majors as often as she swapped out boyfriends, at least until she'd found Harry. Harry brought stability to her life.

Bianca had always been her protector. From the time they were children, she'd stood between Remi and whatever tried to hurt her—words, fists, heartbreak. If anyone so much as looked at Remi the wrong way, Bianca was there, fists clenched and ready for a fight. And she wasn't just her human shield; she was her biggest cheerleader. The loudest voice in the room when Remi doubted herself. The first to celebrate her wins and the last to let her wallow in loss. Bianca believed in her even when Remi didn't believe in herself. It had always been that way between them.

Even now, as Remi looked at her, eyes weary from a night of too little sleep; Remi had kept her up most of the night, venting and reminiscing about Gerard. She couldn't sleep, and so Bianca hadn't either. Her head bounced against the back of the passenger seat, as she stopped the video recording and called Mila.

"Still not answering," she said.

"Maybe she's charging it," Remi reasoned.

"Yeah maybe." Bianca sighed. "Do you know Harry's taking her to Maine?"

Remi frowned. "What's in Maine?"

"He wants her to meet that woman's family."

"The girlfriend?"

"The girlfriend who he intends to propose marriage to this weekend."

"Nooo." Remi glanced over at Bianca; shock rushed through her. Her heart ached for her friend, who was noticeably bothered. She knew Bianca better than anyone did. She loved Harry. And though she would never admit it or say it aloud, Remi knew Bianca always had hopes of reconciling with him. "You know she could never take your place, right? You'll always be Mila's mom."

"I just feel like we're always at odds with each other, Mila and me. She still blames me for the divorce, you know." Bianca sighed. "Harry divorced me. Not the other way around."

"She'll get past it. Just wait until she goes through her own shit—a breakup, a divorce, real life, grown-up stuff. She doesn't understand it now, but she will one day."

"I'm going to try my best to connect with her when she gets here. I'll try to bond; rebuild our mother-daughter relationship. We were becoming closer before the divorce."

"You are a great mother, B. Never doubt that. I saw the sacrifices that you made for her."

"I was so busy building my business. She spent more time with Harry. I feel like I missed those formative years with her, you know?" Bianca was on the verge of tears but fought them. Remi knew she'd never allow herself to feel, to be vulnerable. She couldn't remember the last time she'd seen Bianca cry—always determined to show strength. "We aren't like you and Zoe. You two are the perfect mother-daughter duo."

"We're far from perfect." Remi laughed, thinking of some of the challenges they'd faced.

Zoe had her moments, for sure. There were times when she defied Remi, especially after she turned sixteen and—as

Remi's mother used to say, started "smelling herself," that old phrase meaning she was getting a little too full of herself. Those were trying times, and Remi was grateful they had moved past that phase. Things were easier now between them.

"Overall, she's been a great kid. And we spend a lot of time together. Had to, because Gerard wasn't always there. He worked so much."

"Homeschooling made the difference, too, huh?" Bianca asked.

"It helped."

Homeschooling had given Zoe a good, solid foundation. It also allowed them more time together. But when she decided that she wanted to attend a public high school, Remi wasn't ready for it—not at all. She tried to talk her out of it, but Zoe was adamant that she wanted to spend her last two years in public school, be a normal kid. With that, Remi had to respect her wishes.

"Even after she went to public school, it worked out," Bianca said.

"Yeah, it did. Turned out to be the best thing for her socially. She thrived in public school and excelled academically. She was the most popular girl at the freaking school—cheerleader, homecoming queen, varsity volleyball star. All of it."

But Remi knew it was more about Zoe proving a point to herself, and to the girls at school, who believed she couldn't do any of those things. Zoe never truly cared about pom-poms or crowns. In fact, she hated wearing dresses and heels. She was most comfortable in denim and T-shirts.

"Mila excelled at the private school that Harry insisted upon. But I think she missed out by not being exposed to other things. She was a bit sheltered."

"Mila's a great kid. You both did well with her—you *and* Harry. Don't beat yourself up. Just take advantage of this time with her. When she gets here, make the most of it."

"I will." Bianca gave Remi a half smile. "I really plan to."

Remi turned up the volume on the stereo. Louis Armstrong's "What a Wonderful World" filled the car as she continued to drive the SUV across the Golden Gate Bridge. Bianca lifted her sunglasses from her eyes to get a better look at the stretch of valley, the rows of vegetation, and the mountainous views outside her window.

She glanced over at Remi. "You know we're not listening to this ancient Grandma Lorraine music the whole two weeks, right? I mean, I love Grandma Lorraine like she's my own, but . . ."

"What do you have against old school?" Remi laughed. It was great to laugh, to feel normal, something she hadn't felt in weeks. And it was a genuine laugh. She could be herself with Bianca and be honest. They allowed each other to just *be*. Don't put on a face, just live in whatever you were feeling. That's what she loved most about their friendship.

"That's not really old school, Rem. That's some Louisiana 1940s stuff." Bianca laughed. "We're listening to some rap after this."

"Not rap!" Remi giggled, the sunshine hitting her face. She cracked the window slightly, letting Napa's mild breeze drift in, lifting her curls, and carrying with it the scent of wildflowers.

"Yes, rap." Bianca laughed and then relaxed in her seat, looking out the window. "It's so beautiful up here. I've never seen anything like it. I can't believe it took me so long to get here."

"I can believe it. You're a workaholic."

"Someone has to pay the bills, you know? I'm on my own now."

"Harry left you a nice little nest egg, and I'm sure you invested it well. And you should try to live more, now that you've won your fight with . . . you know . . ."

"You can say it, Remi. Now that I've won my fight with breast cancer . . ."

"Yes, that."

Bianca's breast cancer had been in remission for two years. Remi admired her friend, a survivor who had refused to let cancer steal her light. Bianca was tough. She had battled the disease and endured a painful divorce, all at the same time. Through it all, Remi had stood by her side—every hospital visit, every chemo treatment, every weary moment.

When Harry walked out, abandoning their marriage when she needed him most, Remi was there then too. She'd been her sounding board, her steady place, and the friend who gave her strength when she couldn't muster any for herself.

Remi offered her a warm smile as the sunlight streamed through the windshield of the SUV, casting golden rays across the dashboard. It was a picture-perfect day—eighty-six degrees in California's wine country. The air was rich.

"I know, I should take more time to enjoy life."

Bianca fell quiet after that, her expression distant, reflective. Remi didn't press her. Instead, she kept driving. The SUV rolled smoothly over the winding roads. Finally, they arrived at the vineyard. Remi slowed as they neared the estate, making a right onto the long, gravel entryway that led to their Napa Valley home—a sun-kissed, eighteenth-century gem overlooking a vineyard. The house stood proudly at the top of the hill, its mahogany-brick staircase welcoming them home.

"Is this it?" Bianca adjusted her body in the leather seat and leaned up. "It looks so stately."

"This is it. And it looks that way on the outside, but really very warm and cozy on the inside. It's what Gerard and I loved most about it. It has soul."

"Well, let's go check out this warm mansion." Bianca giggled. "I expected it to be beautiful, but . . . just wow!"

No picture Remi had ever sent could've captured the fullness of the place—the charm, the serenity, the elegance. Towering trees flanked the winding path up to the estate, branches swaying gently in the breeze. The sunlight peeked through the leaves, casting light across the steps leading to the front door.

Remi parked the SUV and shut off the engine. She hopped out and lifted the hatch. She looked around at the beautiful grounds of the vacation home that she and Gerard had purchased three summers ago. She glanced at the vineyard that belonged to Paloma and her family. Paloma was a godsend; a friend Remi had made during that first summer in Napa Valley. She looked after the house whenever Remi and Gerard were back in New Orleans. She lived on her family's land and owned the building between them—the one that once housed a thriving winery, before illness had forced her to close its doors. She had always hoped that Remi and Gerard would buy the old space, restore it, and make it their own. A fresh start for the place she could no longer run. And she would be there, by their side, ready to help them bring it back to life—a silent partner of sorts, but one who expected nothing in return.

"That's it over there—the winery," she said, pointing at the old structure just across the path, nestled between Paloma's estate and their own.

Remi had, in fact, made the purchase, with an online signature and funds from the investor and her own investment. With Paloma's dependable support, transformation of the building had already begun. Contractors were hired, plans were drawn, and the early signs of possibility were already taking shape. Next on the list was the maze of licensing, which she would handle as soon as she was settled. She knew it wouldn't be easy, but for the first time in a long time, Remi felt ready for it all.

"*Joie*'s future home." Bianca grinned widely. "That's so cool. Let's go check it out."

Before Remi could say anything more, Bianca headed toward the building.

"Wait! Let's drop our bags first and . . ."

Bianca kept walking, looked back at Remi, and removed her sunglasses. "Come on, let's see this wonderful dream of yours."

Remi hesitated for a moment before following, the gravel crunching beneath her feet as she trailed after Bianca. The sun was beginning to set, casting long golden stripes across the rows of grapevines. A warm breeze rustled the leaves a bit, carrying with it the faint scent of fermented grapes.

Remi caught up, whispered to herself, "This woman."

Joie. She had said the name a thousand times in her head before it ever landed on paper—before she even shared it with Gerard. It was French for joy. She had no idea how much the name would come to mean to her now. It started as joy in the bright obvious sense, with the balloons, laughter, and champagne flutes raised. But now, after everything in her life had changed, she saw it as the kind of joy that she needed to grow out of pain and the struggle to keep going. It was the kind of joy that she needed to teach her how to breathe again, even as her lungs still ached from losing Gerard.

Bianca reached the old structure first and pulled the door open, peering inside.

"It smells like your wildest dreams coming to life, girlfriend," she called back, grinning. "This place is already beautiful. It's a really good structure."

"Yes, it was once a thriving winery. Just needs a little TLC."

Remi smiled hesitantly, her mind a jumble of doubts as she stepped into the cool dimness of the place. Had she made the right decision? She glanced around the old space. Studied the rawness of it, the weathered stone, the history in the walls.

There was beauty here, a sense of potential, not yet shaped by her vision—but it would be. She had dreamed of blending contemporary with rustic, new with old, youth with wisdom. The interior was rough—exposed beams, an old stone fireplace in the corner. There was light too. Huge windows framed the vineyard like a painting.

"You see the vision, don't you?" she asked Bianca softly.

"I do. I really do." Bianca turned to her.

They stood in silence for a moment, allowing the vision to fill the room around them—the tasting bar here, a gallery wall there. Maybe some live jazz on the weekends. Poetry readings on Thursday nights.

Remi walked to the center of the space and turned in a slow circle. "I thought of giving up on it. I almost did. Still not completely sure of my decision."

"Well, you'd better get sure! You've made the purchase and the contractors are here." Bianca giggled.

She nodded in agreement, but her mind was still hesitant. "Let's go," she told Bianca and headed out the door.

She pulled her hard-shell suitcase out of the SUV, wheeled it into the house, and left it in the entryway. She removed her sunglasses and looked around, taking it all in.

"Oh, how I've missed this place." Remi breathed deeply.

With buffed hardwood floors and the smell of lemon and jasmine trickling through the place, a light breeze blowing through the open kitchen window, she knew that Paloma had been here recently. Remi led the way through the house, taking in the sweeping views of Napa Valley, Mt. George, and the San Pablo Bay from the expansive windows. She peeked at the formal living area, with its cozy fireplace and made her way to the dining room, the large antique table with its wooden double pedestal. They entered the sun-drenched kitchen with the large marble-top island, stainless steel appliances, and a large, walk-in pantry.

"I love this kitchen," Bianca said, and then walked over to the sliding glass door and peeked at the porch that was just off the kitchen. She pointed outside. "That's where I'll be having my coffee in the morning."

"I knew you would love this kitchen. Gerard loved it too." Remi grabbed Bianca by the elbow. "Let me show you the wine cellar."

"There's a wine cellar?" Bianca paused, hand on her hip. "In this house?"

"Yes. It's small, but so perfect," Remi said. "Being the wine lover that I am, you know I had to have somewhere to store my best finds."

They entered the den with views of the vineyard and a walk-in wine cellar. Remi grabbed a bottle of Sauvignon Blanc from its compartment.

"We'll have this with dinner."

Just as they made their way back to the kitchen, Paloma entered, interrupting them. "Hello, Remi. I thought I saw you pull up."

"Paloma." Remi embraced the older Hispanic woman. "It's so good to see you."

"You as well." Paloma smiled warmly, holding on to Remi's hands. "I was so sad when I heard the news about Gerard. I'm so sorry. Such a sweet man. He was always very nice to me, considerate and warm."

"Thank you, Paloma. He loved you like family. You and Bas."

Sebastian, Paloma's son, had been very fond of Gerard. The two of them had spent many hours together—talking, fishing. Bas had been like the son Gerard never had. They'd grown close over the summers in Napa Valley. Gerard had encouraged Bas to attend Harvard in the first place. College hadn't been on his radar at all, but when Zoe helped him to apply for scholarships the summer before their senior year, it showed him that college was affordable, even at an Ivy League school, so he reconsidered. He applied at Harvard and was accepted.

"He was devastated when I told him." Paloma shook her head.

"I'll bet. They were really close."

Paloma lowered her eyes, almost became misty. "He graduates next year."

"Gerard would've been so proud. He would've been at that graduation and the loudest one in the audience."

Paloma nodded a yes. "He's home for the summer."

"Zoe will be happy to see him as well. She'll be here in a few days."

"I'll tell him."

"Those two and their summer adventures." Remi shook her head; a smile crept into the corner of her mouth. She remembered Bas and Zoe—inseparable, wild-hearted—spending endless hours at Sonoma Beach, coming home sun-kissed, forever missing curfews. They had always partied too much and lived like summer would never end.

Paloma giggled, held on to Remi's hands for a moment. Remi's eyes found Bianca.

"Pardon my rudeness. This is my best friend, Bianca," Remi said. "Bianca, this is our beloved Paloma. She takes care of the place while we're away. And she takes care of us when we're here. She and her son, Sebastian—um, Bas—are like family."

"So nice to meet you, Paloma." Bianca reached out her hand. "You're a woman who wears many hats. Kinda like me."

"Nice to meet you as well," Paloma shook Bianca's hand. "I've heard a lot about you."

"Oh no! Don't believe a word of it." Bianca laughed.

"It was all good things." Paloma offered a light smile. "Remi has told me all about her bestie and how you've been like sisters since childhood. What a blessing."

"Yes, she is literally one of my greatest blessings," Bianca said, and then started roaming through the house, peeking into closets and cabinets.

Paloma smiled sweetly. "I took the liberty of putting fresh linens on the beds for you. And if you don't mind, I'm going to borrow your kitchen for a bit. I'm making my Spanish seafood stew. Figured it'd be easier to do it here."

"Don't mind at all." Remi's eyes softened. "And oh how I love your seafood stew."

"Seafood anything sounds wonderful," Bianca called from the pantry. "I might watch you, see what all you're throwing in that pot."

"Feel free."

Paloma and Remi both giggled.

"I see that the contractors have already begun work on the winery."

"Yes, just the floors and walls," said Paloma. "I'm so happy that you've decided to maintain much of its original character."

"It's already a beautiful space."

"The old building has been on this property—in our family for years. I know you'll do it justice."

"I'm grateful for it, Paloma." Remi hugged the woman, then collapsed in her arms. "Thank you for giving me such a great deal and allowing me to make it my own."

"Of course. I'm excited about *Joie*." Paloma hugged her tightly. "And you, my dear, are family. It's just been sitting there doing nothing. It's wonderful to see it being put to use."

"We're just going to get settled in." Remi let her go and then turned to Bianca. "Let me show you to your sleeping quarters."

"It was great meeting you, Paloma. I'll be back for my cooking tutorial." Bianca threw a hand into the air as she followed Remi.

"I'll be starting soon." Paloma smiled.

Remi led the way to a staircase just off the kitchen and up a short flight of stairs and down a hallway lined with gleaming hardwood floors that creaked softly. She paused in front of a spacious room, then pushed open the door to reveal a bedroom bathed in late afternoon light.

At the center stood a king-sized Victorian bed with an ornate headboard, its wood aged. A matching antique dresser rested along the far wall; delicate carvings etched into its surface. The walls were painted a soft peach color, casting a warm glow into the room. Above the bed hung a large portrait of a ballerina in midpirouette—graceful, as though she might twirl right off the canvas.

Bianca drifted toward the window and gently pulled aside the lace curtain. Below, the garden stretched wide, bursting with color and life. A proud magnolia tree stood in the center, surrounded by rose bushes in full bloom and vibrant wildflowers. At the heart of it all sat an iron bench, half shaded by leaves, inviting stillness and reflection.

Bianca sat on the edge of the bed. "Thank you for inviting me to come here, Rem. I love it. I wish I'd come sooner, when you invited me before. I just . . ."

"It's okay. You were busy living life, building your own business. I completely understand. Thank *you* for coming this time. Life is different for me right now, and I really appreciate you helping me get some normalcy back."

Bianca stood up and hugged Remi. "I love you, sister."

"I love you more."

"What a day, huh?" Bianca asked. "I could use a glass of wine before dinner."

"Makes two of us. Let's unpack and then open that bottle."

Bianca walked toward the door. "I'll meet you downstairs in a minute. I'm just going to grab my bag and freshen up a bit."

"Sounds good."

* * *

What made the house so unique, Remi thought, were all the little hideaways—quiet nooks and cozy crannies, tucked into so many corners of the house. The sunporch was her favorite, by far, especially this time of day. It was the perfect spot for a bottle of Sauvignon Blanc before dinner.

She stood at the window, gazing out at the majestic California mountains. Inside, Kenny G's "Summer Song" drifted softly through the speakers, the mellow sound of the saxophone curling around the room, embracing it. From the kitchen, the rich, savory aroma of Paloma's Spanish seafood stew had already begun floating through the air.

Remi's phone buzzed and she answered.

"Well, I'm going to assume that you made it to Napa safely," Zoe said in a motherly tone, as if Remi was the child and not vice versa. She gave Remi a light smile as her face appeared on her phone screen.

"I'm so sorry, sweetheart. I meant to call, but it's just been such a long day. We're just getting settled in."

"That's good. I'm headed there as soon as I finish my last final on Thursday." Zoe, with Gerard's eyes, Remi's skin and cornrows in her chestnut brown hair, said, "Mila and I get into San Francisco around the same time next week, so I'm just going to wait for her. We'll just rent a car and drive up together."

"That sounds good, honey. I can't wait to see you both."

"Can't wait to see you, Mom. Are you doing okay?"

"I'm okay. What about you?"

"I get sad at times, but these finals are a good distraction. I know we have a long road ahead of us. What's your distraction?"

"Bianca's here, and we're going to dive into the business of the winery, maybe do some antique shopping, and we're going to drink lots of wine. I have plenty to keep me busy."

"I'm glad Aunt Bianca's there, but not too much wine, Mom. It's dangerous to drink too much during this time."

Remi laughed heartily at Zoe's lecture. "I'm not going to become an alcoholic."

"I'm just saying."

"Don't worry too much about your mother, sweetheart. Focus on your finals. We will get through this." She said it aloud but wished her words and heart were aligned.

"Okay, Mom. I will. I have to go now. Love you."

"I love you." Remi smiled at her only child. Blew her a kiss. "Bye now."

Remi ended the call with a soft sigh. She leaned back in her chair, stretched her legs across the wicker ottoman, and took a slow sip of wine. The warmth of it lingered on her tongue, but her thoughts had already drifted elsewhere. The thought of being here without Gerard tugged at her heart. This was their space, their home. His absence lingered in every corner of every room. She felt it in the silence where his voice used to be. It especially echoed in the kitchen, where he once prepared their meals . . . the clatter of pots and pans and utensils would already be in full play by now. Even the familiar smells—the Creole spices—that used to linger long after the food was put away. The warmth of his presence was gone.

The road without him wasn't going to be easy, she knew that much. It would be long. It would certainly be hard. But she was ready to face it.

Chapter Five

Bianca

Bianca thought of Harry. The idea of him proposing to a woman he'd only known briefly unnerved her more than she let on. She remembered his proposal to her, on her front porch in Louisiana, twelve roses in his hands, his palms sweating. He hadn't dared ask permission from her Abuelita Josefina, who had insisted they focus on their studies, not marriage. Harry had quieted the chaos inside her. He made her believe she could be okay, normal. Despite all the bad circumstances in her life.

Now, someone else had taken her place in Harry's life. It clawed at her whenever she let down her guard. She hated herself for what she'd done—the thing that had driven Harry away—and she hated the woman he was with even more, though she didn't even know her.

She was shaken from her thoughts by the sliding of the back door. "Here you are." Remi handed her a glass of red wine. "Penny for your thoughts."

"Nothing, really. Just enjoying the night," Bianca lied, stretching out her legs on the lounge chair. The wine helped dull the ache, but not enough. "I needed this getaway too."

Remi sank into the chair beside her. "How many times have you called Amelia since we left?" she teased.

"Not many." Bianca smirked. She'd called the girl three times in the past hour—maybe four. She couldn't help it. Her business, like her life, needed constant control.

"You're too much." Remi shook her head.

"I know it. I can't help it," Bianca replied, leaning back into the cushions.

"I'm a little tired," Remi murmured. "We'll rest tonight, explore tomorrow."

Bianca smiled, but her thoughts had already drifted elsewhere. They lingered, uninvited, on Harry and the woman who now occupied the space Bianca once called hers. A life she had built. A man she had loved. Gone now, yet some part of her *still* refused to let go.

It was her first night in Napa and she couldn't sleep. It was always like this when she traveled—whenever she lay in a bed that wasn't her own. It usually took her a couple of nights before her body settled, before the unfamiliar felt safe enough for rest. She spent most of the night staring at the ceiling, listening to the faint chirp of crickets outside the window. The sheets smelled fresh, clean, but they weren't hers.

Around seven o'clock, she crept downstairs and wandered into the grand kitchen. She needed motion. She rummaged through the cabinets, pulled out a pan, and pulled fresh vegetables from the fridge. She sliced, diced, and sautéed. The garlic sizzled—its sharp, pungent aroma filled the house. The beat of J Balvin's "I Like It" invaded the kitchen. She turned the volume down lower, so as not to wake Remi—but danced, with hips swaying anyhow.

But it was too late. She'd already awakened her.

Remi appeared in a pink robe, rubbing her eyes. "You sure know how to wake up a house."

Bianca twirled and kissed her cheek. "Time to rise and shine, amiga!"

Remi chuckled. "You couldn't resist this kitchen, could you?"

Bianca smirked. "I couldn't wait. And that garden outside? It's paradise."

"Well, welcome to wine country," Remi said, but her tone was off.

"You okay?" Bianca asked, catching the shift.

"Fine. I was thinking we might stay in today."

Hadn't she promised that they would explore the city?

"Absolutely not. We can't sit here all day and allow your emotions to get the best of you. We're going to see what's going on in Napa Valley. Maybe we'll even drive down to Sonoma Beach, show off our bikinis . . ."

"Maybe you'll show off *your* bikini." Remi laughed. "I'm a one-piece girl."

"You could totally do a bikini with that bod, girl—a body that you don't even have to work hard to maintain. God gave it to you just because he felt like it. On the other hand, people like me . . . we gotta work at staying in shape."

"I have my challenges too."

What challenges? Remi had everything, in Bianca's opinion—the perfect home, the perfect child, *had* the perfect husband. Gerard took care of her every need. She never had to think about anything other than keeping house. Her time was hers. Bianca had long envied that life. She used to wish that Harry had been more like Gerard—strong, confident. Gerard had a larger-than-life presence and the ability to command a room like no one she'd ever known. And he never met a stranger. People naturally gravitated to him. He took great care of Remi and Zoe—ferociously protected them.

"What challenges?" Bianca asked, more sharply than she meant to, an edge of jealousy in her voice. "You have everything."

Remi didn't flinch. "I don't have everything. Sure, I have physical, tangible things, but not everything that I need or want. The things that truly matter. And if you've forgotten, my life has changed overnight."

Bianca's tone softened, reminding herself that Remi was still fragile. "You're right, sweetie. I didn't mean to suggest . . ."

Remi offered a light smile. "It's okay."

Bianca forced some cheer into her voice. "Either way, eat up, get dressed and let's go! We're getting out of this house."

"Not taking no for an answer, huh?" Remi asked.

Despite the fatigue that had been pulling at her lately, Bianca held firm. "Not at all."

They drove through winding roads, vineyards stretching endlessly on either side. They had just parked in downtown Napa when Bianca's phone buzzed. A text.

Unknown number: **You're not as invisible as you think, Bianca.**

She gasped. Her fingers trembled against her phone.

"What is it?" Remi asked, peering over at her.

Bianca quickly locked her screen. "Nothing. Wrong number." Her stomach twisted.

Chapter Six

Remi

With straw hats perched upon their heads, Bianca and Remi wandered through the heart of Napa Valley—with its old town, family-run eateries and historical buildings. The first stop was Oxbow Market; a vibrant forty-thousand-square-foot marketplace nestled along the Napa River. The air buzzed with the scent of Moroccan street food, wood-fired pizzas, high-end meats, and the sweetness of freshly picked produce.

They stopped by a vintage candy shop in the heart of Napa and sampled the handmade chocolates. Bianca bought a dozen of their wine-infused truffles and had eaten nearly half of them before they even left the shop. She'd threatened to go back for a dozen more.

"These things are dangerous," Bianca said in between bites.

"Pace yourself, sister," Remi warned with a giggle. "In fact, gimme the bag."

Bianca playfully slapped back Remi's hand. "Touch these and draw back a nub."

They both laughed heartily.

After lingering in the cozy bookstore, they found themselves tucked into an artisan café on the riverside deck, sharing a cheese board and sipping glasses of brandy, the water beside them glistening in the late-afternoon sunshine.

"This is the life." Bianca raised her glass in the air.

Remi raised her glass too. "Can't believe I'm drinking brandy in the middle of the day. I'm going to be an all-out alcoholic, as my daughter put it."

Bianca laughed. "Stop."

"It's true. This place makes you want to drink."

"We're on vacation." Bianca kept a smile plastered on, laughed in all the right places, but her fingers kept brushing against her phone, seemed to be itching to check it.

Remi narrowed her eyes. "Okay, spill. What's going on with you?"

Bianca shook her head. "Nothing. Just tired. Didn't sleep much."

"That's not it. You seem spooked about something."

Bianca hesitated, then she let out a deep sigh. "I got a message from an *unknown number*."

Remi blinked. "What kind of message?"

Bianca lowered her voice. "They told me to stay away. Said I wasn't invisible."

Remi's expression turned sharp, concerned. "That's . . . creepy. Who do you think it was? You think it's Harry's new girlfriend?"

Bianca shook her head. "No."

"Well, who, then? Tell me."

Bianca sighed and hesitated before saying, "I was sort of dating this guy recently, and he wasn't very happy when I broke things off."

"What guy? You haven't told me about anyone new." Remi's eyes settled on her, studying her friend. They had shared everything with each other since childhood.

"We were keeping a low profile. I didn't want to tell you until I thought it was something to tell." Bianca smiled sheepishly. "Plus, you've been busy with your classes and laying the groundwork for your business. Then Gerard . . ."

"Not too busy for you," Remi said. "You should've told me about him."

"He's stalking me."

"Bianca!" Remi's voice dripped with concern. No . . . with fear.

"I know. I didn't want to tell you. Didn't want you to worry."

"Well, now I am worried. Have you gone to the police?"

Before Bianca could answer, a tall, handsome man approached their table and interrupted their conversation. "Remi, is that you?"

"Leo." Remi rose to her feet and hugged the man. "How are you?"

"I'm good." He grinned, showing off a beautiful set of white teeth. With deep curls in his hair, the body of a gym rat, and perfect, flawless skin the color of chocolate, he asked, "Gerard playing a round of golf this morning?"

Remi's face was solemn at the sound of Gerard's name. The painful thought that he would no longer play a round of golf ever again pierced her heart. The more days that passed, the reality of his absence was becoming even clearer, and with Leo standing in front of her asking a question that she so desperately hated answering—awaiting an explanation that she was already so tired of repeating, caused her further pain. Her shoulders were slumped, and with a toneless, quiet voice she said, "Leo . . . Gerard had a heart attack last month. We lost him."

The color left Leo's skin immediately. His face became a dull, grayish color. He stared at Remi for a moment, as if he expected her to tell him something different.

"Oh no, Remi. I had no idea. I'm so sorry." His hand stroked her arm. The genuineness of his tone was clear, and without hesitation, he pulled her into a firm hug; a solid, endearing one.

As Leo wrapped his arms around Remi, she caught sight of Bianca just over his shoulder. Her friend's eyes flicked to the bare ring finger on Leo's left hand, then back to Remi with a lifted brow. The gesture was small but unmistakable. Remi knew that look. Bianca's curiosity was piqued, her silent question loud as hell: Who exactly is this man, and is he single?

"Thank you." Remi rested her palm against Leo's chest. She took her seat.

"Gerard was a great guy. He'll certainly be missed. I wish I had known. I'd have flown to New Orleans for the services."

Remi offered a light smile. There were times when she could live in the moment and not think about Gerard's death, or the services, or the grief that consumed her at least twenty-three of the twenty-four hours in each day, but this wasn't one of those moments. No, at this moment she was back in New Orleans at the funeral.

"I know you would have. And I'm so sorry I didn't call. It just all happened so quickly. The heart attack, the services . . . everything. And it was an intimate service."

Remi was still fragile, triggered. And suddenly she felt guilty for not reaching out to Leo after Gerard's heart attack. She'd been wrapped in her own pain, but it was no excuse. They had been like brothers.

"I'm Bianca," she interrupted, and reached her hand to Leo. "Remi's oldest and fiercest ally."

"Pleased to meet you, Bianca. I'm Leo."

Remi gathered her emotions. "Leo is a good friend and he owns the property next to ours."

"Oh, the one with the massive wraparound veranda." Bianca's eyes lit up. "Gorgeous spot."

"That's the one." Leo chuckled, then looked at her. "A pleasure meeting you, Bianca."

"You as well." She leaned forward, a little coy. "Let me guess—your wife insisted on that big veranda?"

Remi shot Bianca a look, eyes wide, her brows raised.

Leo's expression shifted. "I'm a widower," he said quietly. "I lost my Vivian two years ago."

Bianca's flirtatious edge dropped instantly. Regret shone on her face. She seemed a bit embarrassed, too, and pulled back. "I'm so sorry. I didn't know."

"Viv was a wonderful woman," Remi said softly, offering Leo a smile of remembrance.

"She really was. Kindest soul I've ever known," Leo said, his eyes a little sad. He recovered quickly. "I see they've started work on Paloma's old winery. I'm guessing you bought the place. I remember you talking about it last summer."

"Yes, I did. Hoping to have my first tasting by the end of the summer; if not, early fall. It will be a big to-do. I hope you'll be there."

"You know I will. Wouldn't miss it," Leo said. He glanced at his watch. "Listen, I'm picking up a few things for a barbecue tonight. Just a casual thing—music, some food, good people. You know, the usual crowd. You're both more than welcome to come by. I'd love to catch up properly."

Remi's smile returned, this time a little easier.

"Gerard and I used to love your parties. We might stop by."

"I hope you do." Leo gave a nod and turned, his oak cologne lingering behind. He raised a hand in the air. "See you soon."

Bianca watched him walk away, then looked at Remi with a grin. "He's cute."

"He's kind," Remi said, eyes still on the path Leo had taken. "He and Vivian were some of the first people to welcome us here."

She remembered how the pair had shown up on their doorstep with a bottle of cognac and a homemade sweet potato pie that Vivian had baked. She and Gerard invited them in, and the four of them talked for hours, drank cognac, and ended up playing cards for most of the night. Loud music played on the stereo. Gerard and Leo remade their own rendition of Boyz II Men's "On Bended Knee", as they all became fast friends in a single evening. They were family, and when Vivian died, Remi remembered grieving her death as if she had been her own sister. She had worried that Leo wouldn't recover, and she and Gerard took turns checking on him in the months that followed. He had grieved for so long.

"Seems like a nice man," Bianca said.

"He is." Remi exhaled slowly and looked out over the hills.

"Rem, a great party is exactly what you need."

"You might be right."

"I know I'm right."

It was a full moon, and Boney James's saxophone seemed to echo through the dark, moonlit night. Laughter and conversation mingled in the air, rising above the low hum of voices and the sexy rhythm of "All I Want Is You." Leo's backyard pulsed with life, as it always had, with people holding glasses of wine or cognac, dancing, chatting, or simply soaking up the evening.

Remi wore a colorful summer sundress paired with embellished flat sandals. The coolness of the night caused goose bumps to race up and down her arms, and she wished she had worn sleeves or brought a sweater. Flames from the firepit danced and mesmerized her as she reclined on the outdoor sofa. Across the patio, Bianca danced with one of Leo's handsome friends, her sleeveless minidress hugging her curves. The chill didn't seem to bother her at all—likely thanks to the tequila on the rocks, of which she'd had at least three glasses.

Remi had spent much of the evening mingling, making polite conversation with neighbors she and Gerard had come to know during their summers in Napa. Most of them hadn't heard the news. So, over and over again, she'd answered the same painful questions—"Where's Gerard?"—and watched faces fall as she explained that he had a heart attack. Their reactions—"Oh no," "Why didn't you call?" "We would've come"—were kind but exhausting. She was grateful to have them all in one place, though. At least it spared her the trouble of having to offer them individual explanations when she bumped into them later. She finally managed to sneak away for a moment of peace, but Leo found her.

He slid onto the sofa next to her, glancing toward the dancing crowd. "Your friend seems to be enjoying herself."

"Looks that way." Remi smiled. "I'll be hauling her home, putting her to bed soon."

Leo chuckled, his eyes warm. "She's in good hands. But how about you, Rem? How are you *really* doing? And don't give me the bullshit answer that you've been giving everyone else all night. It's me, Leo. Give it to me straight."

She looked at him, then away. She remembered the times she had sat with him like this after Vivian's passing, when his grief had nearly consumed him. Now it was her turn.

She exhaled deeply. "Every day is a struggle just to get out of bed and keep going. I keep thinking I'm going to wake up one morning and he's in the kitchen cooking me one of his world-famous Creole dishes, and all of this is just a bad dream."

"I feel that." Leo nodded, his expression solemn. "You know I'm here, right? Anything you need, you just say the word. You and Gerard were so good to me."

Remi swallowed hard. "Gerard handled everything—our finances, our bills. I feel like I'm drowning in the details while trying to catch up on a life that was running fine without me."

"I can help," Leo said softly. "Anything you need, I'm here."

She hesitated, then admitted, "I brought his laptop. Stuffed every document I could into my suitcase. I just haven't had the chance or energy to dig into it yet."

"I'm here when you're ready."

Remi turned to him, her eyes glistening. "Thank you for letting me be honest. I can't tell you how much that means."

"Always." Leo gave her hand a gentle squeeze, then nodded his head toward her empty wineglass. "Can I refresh that for you?"

Remi smiled. "Sure, why not?"

He reached for her glass. "Merlot, right?"

"You know that's my fave."

"You with the Merlot, Gerard with the yack."

"And you with the whiskey and Viv . . . well, Viv with the sweet tea, because she was likely your designated driver."

Remi laughed and Leo joined in, his grin wide. The white linen shirt he wore seemed to glow against his smooth chocolate skin, catching the firelight just right. He was always handsome.

"Exactly. One of us had to stay sober," Leo said, still smiling. "I'll be right back."

Remi watched as he walked across the patio and exchanged a quick word with the bartender. Then, out of nowhere, Bianca rushed from the dance floor, leaving her dance partner confused and standing alone. She made a beeline for the bar, sliding up next to Leo like she'd been waiting for her cue.

Remi's eyebrows lifted. She shook her head. "This girl," she whispered to herself.

Bianca touched Leo's arm and whispered something in his ear. What she said made him laugh. She lingered beside him, smiling up at him with a look that was too eager. A schoolgirl crush, Remi thought, or something more desperate. Ever since her divorce, she thought Bianca had been too eager for attention. Remi shook her head. Her friend could be persistent, sometimes too much so. She often wondered how she'd managed to lose Harry in the first place. He had doted on her, adored her . . . until, suddenly, he didn't. One day he was gone, just like that—moved out, with no real explanation. Bianca had just blown it off as they had grown apart. Yet she seemed jealous about the woman he was currently dating. It just didn't add up.

Bianca never gave Remi full details about what happened. She'd been vague, evasive, which pissed Remi off, because they'd always been straight with each other about everything—or so she thought. The secrecy had caused Remi to draw her own conclusions. Watching her now with Leo, she couldn't help thinking it was this same behavior that had driven Harry away. And while Remi didn't want to judge her best friend, she couldn't help feeling a bit of embarrassment in this moment. She didn't have the heart to tell her that she wasn't at all Leo's type. She was nothing like Vivian, who had been quiet, poised. Bianca was neither of those things. Still, she clung to Leo's arm, laughing, wobbling slightly as he steadied her with one hand and walked back toward the sofa.

"I'm going to walk her home," Leo said, and handed Remi the glass of wine. "Looks like she's had a little too much."

"Looks that way." Remi gave Bianca a pointed look.

"I'm calling it a night, Rem. Had a bit too much tequila." Bianca winked, barely able to stand. "I'll see you at home."

"Fine. I'm going to finish my wine first and then I'll be home soon." Remi took a long sip as she eyeballed Bianca.

"No rush, honey. Enjoy yourself. I'm in good hands."

Remi raised her glass "Indeed, you are."

Remi watched as the pair crossed the patio and disappeared into the night. Then, at last, she leaned back and closed her eyes. The breeze was soft against her skin as she breathed in the beautiful California night air. The fire danced beside her, its scent mingling with the warm, woodsy candle burning on the table. Somewhere in the background, the sound of Michael Franks's "The Lady Wants to Know" played, mellow and teasing. It wrapped itself around her, pulled her deeper.

Chapter Seven

Bianca

Bianca opened one eye as the sunlight crept through the sheer curtains and unforgivingly struck her face, causing her to squint. She winced, groaned, and pulled the covers over her head, trying to hide from the intrusive sunlight. Too late. There was no escaping it. Her head throbbed like a distant drum, dull but persistent. She wasn't ready to face the morning, not with this hangover.

Laughter trickled in from the kitchen—light, familiar, high-pitched giggles.

She sat up slowly, the room tilting for a moment before settling. "Shit," she muttered to herself, her voice hoarse from last night's shenanigans. "Are the girls here already?"

The last thing she needed was Mila seeing her like this—disheveled, groggy, still smelling faintly of last night's tequila. She had hoped for more time to collect herself, scrub her conscience clean a bit, and pull it together before Mila arrived. The tension between them was already thick enough. Mila still hadn't forgiven her. And maybe she never would.

That laugh was definitely Mila's.

Bianca dragged herself out of bed and stumbled toward

the bathroom, flicking on the light. Her reflection stared back at her—mascara smudged, eyes puffy, hair matted on one side. Her gaze dropped lower, tracing the lines of her body. She looked thinner . . . slimmer in places she hadn't noticed before. She touched her neck gently. Her lymph nodes felt a little swollen again, just like they had before she'd left New Orleans. That, along with the recent night sweats and fatigue had prompted her to see her oncologist before this trip to Napa—for tests, just to rule out any issues. She told herself it was nothing. It was just a routine checkup—a precaution. But the what-ifs crept in anyway. She'd been cancer-free for some time, but in the quiet corners of her mind, she knew it carried with it the potential for return.

She grimaced and reached for the faucet. And now, with cold water on her face and a toothbrush inside her mouth, she needed to look better than she felt.

Downstairs, Zoe, Mila, and Remi were gathered around the island laughing and talking. The warmth of their voices drifted upward, and for a moment it felt like a party she hadn't been invited to. She leaned against the banister, listening. Her daughter's laughter was easy and effortless, like she belonged in a way that Bianca didn't. It wasn't jealousy, not exactly. It was more like grief for a closeness she hadn't earned with her.

"Oh, there she is." Zoe spotted Bianca first, hopped down from the stool, and hugged her. "Good morning, Aunt B."

Mila was slow to greet her—gave her a weak hug, almost pitiful. "Morning, Mom."

Bianca studied her daughter carefully. The front of her dark hair streaked with subtle highlights—likely a summer experiment. But that toboggan still covered the rest of her head like it did when they'd video-chatted a few days ago. *A new fad?* Bianca wasn't sure. And she looked slimmer than usual, almost too much so, as if food had escaped her for weeks. Her tight, distressed jeans that usually clung to generous hips—like her mother's—weren't so tight. Though a cropped vintage graphic tee revealed a sliver of her toned midriff. Her rich, caramel skin had taken on a golden glow, kissed by the sun, but beneath it all, something about her seemed . . . off.

"Good morning to both of you! We weren't expecting you until Friday."

"I didn't go to Maine. Daddy understood that I needed to come here for Aunt Remi." Mila gave Remi a sweet smile. "I'll join him and Jen in a few weeks, I guess."

Bianca cringed when she heard Jen's name. Jealousy rushed through her. "That was big of him."

She remembered the first time she'd ever heard the woman's name, or even knew she existed. It had rocked her to her core. She'd have been better off not knowing that someone new was quickly becoming a permanent fixture in Harry's life.

Mila ignored her sarcasm. "You slept in this morning, I see."

"Had a late night, honey." Bianca walked over and stroked Mila's brown tresses, the part extending from the toboggan. "What's with this winter hat? You should let your hair breathe. It's summertime."

"My hair is fine, Mom."

"I see." Bianca didn't press.

Mila leaned against the island, arms crossed. "Aunt Remi said you guys had a night out. Was it worth the headache?"

Bianca raised an eyebrow, brushing past the judgment in her tone. "Depends on who you ask."

Remi stepped in with a grin. "She was the life of the party, as usual. You know your mother."

"I *do* know my mother," Mila mumbled, turning to pour herself some orange juice.

Bianca watched her daughter's back as she moved. There was distance in every gesture, every word. It wasn't just about last night—it hadn't been for a long time.

Bianca leaned against the counter, arms crossed. "So . . . what's the real reason for the early arrival?"

Mila sipped her juice, then set down the glass with a soft clink. "Why does there have to be another reason?"

"I don't know," Bianca said, trying to keep her tone light. "You were just so excited about going to Maine with your father and . . . *what's her name*."

Remi shot her a look—part warning, part curiosity—but said nothing.

Mila rolled her eyes. "I wanted to be here, for Aunt Remi. That's it. That's the reason."

Bianca flinched inwardly. There was no mention of her in Mila's wanting-to-be-there for other people. "Right. Of course. Well, it's good to have you here." She paused, glancing at Mila's face for some softening. There was none.

Zoe, sensing the shift in energy, attempted a distraction. "Can we go to the flea market later, Aunt B? I want to find some vinyl so I can break in this new record player I got for Christmas."

Bianca smiled at her, grateful. "Vinyl? Oh, you're speaking my language now. You should see my record collection the next time you're in Louisiana."

"I would love to."

"Of course we can check out a flea market, sweetheart. We'll go after breakfast," Bianca answered. "Remi, you coming?"

"Wouldn't miss it," Remi said, glancing at Mila. "Might be good for all of us to get out."

Mila offered a tight smile. "Sure thing."

Remi wrapped her arm around Mila's shoulder. "Come on, it'll be fun."

Bianca turned to the coffee maker, her hands gripping the counter as it buzzed to life. She grabbed a coffee cup from the shelf. Her hangover was fading, but a different kind of ache was settling in—the one that came from having her daughter close by but a million miles away.

The sun was already high by the time they pulled into the dusty lot behind the flea market. The place was alive with color, mismatched tents, tables full of old books, hand-painted signs, and the sound of someone strumming a guitar for tips.

Zoe hopped out of the car first, her black tank hugging her slender frame, a pair of baggy camo pants hung low on her hips, a leather backpack slung over one shoulder. "Okay, I want vinyl, vintage sunglasses, and maybe a fake fur coat for the winter." She laughed.

"Very practical," Remi said, locking the car with a chirp.

Bianca adjusted her sunglasses, grateful for the fresh air and the chance to pretend everything was fine. "Let's stick together for the first half hour, then we can split up."

Mila lagged behind, arms folded, her expression unreadable. She had on oversize sunglasses and earbuds in.

They walked in silence at first, past booths selling incense, mismatched jewelry, and faded comic books. Zoe darted ahead, pulling Remi with her, leaving Bianca and Mila alone.

Bianca glanced over. "You always do this thing when you're mad at me. The sunglasses. The silence. The distance."

Mila didn't stop walking. "Maybe because I don't want to have the same conversation for the thousandth time."

"I'm not trying to fight with you."

"Then don't turn everything into a fight," Mila said, voice low but sharp. "Not everything I do is about you."

Bianca stopped at a booth full of antique picture frames, pretending to study them. "Sweetheart, I don't know how to read you, but I'm really trying."

Mila finally turned to face her, arms still crossed. "You

want to know the truth? I didn't come early for Aunt Remi *necessarily*. I came because I'm not particularly happy about Dad proposing to Jen. I don't like her." She said it emphatically.

Her words sent shock waves through Bianca, and she wanted to ask why—why her daughter disliked this woman her father was preparing to marry? Was she jealous of having to share her time with Harry, or was it something else? What had Jen done to make Mila feel this way, and express it so emphatically?

Bianca's heart pounded. The air felt too thick. Mila had always been perceptive, but she rarely voiced her feelings this directly. Bianca had assumed she was adjusting, maybe even indifferent. But this? *I don't like her.* The words looped in her head. She wanted to press, to understand why, but a part of her was afraid of the answer. What if Jen had said something cruel? What if Harry had allowed it? What if her daughter was navigating some silent grief alone?

"I think it's too soon for him to be thinking about marriage," she finally said. "But I didn't come here to fix things with you either. I have my own issues."

Bianca blinked, the words settling like dust in her chest. Concern rippled through her.

"I just wanted to be somewhere I didn't have to smile so much."

They stood in silence as a breeze picked up, rustling a row of dream catchers in all sorts of colors hanging from a nearby booth.

What issues did her daughter, who was so carefree, have? She wanted to know but didn't dare ask that either. Not yet, at least.

Remi called from a few rows down, "Hey! Zoe found a crate of old Prince albums—B, you'll lose your mind."

Bianca waved half-heartedly, eyes still on Mila.

"Thanks for the honesty," she said finally, quietly. "Even if it stings."

Mila looked away but this time didn't walk off. "I'm not trying to hurt you. I'm just tired of . . . pretending too."

Bianca gave a small nod, and they started walking again—not quite side by side but not far apart either. They caught up with Remi and Zoe. They were rounding a corner near a booth of secondhand leather goods when Bianca stopped short, nearly bumping into a tall, handsome young man—clean-cut, in khakis and a Marvel T-shirt, mirrored aviators perched on his face, and a fresh-squeezed lemonade in his hand.

Zoe nearly screamed.

"Bas!" She threw her arms around his neck. "When did you get here?"

"This morning." He smiled, surprised. He hugged her small waist. "Your mom told me you weren't coming until the weekend."

"Well, I'm here now . . . earlier than anticipated," Zoe offered him a wide grin.

"I haven't talked to you in . . . a good while. No calls or text messages."

"You're talking to me now," Zoe said, beaming.

Remi stepped in for a hug. "Hello, Bas. So good to see you."

"Hello, Remi. So good to see you." His voice softened, and a shadow passed over his face. "I was numb when I heard about Mr. G. Still trying to wrap my head around it. I'm so sorry."

"I'm still trying to wrap my head around it too. Thank you," Remi said gently, brushing his arm. "Where are our manners? Bas, this is my best friend, Bianca, and . . ."

"And you must be Mila." Bas extended his hand toward her first. "Much prettier than Zoe said."

Mila managed a half smile as she took his hand. "Thank you, I guess."

Zoe playfully punched him in the arm.

Bas laughed. "Zoe used to talk about you all the time. Good to finally meet you. And you as well, Bianca."

"You are so cute. And so very sweet." Bianca smiled, her mood clearly lifted.

Zoe tugged on Bas's arm, excited. "Ooh, we should drive down to the beach later—have a bonfire. I have so much to tell you—"

A beautiful young woman approached, wearing cutoff denim shorts and a colorful halter top. Her eyes were the exact shade of the emerald ring Bianca wore on her finger—an inheritance from her *abuelita*. Her hair, wild and fire red, framed a pretty face of smooth brown skin that glowed in the sunlight, striking and unforgettable. Without hesitation, she slipped her hand into Bas's and laced her fingers with his.

"Did someone say beach?"

Zoe froze. Her smile vanished. Her hand slipped from Bas's arm. The color drained from her face quickly. Bas seemed frozen too—caught midthought, midmove—so the young woman took the lead. She stepped forward and extended a hand out toward Zoe.

"I'm Sage. Bas's girlfriend." Her voice was bright. A deep smile revealed flawless dimples. She didn't just say it—she announced it, her tone laced with pride, as if claiming territory. The word *girlfriend* hung in the air like a slow echo, loud enough for everyone nearby to hear. Her fingers still reached forward, waiting.

Zoe's eyebrows lifted at the declaration.

"Wow—girlfriend," Zoe repeated, letting the word land hard. She didn't take Sage's hand. Instead, her eyes shifted to Bas. "Seems we do need to catch up."

An awkward silence rippled between them, cut swiftly by Remi, who stepped in with practiced grace.

"Pleased to meet you, Sage," she said, offering a warm but neutral smile and a handshake.

Bas cleared his throat, his grip tightening slightly around Sage's hand. "Yeah . . . we've been seeing each other for a couple of months now. Kind of unexpected, but—" he offered Zoe a tentative smile "—it's been good."

Zoe nodded slowly, jaw tight, her gaze flicking from Bas to Sage and back again. "Well. That's . . . great. I'm happy for ya," she said sarcastically.

Bianca watched her carefully, her earlier warmth now replaced by wariness. She stepped closer to Zoe, a subtle show of support. Mila, ever observant, tilted her head slightly, studying Sage with open curiosity.

Sage, oblivious—or pretending to be—laughed lightly. "I've heard so much about your family. Bas talks constantly about spending the summers here, especially with you, Zoe."

Zoe's smile returned, but it was all teeth now, sharp and too bright.

"Funny," she said. "He never mentioned you at all. Even when we talked during Christmas break." Her eyes veered to Sage.

Bas winced. "Zoe—"

"It's fine," she said quickly, waving it off like it didn't sting. She turned to the group, already stepping backward. "Actually, I think I'm going to grab an iced coffee."

"Zoe," Remi said gently.

"I'm fine, Mom," Zoe said. "Does anyone else want coffee?"

Before anyone had a chance to answer, she'd turned and walked off toward the café across the street. Bianca watched her go, wondering what was really going on between Zoe and Bas. They were clearly more than summer friends.

Chapter Eight

Remi

Remi's bare feet were cold against the hardwood floors as she scampered outside to the patio, carrying a glass of lemonade. Zoe was stretched along a lawn chair in her gray lounge shorts and tank top, her eyes lightly closed. Remi plopped down beside her.

"Hey honey, you feeling better?" she asked, handing her the glass.

Zoe took the lemonade without opening her eyes. "Thanks, Mom. I'm fine. Really."

Remi hesitated. "What was that back there at the flea market? With Bas?"

Zoe blinked at the sky. "I didn't know he was bringing someone for the summer. It's always been just me and him."

Remi softened. "Well, you've got Mila here now. Maybe all four of you can hang out."

Zoe shrugged, lips tight. Her gaze drifted to the pool.

Remi studied her daughter. "There's more to it, isn't there?"

Zoe didn't answer right away. She sipped her lemonade. "Can we just drop it? I'm really okay."

Remi didn't push the issue any further. She just gave Zoe's leg a gentle pat, then rose and went back inside, the sliding glass door swooshing softly behind her. She watched from the door as Zoe seemed to exhale as if she was grateful that Remi had left. She tilted her head back and closed her eyes. Remi headed to the kitchen.

She washed the few dishes left in the sink, her hands moving on autopilot. Through the window she caught a glimpse of Zoe—still guarded, too quiet for summer. By now she and Bas would've been headed to the Sonoma Coast for a dip in the ocean. They'd have stayed gone most of the day, only to return home in the wee hours of the night. They spent just about every waking hour together during the summer, exploring both Napa Valley and the stunning coastal scenery. It amazed Remi how they found so much to do. And when they weren't exploring, they swam in the pool or spent hours under the moonlight swatting mosquitoes and talking about only God knew what.

She dried her hands on a dish towel and leaned against the counter. The girl was trying so hard to hold it together. Just like her father, Remi thought. So strong, or at least pretending to be. She had Gerard's confidence.

Remi shut that door in her mind. Thinking about Gerard always brought pain—pain she didn't really feel like dealing with at the moment. In fact, she was learning to numb herself to it. It was easier that way.

She opened the fridge, not really hungry, and closed it again. Then she walked over to the dining table where Zoe's sunglasses were left. Purple frames with a tiny scratch on the left lens. She picked them up and turned them over. She remembered Zoe at ten—running down the hallway of their Louisiana home, barefoot, crying over some girl at school who said she wasn't cool enough to hang out with. Remi had made popcorn, curled up with her on the couch, and played Disney Channel reruns until Zoe was okay again.

By the next morning, Zoe had bounced back like she always did. She'd returned to school with her chin a little higher, her ponytails a little tighter, and, by lunchtime, had gathered a group of her own. Remi hadn't been surprised. Even then, Zoe—like her father—had a way of commanding space, of turning rejection into resolve. She was a leader, even then.

Now, watching her daughter move through grief—*and something else*—with a quiet strength, Remi saw that same spirit shining through . . . like when she was younger. Different challenges but the same core. She was still that brave little girl—just older now, more layered, and more aware of the weight of things.

Remi took a deep breath, went back to the kitchen, and slid the leftover pizza in the fridge. The house had begun to settle into its evening hush. She made herself a cup of tea. Bianca had turned in early—finally catching up on the sleep she'd missed earlier. Mila was tucked away in her room, bingeing on one of her popular TV series. There was a quietness, not unusual, but different somehow. Distant, like she was hiding from something, but Remi didn't put much thought into it. Mila had always been a little reserved, often disappeared into her own world. She was more introspective than outspoken. Not like Zoe, who said exactly what she meant. Mila held things closer, but perhaps she just needed the space.

Tomorrow morning would be full of activity. Paloma had organized an early staff meeting at the winery to go over timelines for the new tasting room, and delivery of the fermentation tank was scheduled before noon. She was tempted to call it a night herself, to retreat into the quiet of her bedroom. But first, she wanted to check on Zoe again; she was still out on the patio. Something in her motherly instinct told her that her child needed a little extra affection tonight.

She stepped outside, letting the glass door ease shut behind her. Zoe sat cross-legged in the same spot, earbuds in, scrolling her phone. She looked up when Remi approached but said nothing.

Remi eased down beside her. "You hungry? You didn't eat any pizza tonight."

Zoe shrugged. "Not really hungry."

Remi nodded but didn't press her about it. "I thought maybe we could drive into town tomorrow afternoon, after my meetings. Walk the square. Maybe hit up that little bookstore you love."

Zoe glanced over, cautiously. "Just us?"

Remi smiled. "Just us."

For a moment neither of them spoke. A cool breeze blew across the patio and caused Remi to shiver.

"I miss Daddy," Zoe finally said, voice barely above a whisper.

"I know," Remi replied, her throat tightening. "I miss him too."

Zoe looked down at her hands, fingers fidgeting with the bracelet Gerard had given her on her fifteenth birthday—a small gold charm shaped like a sunflower. She never took it off. "Do you ever . . . feel like just giving up when things get too hard?"

Remi reached over and gently took Zoe's hand. "Sometimes. But then there are moments like this—sitting here with you, and I remember why I have to keep going."

Zoe nodded slowly, not quite ready to smile but close.

"We'll get through this," Remi added. "In time."

Zoe leaned her head back against the lawn chair. "Okay."

"And whatever you're going through with Bas. It'll work itself out too."

Zoe didn't agree or disagree. She just looked out at the pool.

* * *

Downtown Napa was already alive by the time Remi and Zoe arrived. The streets hummed with Monday afternoon energy—locals carrying baskets from the farmers market, tourists snapping photos of historical brick buildings framed by flower boxes and wrought-iron balconies. The scent of espresso and buttery pastries floated from a corner café where two musicians played an upbeat acoustic set.

It was the first time Remi and Zoe had some time to themselves. They'd always spent a good amount of time together when they visited Napa for the summer.

Remi parallel parked beneath the canopy of a large oak tree. Zoe was out of the car before the engine stopped, adjusting her sunglasses and tucking her braids behind her ears, her leather backpack in tow. Remi often wondered what all she carried in that thing and shook her head at the thought. She stepped out of the car more slowly than her eager child, soaking in the sun and the buzz around her.

"Where to first?" she asked.

Zoe hesitated for a moment, then pointed toward the bookstore with its ivy-covered awning and weathered wooden sign.

Remi smiled. "Of course."

There was a hot new series that all the young readers were raving about—the author was edgy and funny and had garnered a massive following of twentysomething-year-olds. It was the talk of the book world. The fourth book in the series had just been released and Zoe couldn't wait to get her hands on it—to lose herself between the pages, as she did with so many other books in the past. She was a ferocious reader. Asking Zoe to come to a bookstore was like inviting her to a full course meal or a concert with her favorite artist. She was just that excited about books.

Inside, the shop was quiet, cool, and fragrant with old paper and cedar shelves. The owner, a soft-spoken man named

Theo, waved from the counter and said nothing more. He knew them both well—she and Zoe had spent countless hours in his shop. He knew them well enough to give them space to explore too. They would ask questions if they needed to.

Zoe immediately found the book she was looking for—the coveted fourth book in the series. She held on to it as if it were the last copy on the shelf. Then she drifted toward the back, where vintage vinyls, poetry collections, and obscure zines lined the shelves. Remi moved slower, in a different direction, trailing her fingers across the spines of books she'd read years before—Toni Morrison, Maya Angelou, Edwidge Danticat—authors and characters who felt like old friends.

From a nearby shelf, Zoe called softly, "Mom."

Remi turned as Zoe held up a slim book—*On Grief and Grieving* by David Kessler and Elisabeth Kübler-Ross.

Remi's heart clenched. "You want to get it?"

Zoe nodded, her voice barely audible. "Yeah."

They didn't say anything else. Just brought it to the register along with a few other finds—an art book for Remi and a record—*Scratch* by the Crusaders—for Zoe. Her taste for old music and vinyl records had come from her father, who'd been spinning records since she was barely able to walk. They both had a deep love for classic jazz—Miles Davis, Herbie Hancock, Sonny Rollins—and Zoe had built an impressive collection of her own, filled with artists like Earth, Wind & Fire, Marvin Gaye, Steely Dan, James Brown, Aerosmith, Elton John. An unusual mix, but Zoe had never been a typical child. Her musical palate was far from typical for someone her age. Gerard had made sure she grew up with soul, funk, and grit in her ears.

After the bookstore, they wandered to Honeybee, a tiny boutique where Zoe tried on two pairs of retro sunglasses and modeled them in the mirror while Remi gave opinions.

"These," Remi said, pointing. "Very Hollywood . . . *I mean*, very Louisiana film student."

Zoe's love for the arts, for film, was strong. She was thriving in Xavier's film program. She grinned, grabbed the glasses from her mother, and bought them. By noon, they were seated at a small riverside café with linen umbrellas and glasses of cucumber water. A summer salad was shared between them—arugula, peaches, and candied pecans.

"You okay?" Remi asked softly, watching her daughter.

Zoe stared across the water, sunglasses pushed up onto her head. "I've enjoyed today." She said it with a light smile.

Remi reached for her hand across the table. "Me too."

The sunlight, the river, the stillness between them was therapeutic for them both.

Chapter Nine

Bianca

Bianca's phone buzzed on the patio table.

She ignored it at first—assuming it was Amelia, checking in. She just continued to watch as Mila and Zoe played Marco Polo in the pool. Remi sat on the edge in her one-piece black-and-white swimsuit, sunglasses on her face and a book in her hand. A lemon drop martini rested next to her on the concrete.

A second buzz. Then a third.

Bianca adjusted her bikini top before picking up the phone. She glanced at the screen.

Unknown Number: **Still pretending you're someone you're not?**

Her breath caught in her throat. She hadn't heard from him in a few days—her annoying stalker. She thought maybe he'd moved on or vanished, like the mistake he'd always been. But here he was again. A ghost she hadn't yet figured out how to bury.

Unknown Number: **You're not as untouchable in Napa as you think.**

Bianca's fingers trembled as she locked the screen and

placed the phone face down. She took a sip of the lemon drop martini that she and Remi had spent the afternoon whipping up in the kitchen—with fresh lemons, vodka, and simple syrup. She looked over her shoulder, as if someone might be watching from the window inside the house.

When she looked across the pool, Remi was observing her with skeptical eyes, her eyebrows furrowed. She gave her a light smile, hoping to ease her concern. Remi didn't return the smile. Instead, she closed her book slowly and slid her sunglasses down her nose just enough to see Bianca's face clearly.

"You good?" she called out.

Bianca nodded too quickly. "Just Amelia checking in again," she lied, her voice breezy. "That girl acts like I'm going to vanish if she doesn't text me every two hours."

Remi didn't laugh. She watched her friend for a moment longer, then turned her attention back to Zoe and Mila, who had collapsed in laughter at the far end of the pool. Still, Bianca could feel the weight of Remi's gaze, even after she looked away.

She glanced down at her phone again. No new messages. Not yet. But she knew more would come. She shuddered at the thought. Her heart raced.

Bianca stood up, wrapped the towel around her hips, and reached for her sunglasses. "I'm gonna lie down for a bit," she said in Remi's direction, voice flat. "Too much sun."

Remi nodded slowly, still studying her. "You sure?"

"Yeah." She mustered a smile that didn't quite reach her eyes. "Just tired."

She walked through the patio doors, heart pounding against her ribs. The cool air inside the house was a stark contrast to the heat rising in her chest. She looked at her phone again.

Unknown Number: **That little vineyard won't protect you. I know everything. And I bet your daughter would love to know too.**

Bianca's hand clenched around her phone. Her jaw tightened. This wasn't a stalker who couldn't let go. No . . . this was much more. This was someone who knew too much.

Chapter Ten

Remi

The sound of laughter echoed across the patio as the side gate creaked open. Remi glanced up from her book just in time to see Bas step inside their yard, followed by Sage. The late-afternoon sun gleamed off the water, casting a shimmering light onto their faces.

Bas was barefoot, wearing swim trunks and a sleeveless shirt, a towel tossed over one shoulder. He flashed that easy grin, charming and warm. He was just as comfortable at their pool as Zoe was. Their pool had been *his* through several summers. He had even become so comfortable with their family that he barely knocked before entering their home. And they were fine with it. Bas had become family. But Sage . . . not so much. Still, she trailed behind him in a bright yellow bikini, her deep red tresses pulled up into a bun, sunglasses perched on her nose.

"I thought I heard some Marco Polo going on over here," Bas called, already heading toward the pool steps.

Mila popped up from the water. "Bas!" She squealed, as if she hadn't just met him and behaved as if she'd known him forever. Then she splashed toward the edge.

Sage gave a polite wave. "Hey everybody."

"Hello, Bas. Hello, Sage." Remi gave a light smile, returned Sage's wave, but her eyes lingered just a second too long, flicking from Sage to Zoe, who had remained still in the pool and said nothing. Her daughter's expression was unreadable, casual on the surface, but Remi saw the way her jaw flexed, the way she avoided looking directly at Bas or Sage.

"Room for one more?" Bas asked, already peeling off his shirt.

Zoe shrugged, but Mila piped up with a cheerful, "Of course. Come on in, the water's great."

Sage settled into one of the pool chairs, stretching out like she owned the place. She rested her sparkling water on the table, crossed her legs as if she was at a fine resort. "This is nice," she said. "California's sun is something amazing."

Remi felt the shift in the air—the subtle tension that Bas seemed to be trying to ignore. He had to feel it. He and Zoe had always been so easy with each other—like best friends. But there was no mistaking the thickness. Something was brewing just beneath the surface, and not just in Zoe's narrowed eyes, or the way Bas avoided looking at her for too long.

Zoe sank beneath the water, disappearing into the turquoise ripples. When she resurfaced on the opposite end of the pool, there was a wrinkle on her forehead—a frown on her face. She swam toward the edge and pulled herself out, water cascading from her gym shorts as she grabbed a towel and wrapped it around her shoulders.

Bas watched her. His grin faltered, eyes trailing her every movement. "Zoe," he said, barely above a whisper. She didn't turn around.

Remi hadn't stopped watching. The invisible threads between her daughter and Bas were still there—stretched now, maybe fraying, but definitely not severed. She saw it in the way Bas shifted uncomfortably in the pool, the way he laughed at something Mila said but didn't take his eyes off Zoe. Sage noticed too. Her mouth curved into a sly smirk as she leaned back further into her lounge chair, clearly enjoying Zoe's discomfort—staking her claim.

"You should've been here this morning, Bas," Mila said, pulling herself out of the pool. "My mom made beignets. Like, real New Orleans ones. Powdered sugar and all." She was clearly trying to lighten the mood because giving her mother any sort of compliment was unusual, particularly for her.

Bas chuckled. "I'll take that as a challenge to make breakfast tomorrow."

"You cook?" Sage asked, lifting her sunglasses—raising a brow.

Remi wondered just how much this girl knew about Bas, and what possessed her to follow him home to Napa Valley. Where exactly was her home, and why wasn't she there for the summer?

"Heck yeah!" Bas gloated. "Learned from the best—both my mom and Mr. G. My mom taught me to use only the freshest ingredients in an omelet, but Mr. G taught me how to make some of the meanest shrimp and grits you will ever taste."

Zoe sat at the edge of the pool now, legs dangling into the water, her face turned toward the vineyard. Her thoughts seemed far from the casual conversation behind her. Remi could see that, for sure.

"We're headed down to Bodega Bay . . . for a bonfire later," Bas announced as he hopped out of the pool. "Mila, you coming?"

"No, I'm stuck on this series I've been watching. In fact, it's about to come on. I'm going in for a bit." Mila placed her hand on the handle of the patio door. "Next time, though."

"Cool. You, Zoe?" He was grasping for straws—knew it was a long shot.

Zoe didn't even look his way, just said, "No thanks."

As the sun dipped lower in the sky and the chill of the evening began to set in, Remi reached for her book again but didn't open it. She watched her daughter instead. Watched as Bas and Sage left through the same gate on the side of the house that they had entered earlier. She watched the small silences that said everything.

Remi placed a tea bag in her mug and pulled honey from the shelf. She stood in the kitchen, watched as Zoe sat on the sofa, her legs curled underneath her, flipping through the pages of the book she'd purchased at the bookstore earlier. Just as the teakettle let out a sharp whistle, she heard a buzz—the digital sound of Zoe's phone vibrating on the island. She glanced at the phone as the screen had lit up with a message from Bas:

I wasn't trying to hurt you with Sage, but you haven't taken any of my calls for weeks. Honestly, I thought you moved on. You were so different after we lost the baby . . .

Remi froze. *The baby?*

A cold wave swept through her. Her hands went numb, the mug nearly slipping from her fingers. She turned toward the living room. Zoe sat curled up on the sofa now, cradling her knees, her face turned away, the book turned face down on the coffee table.

Remi stared at her daughter—her child—and suddenly did not recognize her. A thousand moments replayed at once: the mood swings, the quiet disappearances, the unspoken grief.

There was a time when Remi had noticed a change in her daughter that she couldn't quite put her finger on.

It all made sense now.

Why she had come unglued at the flea market. Why Sage's presence had felt like a betrayal. Why she'd pretty much acted as if Bas was invisible at the pool this afternoon. Why she'd come home this summer with silence folded tight around her like armor.

Remi pressed a hand to her chest. The air felt thin.

Her baby had lost a baby. And she hadn't even known.

Remi stood at the island for a long time, one hand still on her chest, the other wrapped tightly around the back of the kitchen chair. Zoe's phone buzzed again, but she didn't look this time. She didn't need to.

She breathed in slowly, then walked past Zoe to the patio door. Outside, the sun was beginning to slip behind the cypress trees, casting long shadows inside, across the room. Zoe hadn't moved from her spot. She paced a couple of times, trying to decide if the time was right to mention it, or if she should wait for a better time.

Remi slid next to her on the sofa. Her voice was soft but steady. "Zoe."

Zoe looked up at her mother, sat up a little straighter. "Yeah?"

Remi's fingers massaged her temples. "I saw your phone. Bas texted you." She breathed in deeply. "I wasn't being nosey. Well, maybe I was . . ."

Zoe blinked. Her lips parted. She looked away from Remi. "Oh." Her voice was barely audible.

"Why didn't you tell me?"

Zoe shook her head, eyes locked on the blank television screen, as if it were on. She seemed to know exactly what Remi was referring to.

"I didn't want you to worry," she said quietly. "I didn't want to disappoint you and Daddy. There was already so much going on—with school and everything. I was scared you'd think I wasn't going to finish. That I might drop out."

"Zoe." Remi's voice caught. "You lost a baby."

"I couldn't even say it out loud, Mom. Not then. Not even to Bas at first, not really. We didn't even know what we were doing. We were irresponsible." Her voice cracked. "I just . . . wanted it to go away."

Remi moved closer, but not too much. "You didn't have to go through that alone."

Zoe's eyes shimmered, but she didn't cry. She hugged her knees tighter.

"I didn't feel like anyone would understand. You always look at me like I'm that little girl with the scraped knees and Glitter Glue. I didn't want you to see me like this."

Zoe was wrong about one thing: Remi would've understood—all too well. It was raining the day she had found out *she* was pregnant—a baby boy—before she and Gerard were even married, long before Zoe. She was just a freshman at LSU. Warm Louisiana rain, heavy and slow, slid down the windows of Gerard's apartment. She sat on the edge of the tub, arms wrapped around her stomach—not protectively, but just anchoring herself. The test stick lay on the bathroom counter showing two lines, blunt and unapologetic.

Gerard had gone for beignets. She hadn't asked him to. He just said he'd be back in twenty, and he kissed her cheek like it was a normal morning.

It wasn't.

She kept staring at the pink lines like they might change if she waited long enough.

Gerard's phone rang—his landline. She thought it was probably him, wondering if she wanted coffee with the beignets.

She didn't answer. Her throat was dry and her skin felt tight. She hadn't pictured herself holding a baby or telling anyone. She couldn't even wrap her mind around it.

Gerard came back with a white paper bag and two cups of coffee.

"Brought extra. They're fresh too," he said, smiling.

Remi remembered having really looked at him. The crooked grin. The way he always leaned too casually against the doorframe. The smell of beignets that lingered in the air mixed with the cold bite of realization that had just settled in her lungs. She was thankful his roommate wasn't there. She might've come unglued had he been.

"I need to tell you something," she said just above a whisper.

He sat beside her on the bathroom floor. She didn't cry and neither did he. He just pulled the test toward him and stared at it as if it were a language he didn't understand. When he finally looked up, he didn't say anything profound. Just, "Okay, baby. We'll figure it out."

But the truth was, they didn't need to figure it out. Because all too soon, it was over. They both cried the day they lost Gerard 2.0, the nickname they had both agreed on for the baby boy who would never make it into the world.

Remi was never the same after that.

She let Zoe's words settle. *I didn't want you to worry. Didn't want to disappoint you and Daddy.* Then she reached over, slowly, and placed a hand over Zoe's.

"I don't need you to be okay. I just need you to be honest with me. When I know what's going on, I can help you. And you don't have to protect me, sweetheart."

There was a long pause between them.

Finally, Zoe whispered, "I thought if I came back here to Napa—maybe if I saw Bas, we could forget it happened. Maybe I could get past it. But I don't think I can, Mom."

Remi gave her daughter's hand a tight squeeze. "No, you won't ever forget. But you don't have to carry it alone anymore."

Zoe didn't say anything, but she didn't pull away either.

Remi wouldn't tell her about Gerard 2.0. Not yet. Not tonight. But one day she would.

Chapter Eleven

Bianca

After both girls had gone upstairs, Bianca and Remi enjoyed a bottle of Chianti on the veranda, the night's chill softened by the wine and a throw blanket draped over their laps. Crickets hummed from the trees beyond the vineyard. Somewhere down the hill, soft music played lightly; it seemed to be coming from Leo's veranda. Bianca had to admit she found him handsome but knew he hadn't quite moved past his wife's death. And she wasn't looking for a man with that kind of baggage—not that she was all that interested anyway. Besides, he didn't seem particularly interested in her, either.

Remi poured the last of the bottle between their glasses, swirling hers before taking a slow sip. "It feels good to just relax and do nothing," she said.

Bianca nodded. "Feels like we're always putting out fires lately."

"Or hiding the smoke," Remi said.

They both laughed.

The light flickered above them—the room where the girls were. Bianca shifted in her seat. "Is everything okay with Zoe?" she asked quietly.

Remi's glass paused halfway to her lips. "She'll survive."

Remi had shared a bit about Zoe's situation with Bianca.

"She's been through a lot." Bianca glanced upward, a faint yellow light glowing.

Remi exhaled slowly. "More than I realized."

A stillness settled between them for a moment.

"I can't believe I didn't know about the baby," Remi said softly, as if the night itself might be listening too closely. "All the signs were there. I knew something was going on . . . but I didn't know what." She hesitated. "I stumbled on a message on her phone. Can you believe that? It was like . . . it was meant for me to see."

Bianca didn't answer right away. She just reached over and placed a hand on Remi's arm. "She's young, Rem. Scared. Probably didn't have the right words to share with you. And she sure as hell didn't want Gerard to find out. She was his baby girl. And let's be honest—Gerard thought the world of Bas. She probably didn't want to blow that up either. You know how he was . . . he might've taken that boy's head off."

Remi gave a faint, bitter laugh. "You're right. Bas would've been in deep trouble."

"You know your husband didn't play when it came to his favorite girls."

"He did not. He would go to war over us." Remi blinked at the stars above. "But it still hurt that I didn't know. That she had to endure it alone. At least I could've had her back."

"Did you tell her about Gerard 2.0?"

"Not yet. That's a conversation for another time. But I will tell her. I think it will free her, in some ways."

"I think so too."

Bianca looked at her glass, then up at the sky. "Funny how we thought that grown-up life would be . . . easier. Like once we hit our forties, everything would just line up."

"We were crazy." Remi smiled weakly.

The girls' laughter drifted down from the upstairs room—brief, high-pitched, untouched by the weight below. And for a moment, the world felt normal. But the feeling passed in a flash.

They sat for a while in silence; the kind only old friends can share comfortably.

Then Remi turned toward her. "What about you? Any more messages?"

Bianca nodded slowly. "Just one earlier today, when we were by the pool—when you were quizzing me."

"I knew something was up."

"I didn't want to alarm the girls. Then there was one later, from a blocked number. It said, *I know where you are. How's the weather in Cali?*"

"Shit, Bianca! That's it, you're calling the police in the morning. For all we know, he could've followed us here. He could be lurking in the shadows right now." Remi's voice was low but firm.

Bianca stared off into the darkness, as if she were looking for someone to emerge from the rows of vegetation. She didn't tell her about the one that really shook her—the one that read: **That little vineyard won't protect you. I know everything. And I bet your daughter would love to know too.**

"I promise I will tomorrow," Bianca said.

"How long has this been going on?" Remi asked.

Bianca hesitated. Ever since the text messages began, she'd been hyper aware of her surroundings—on edge, spooked. And just as she opened her mouth to answer, she gasped, as if her breath had tangled in her throat. "A month. Maybe a little more."

"Bianca, that's a long time without getting law enforcement involved."

Bianca gave a soft, nervous laugh. "I know how it sounds. I just . . . he wasn't always like that. At first, he was kind. Attentive. Thoughtful. You know how it goes." Remi had enough in her heart, dealing with grief. Bianca wouldn't put this on her too.

They sat in silence for a moment, the air thick around them.

"You need to report this. Tomorrow," Remi said, her voice firmer. "I feel like if he knows where you are, we're all involved now. You, me . . . the girls."

"I promise."

"We'll call together. You're not doing this alone. We'll make a plan. I mean it."

Bianca's mind drifted to the guy who she first thought might be her stalker. Luke had been something out of a dream when he waltzed into Chic Threads. He wore all black that day—dark jeans, a slim button-down, and a thin silver ring on his pinky finger. He was looking for something for his mother—a blouse, a piece of jewelry—anything. Her birthday was approaching, and he needed something special right away.

"What would you suggest for a seventy-eight-year-old woman who has everything?" he asked her with a beautiful wide smile.

Bianca didn't hesitate to answer. "A fine piece of jewelry."

She showed him a necklace that she had picked up at one of the trade shows a few days before—a beautiful piece with rare stones. She rambled about how the piece was of a historical nature, a rare find. His mother would love it. He listened intently, like her opinion genuinely mattered.

"Can you wrap it nicely for me?" he asked. Then in a flirtatious manner, he said, "The way something beautiful is packaged makes all the difference. Wouldn't you agree?"

"I do agree, and certainly I can wrap it for you."

That was the first hook.

They had coffee two days later. A week after that, dinner. It was easy—effortless. He was older, yes—but it gave him a kind of allure. He paid attention. Sent flowers. Walked her to her car when she closed the boutique in the evenings. He said all the right things. Until he didn't.

He made a comment about her dress. "You don't need to show off so much, not for anyone else." Then came the questions about where she went, who she saw, why she hadn't answered his text. On some nights he started to show up uninvited under the pretense that he just happened to be nearby. At first, she told herself it was passion in him coming out. She hadn't had someone this interested in her since Harry. But the warmth soured fast. One night, he showed up at the boutique after hours. He was drunk—whiskey on his breath. He cornered her in her back office; told her she didn't appreciate him. That she liked to play innocent, but she wanted the attention, with the tight jeans and sexy dresses. She was nothing but a tease and she owed him. She'd left shaking that night, keys clutched in her hand like a weapon. She blocked his number immediately.

But the messages kept coming. Weird ones, from anonymous numbers. But nothing compared to the message she'd received earlier that made her stomach twist. She didn't think it could be Luke anymore. No, this was someone different.

"I'm going to grab us another bottle," Bianca told Remi while standing up.

"Bring the fresh fruit from the fridge."

Bianca went into the house, opened the refrigerator door, and pulled out the bowl of cantaloupe, honeydew melon, and kiwi, and placed it on the countertop. She made her way to the wine cellar and grabbed another bottle of Chianti. When she returned to the kitchen, she heard giggles from the girls. They were still awake. She started up the stairs to check on them but stopped in midstride.

"What is it with you and your mother? You always seem so tense around her," she heard Zoe say.

"It's her fault that my life is so fucked up."

Bianca stiffened when she heard Mila's words. She rested her back against the wall and continued to listen.

"How do you mean?"

"She's the reason my dad left. She was sleeping around with someone. I know because I heard them arguing about it one night."

"Do you know who the guy was?"

"No, but my dad was pissed. He moved out after that."

Bianca's heart started to beat rapidly. She stood frozen at the foot of the stairs, the slightly chilled bottle of wine slick in her hand, her mouth suddenly dry. The soft light from the hallway painted long shadows against the wall, and the sound of her own pulse belted loudly in her ears.

Mila's voice floated down again, quieter this time. "She thinks I don't know, but I do."

"Have you ever asked her about it?"

"No," Mila answered quickly. "What's the point? She'd just lie like she always does. She just pretends everything is fine, like she didn't wreck our family. Why won't she just tell the truth?"

Bianca couldn't move. Her spine pressed against the wall like it might hold her up. That night—*the night*—flashed through her mind: the shouting, Harry slamming the door. Bianca had thought she'd hidden it all from Mila. Apparently not.

The floor creaked beneath her, and suddenly the girls fell silent upstairs. Bianca straightened quickly and cleared her throat.

"Girls?" she called lightly, forcing calm into her voice. "Everything okay up there?"

Mila called back, her voice sharp with defensiveness, "Yeah, we're fine."

Bianca waited another second, then stepped back into the

kitchen, placing the bottle on the counter next to the fruit. She braced her hands on the edge of the sink, staring out the window into the darkness of the night. Her stomach turned.

So, Mila knew why Harry left. She knew the truth, and Bianca was the villain.

She closed her eyes.

Behind her, the screen door creaked. Remi walked in with their empty glasses. "Everything okay?" she asked.

Bianca nodded quickly. "Yeah. Just . . . still spooked from that text message."

"And rightly so," Remi said, placing the glasses on the counter.

She couldn't stop hearing Mila's voice. The words echoed loudly in her head, sharp and unforgiving. Her eyes widened, as if she'd seen a ghost. She shivered from the chill bumps racing up and down her arm. How much did Mila know? Had she heard all of it or just bits and pieces?

She wrecked our family.

The sad part was, she truly had.

Chapter Twelve

Remi

The sun hung low, casting a golden light across the vineyard. Rows of grapevines shimmered in the breeze. Remi walked the length of the future *Joie* property, clipboard in hand, sunglasses perched on her head. She paused in front of the old stone building that would become the tasting room, its weathered charm undeniable. Bianca joined her, nursing a bottle of mineral water and wearing oversized sunglasses.

"You got that woman-on-a-mission look on your face again," Bianca teased.

Remi smiled faintly. "Talked to Leo this morning. He connected me with his architect friend. Really sharp guy. We already had a phone call. He gave me some solid advice about the tasting room."

"Damn. That was fast."

"I've got a pre-application meeting with Napa County next week," Remi added. "They'll walk me through the whole permitting process."

Bianca smiled. "I'm so glad you're doing this."

Remi looked around at the building. "Me too."

"Regardless of what happened that day, Gerard would be

proud. He would want you to move forward, even if it's without him."

Remi didn't answer right away. Her throat tightened as she thought of that last argument with Gerard.

"He loved the name—*Joie*. Said he could see me here, barefoot in the vines, pouring wine and laughing." Remi giggled. "I told him I don't see myself barefoot in anybody's vines. Not this girl."

Bianca laughed. "No, not at all. Not Remi, who was afraid of playing in the mud when we were kids—too afraid of getting your hands dirty."

"I wanted to be a little lady, not a mud dobber."

"You're still that way. Afraid to let your hair down. Sometimes you just need to throw caution to the wind."

"Sometimes throwing caution to the wind gets you in trouble. People need to think things through."

Bianca narrowed her eyes playfully. "Agreed. Sometimes they do. But sometimes you need to just go with your gut."

Remi looked away for a moment, then at Bianca. "And where exactly has throwing caution to the wind gotten you?"

Bianca chuckled. "Somewhere between freedom and heartbreak."

They both laughed.

Bas peeked through the glass and then tapped on the window. Remi waved him inside. He stepped into the building, his hands locked behind his back like a guilty teenager.

"I've been looking for Zoe, trying to see if she wanted to drive down to the beach today."

"Have you tried calling her?"

"Multiple times, but she won't answer. She won't talk to me at all, not since . . . Sage—"

"Do you blame her?"

"Sage is . . . I don't know. Things with her are not really that serious," he rambled.

Remi breathed heavily and then removed her sunglasses. She spoke in a calm, but heavy voice. "Bas, I know about the baby."

Bas froze. A flicker of panic crossed his face. He seemed to be caught somewhere between denial and wanting to ask how she knew.

"Oh," he finally muttered.

"Yes. I had no idea that she was going through something so painful, nor that she was so alone. While Zoe was slowly falling apart, you were in Boston at Harvard, cozying up to your new girlfriend . . . ."

"Sage and I—"

She didn't give him a chance to finish. "And where is she from anyway?"

"Her family lives in Virginia," he said.

"Why isn't she in Virginia for the summer?" Remi asked but didn't give him an opportunity to respond. She realized she was getting too worked up—too invested. "Never mind."

He paused, shaking his head. "We've only been seeing each other for a couple of months. She's barely even—"

"Barely even what? Your girlfriend?"

"Barely."

"But you can understand how hard this is for Zoe, watching you show up here with someone new, while she's still grieving a baby and now her father."

"I didn't realize that Mr. G—"

Remi interrupted. "Seems you didn't realize a lot of things!"

"I thought she was done with me," he said, his voice barely above a whisper. With pain in his voice, he continued, "I tried calling her over and over again, since Christmas."

"You haven't tried hard enough," Remi snapped. "You know Zoe; she's guarded."

"I'm so sorry."

"Does your mother know about this? About the baby?" Remi crossed her arms.

"No," he said quickly. "And I really don't . . ."

"What?" Remi stepped closer, getting in his face. "You want her in the dark like I was?"

Bas dropped his head; his six-foot frame seemed to slump under the weight of guilt. He ran a hand through his dark curls, then looked up at Remi with wet, red eyes. "I guess I should tell her, huh?"

"Best it comes from you and not me."

He nodded slowly. "Okay."

He started toward the door but turned back. "I really do love Zoe. I would never hurt her on purpose."

Remi raised her eyebrows. She believed him but wouldn't give him the satisfaction of him knowing that. She wasn't going to let him off the hook—not yet. Not while her baby was hurting.

"You'd better tell Paloma. She has a right to know too. Or I will."

"Okay," he said, giving her a faint, nervous smile. "Thank you for not killing me."

Remi didn't smile back. "It's not off the table."

After Bas left, Remi and Bianca laughed.

"That poor boy probably wet his pants."

"He needs to feel what Zoe's feeling and share the responsibility. That's some heavy stuff my baby is dealing with."

"Agreed." Bianca sipped her mineral water.

The sun had long dipped below the horizon, casting a deep indigo sky above the vineyard. Inside the house, Remi sat cross-legged on the living room floor surrounded by stacks of folders, envelopes, and Gerard's brown leather laptop bag. A fire burned gently in the fireplace, creating flickering shadows against the walls. She was grateful for the quiet—everyone had opted for an afternoon nap that lasted long into the early evening.

Zoe startled her when she walked into the living room, cradling a mug in her hands. Her fingers trembled slightly. She sat on the sofa, curled her legs beneath her bottom. Remi sat across from her, silent, patient, her eyes steady but not pressing. She opened Gerard's laptop and began trying to retrieve his password.

The silence stretched, thick but gentle.

Finally, Zoe exhaled. "I found out I was pregnant right before Thanksgiving break."

Remi didn't flinch. She only nodded slowly.

"I didn't tell anyone. Not even Bas, at first. I couldn't. It didn't feel . . . real, at first. A real little one growing inside of me." She paused, her voice catching. "I was so scared, Mom. Not just of being pregnant, but of what it would mean. It would change everything."

Remi reached over, placed her hand lightly on Zoe's leg.

"Then I told Bas I was pregnant. He was so happy. Such an idiot." She smiled a bit, forcing the tears to restrain themselves.

Remi couldn't help but smile too.

Zoe swallowed hard. "He kept saying it would be okay, we would figure it out, together. He said we'd get through it, that we needed to come up with a plan. I thought we had time to figure it out. But then I started bleeding . . . and suddenly the baby was gone. That was terrifying."

Remi's lips parted, but she didn't speak.

"It happened so fast," Zoe said, her voice barely above a whisper. "One day I was pregnant, and the next . . . I wasn't. I didn't tell anyone; I just went to the student health clinic and got checked out. Then I came back to my dorm like nothing happened. I didn't even cry that day. Not really. I just felt empty."

Remi moved to the couch next to Zoe, grabbed her hand and gripped it tightly.

"It was like this invisible loss," Zoe continued. "Like no one would believe how much it hurt because it was over before anyone even knew. And Bas . . . he kept calling, texting, wanting to know what was going on with me. I just . . . I told him that I lost the baby, but then I shut him out. I didn't know how to be with him anymore without falling apart."

Tears finally welled in Zoe's eyes. She blinked them away. "I didn't know what to do . . . so, I just carried it alone. Told myself I was strong enough. But I wasn't."

Remi didn't hesitate. She pulled Zoe into her arms and held her tightly; fiercely, like she was trying to protect her from every hurt she couldn't undo. Her own eyes stung, her throat thick. The ache in her chest swelled.

"You should never have had to go through that alone," she whispered, her voice shaking. "I would've carried it with you. All of it."

Zoe broke down. The tears came hard. The sobs shook her shoulders. She seemed to bury the pain into her mother's embrace. Remi held her like she was five and scared of a thunderstorm.

"I'm so sorry you went through this alone," Remi murmured. "So sorry I didn't see it."

Zoe shook her head. "You couldn't have known. I didn't let anyone in."

"But I'm in now. You hear me?" Remi pulled back just enough to see her face. "Whatever this next chapter looks like—for both of us, we'll do it together."

Zoe nodded, tears streaking down her cheeks.

Remi kissed her forehead, then stood up, wiping her own eyes.

They stayed like that for a while, both trying to catch their breath from the heaviness of what had been shared. Remi held her baby just a little longer. "I have something I need to tell you, sweetheart."

Zoe wiped her tears, her eyes widening. She looked up at her mother, searching her face. "What is it, Mom?"

"I can completely relate to what you're feeling," Remi said softly, "because I've been there, where you are now. When your dad and I were in college, I got pregnant. It was before you. Before we were married."

Zoe blinked. "What?" she whispered.

Remi's voice cracked, and she swallowed hard. "It was a boy. We were going to name him Gerard, a junior. Gerard 2.0 was the silly nickname we'd come up with." She chuckled, tried to catch her breath. "But—" her voice broke.

Zoe reached out, gently placing her hand on her mother's cheek.

"He didn't make it," Remi whispered, closing her eyes like it might soften the memory. It didn't. "He was gone before we ever got to meet him."

"Oh, Mom . . ." Zoe breathed.

"It was probably the hardest thing I've ever had to endure," Remi said, her voice thick. "Aside from losing your dad."

"What did you do?" Zoe asked. "Did you tell anyone?"

"I told Grandma Lorraine. She helped me through it. She let me talk about it as much as I needed to, until I was better. The pain never completely went away, though; it just got better over time."

Zoe nodded slowly, tears slipping down her cheeks. "It hurts so bad sometimes," she admitted. "Some days, I can't even breathe."

"You can talk to me about it as much as you want. I'm here." Remi cupped her daughter's face gently. "Therapy is an option, too, baby. Would you be open to that?"

"Maybe," Zoe said in a small voice. "I never really thought about it."

"Okay. We can talk more about it," Remi said. "You don't have to make any decisions right now."

Zoe gave a faint nod. "Okay."

Remi gave her a soft smile, brushing a tear from Zoe's cheek with her thumb. Then she rose to her feet, taking a deep breath. Her heart felt better, having gotten things off her chest. "All right. Enough heaviness for tonight. Let's play some music—something upbeat."

Zoe let out a weak laugh. "Mom, you know our taste in music is way different."

"Well, you play something."

Zoe reached for her phone, connected it to the Bluetooth and to the speaker. A beat dropped—Kendrick Lamar's "Not Like Us" filled the room with energy. Remi pulled Zoe up from the sofa, and they danced in the middle of the living room, clumsy and carefree.

"Oh wait, nobody told me there was a party going on." Bianca stepped into the room, a brightly colored casual romper hugging her curves. They hadn't even heard her coming.

She joined them on the floor, hips swaying effortlessly to the rhythm. Soon, Mila wandered in and, without a word, slipped into their circle. The four of them danced like it was the only thing holding them together. It was pure joy and beautiful energy until the doorbell rang.

"I'll get it," Bianca called, slipping from the rhythm and heading toward the door.

The others kept dancing and *singing*, the music pulsing through the room as Bianca opened the door and exchanged a few quiet words. She signed for the package, a box tucked in her arms.

"It's for you, Rem," she said gently, carrying it over to her.

Remi, catching her breath from dancing, sat on the sofa. Her laughter faded, the light in her eyes dimming as she glanced down at the return address on the package: New Orleans Funeral and Cremation Service.

The breath left her body. Not in a gasp, but as a slow, sink-ing exhale, like something had been pulled from her. She sank deeper into the cushions, her arms suddenly so heavy, her chest felt hollow.

"What is it, Mom?" Zoe's voice broke the silence. She stepped forward, concerned. "Who's it from?"

Remi didn't answer right away. Her fingers hovered over the edge of the box, frozen in place. Her throat tightened. When she finally spoke, her voice was barely a whisper.

"Gerard," she said. "It's his ashes."

The room went completely still.

Remi's fingertips trailed across the label on the box like it might vanish. Her eyes filled, but she didn't cry. Not yet. This was a different kind of grief. The final kind. The kind you could feel . . . deeply in your bones. She held the box in her lap and bowed her head. She held it like she was protecting him.

"I wasn't ready for this," she said, barely audible.

The music kept playing, as if unaware that the atmosphere in the room had changed. Zoe moved first, walked over and turned down the volume. The bass faded into a quiet hum. Remi sat frozen, the box resting on her lap like it might shatter if she moved suddenly. Her hands gripped the sides. She wasn't ready to open it—not yet.

Bianca sat beside her, wrapped her arm around Remi's shoulder. She whispered, "You don't have to do anything right now."

"I know," Remi said softly. "It just makes it so final."

Remi knew that Gerard was gone, but something inside of her still held out hope that he might walk through that door—as crazy as it may have seemed. The chances of this being summed up as a bad dream—well, receiving those ashes crushed all of that. It was real. His death was real. And the evidence was inside this box that she held in her hands.

Zoe knelt down in front of her mother, her eyes soft. "You don't have to open it tonight, Mom. Let's just sit for a bit."

Remi looked down at the box again, then at Zoe. "He

wanted to be here. This was his happy place." Her voice trembled. "I thought I was doing better, burying myself in bringing *Joie* to life."

Mila, who had been standing nearby, crossed the room and leaned down to kiss the top of Remi's head. "You *are* doing better, Aunt Remi," she said softly.

They sat still for a while. Four women. Two generations of love, heartbreak, grief—and unspoken strength.

Remi decided not to open the box that night. Instead, she placed it on the mantel and told Zoe to turn the music back on. She played something slower this time—Sade's "By Your Side." And Remi thought of Gerard and smiled. It was their song.

Chapter Thirteen

Bianca

She kept her voice low and tiptoed downstairs ever so quietly. She slid the glass door open and stepped outside. The morning chill crept beneath her robe as she pulled it tighter.

"So, you're saying that it's back—the cancer?" she asked in a quiet voice.

"I'm so sorry, Bianca. I wish I had better news. I wanted to wait for all your results to come back before I called, but the biopsy results confirm that the cancer has returned and is in your lymph nodes now." Dr. St. James paused for a moment, giving Bianca time to process the information. "I'd like to see you in my office—talk about some treatment planning. How long will you be gone?"

Her hands trembled as she struggled to hold the phone. Her breathing became erratic. Her chest tightened; a knot began to form in the pit of her stomach. She almost whispered, "Another week, maybe two."

She had promised Remi two weeks, but the third had already begun, and she'd quietly decided to stay a little longer. She hadn't said it aloud, but the peace and calmness of Napa had grown on her.

"I'm going to have my nurse call you to schedule an appointment. Or would you like for me to refer you to someone there in Napa? I have a colleague in the area—a woman. She's very good."

"I don't want to see anyone else," Bianca said. "How bad is it?"

"Honestly, I think with a good game plan we can tackle it."

Bianca stood. The weight of the world pressing into her chest. Her eyes stung, but no tears fell—yet. She looked out at the pool and then turned to look at the rows of vines. A breeze rustled the trees, then brushed against her cheeks.

"Are you still there?" Dr. St. James interrupted her jumbled thoughts.

"Yes," she said finally. "I'll be back in New Orleans in a few days."

Before her doctor responded, Bianca was already ending the call. She slowly slipped the phone into the pocket of her robe and lowered herself onto one of the patio chairs. Her hands gripped the arms of the chair tightly. A million thoughts filled her brain. Her heart ached, and fear rushed through her. Her shoulders slumped for a few moments, and then she pulled herself together.

The door creaked behind her, and she didn't have to turn around to know who it was.

"What are you doing out here?" Remi's voice was groggy and laced with concern.

Bianca wiped her eyes with the sleeve of her robe and stood. "Just didn't sleep very well last night. I decided to get some fresh air."

Remi stepped closer, watching her with quiet intuition. "Bianca—"

"I'm fine, friend," Bianca interrupted her and forced a smile. "I promise."

Remi didn't force the issue, but her eyes lingered. "Come inside. I'll make us some coffee."

"That sounds good." Bianca nodded, then tried to lift the mood. "Let's get this morning going and figure out what we're getting into today. What's on the agenda?"

"I have that meeting with Napa County officials," Remi said. "Licensing, permits . . . all the fun stuff."

As they walked inside together, the first light of day cast a shadow across the floor. And Bianca, still holding the weight of the secret in her chest, knew that soon she would have to tell her friend the truth. But not yet. Not while she was still recovering from receiving Gerard's ashes. Not this morning. Not while the world was still quiet. Not until she figured out her plan of action.

Remi moved with quiet purpose in the kitchen, pulling down mugs from the cupboard, setting the kettle to boil on the stove. Bianca leaned against the counter; arms folded lightly against her chest, as if holding herself together.

"You know," Bianca said after a moment, her voice casual but with the edge of something much heavier, "I used to think this wine country life was something of a fantasy. Too quiet. Too still for my taste."

Remi glanced at her. "And now?"

"And now it seems like the type of stillness I need."

Remi poured hot water into the French press, her back to Bianca. "Funny how that happens when life shakes you up a bit."

"Yeah."

Silence settled between them as Remi stirred the coffee in the French press. She turned to Bianca, her eyes warm and steady. "You know you don't have to pretend with me, right?"

Bianca hesitated for a moment. "I know. I'm just not ready to say it out loud yet. Because when I say it out loud—"

"It's real." Remi finished gently.

Bianca nodded with her eyes lowered.

"Okay, well, whenever you're ready I'm here." Remi handed

her a mug. "No rush. And don't worry about putting too much on me. I know that's what you're doing."

Bianca smiled at Remi's intuitiveness. She held onto the mug and nodded. "I'm going home for a bit, but I'll be back. There's something I need to handle."

Silence lingered between them for a moment longer.

"Okay. When are you leaving?" Remi asked.

"Within the next couple of days. Plus, I'd like to check on Chic Threads, make sure things are running smoothly."

"Okay," Remi said. "The girls are here. We'll hang out—keep one another company while you're gone."

Bianca smiled faintly. "Don't have too much fun without me," she said with a slight chuckle. "I'll be back."

"When do you think you'll return?"

The truth was, she wasn't sure how long she'd be gone. She didn't know what would unfold once she returned to New Orleans and met with her oncologist, but she needed to give Remi something. A timeline. "A week, tops." Bianca's smile deepened. "This place has grown on me."

Mila appeared in the doorway of the kitchen. "Are you leaving, Mom? Why?"

Bianca looked at Mila, that toboggan still covering her head. "Just for a little while, baby. I need to handle something in Louisiana."

"You made this big deal about me coming here to spend time with you. I put Dad on hold to come here, and now you're leaving. That's so messed up." Mila stormed from the kitchen in a huff and went back upstairs.

Bianca glanced at Remi. "That went well," she said sarcastically, but deep down her heart ached. Her daughter's disappointment made her feel helpless, like she would never be able to fix what was broken between them. It made her feel useless as a mother. What did she have to compare motherhood to, after all? Her own mother hadn't been there to teach her what it should look like.

"She'll be okay. I'll talk to her. Try to pick her brain."

"It's an uphill battle with her. But thanks. Maybe you can gain some insight." Bianca sighed heavily. "And what the hell is up with that toboggan? It's not even cute."

Remi laughed, sliding a mug of hot coffee in front of her. "No clue about that one."

The doctor's office was able to get Bianca in sooner than expected, and she didn't waste any time booking a flight back to New Orleans. Leaving felt strange—unsettling—but it was necessary. She needed to meet with Dr. St. James to map out a treatment plan.

She could hardly believe she was facing it all again—chemo, radiation, hormone therapy. The words alone made her chest tighten. She had been cancer-free for so long that the thought of going back to that world was surreal. No, not surreal—a nightmare. She had allowed herself to believe she was in the clear. So confident that it was behind her. But deep down, she always knew that it would return—uninvited, unwarranted, unfreaking welcome!

The first time had been three years ago—right after the divorce. Her body had betrayed her at the exact moment her life was falling apart. Harry had barely moved out before the diagnosis arrived. She remembered sitting in the exam room, still wearing her wedding band, as if it might offer some protection. It hadn't.

She was determined not to tell Harry, at first. She didn't want his pity, or him to return just because he felt sorry for her. Bianca had done her best to shield Mila from the worst of it, covering up the nausea, turning hair loss into a game of colorful scarves. But the exhaustion and the toll from the chemo, the fear, all of that was harder to hide, and soon Mila and then Harry became aware of it. However, it was Remi who had been there through it all. Her ride-or-die had helped her through the worst time in her life.

This time felt different, though. Not just because she was older, but because she was alone in a different way. Mila was grown now and pulling away. And Remi, her best friend, her anchor, was a thousand miles away dealing with her grief, while simultaneously chasing her own fresh start. She'd admired her friend, her sister, since the beginning of time. But the fact that Remi had her own stuff made this trip home that much heavier.

She peered out the window as the plane ascended, earbuds in her ears, the California vineyards slowly shrinking beneath her. Napa had felt like a cocoon, an escape from reality. But now, reality was waiting for her in New Orleans. And she'd face it too. It was what she always did. It was who she was, a fighter. And she planned to fight like hell.

Chapter Fourteen

Remi

Remi was at it again. She sat on the floor, her back against the sofa, surrounded by stacks of folders, documents, and Gerard's laptop, which she'd had Bas break into for her. It was amazing how kids knew how to get past passwords yet couldn't manage to fold their own clothes and put them away.

Zoe had agreed to drive down to the beach with Bas for a conversation, to hash things out, finally. On one condition: Sage wouldn't be there. Meanwhile, Mila was tucked away in her room, completely absorbed in the series that had her in a chokehold. She had barely emerged for food or daylight since Bianca left.

Leo had stopped by, making good on his promise of helping her sort through Gerard's documents. He emerged from the kitchen with two steaming cups of chamomile tea. "Tea break," he said gently, setting one mug beside her.

Remi glanced up with tired eyes. "Thanks. I've been at this for hours and I'm still not through half of it."

He settled beside her on the floor, stretching his long legs across the hardwood and moving some tax documents out of the way. Their shoulders touching. The smell of his cologne trickling across her nose.

"I know things are hard right now, but they'll get better. Grief doesn't leave, it just changes. The memories are what will keep you going."

"How long did it take for you to get some normalcy in your life?"

"'Bout a year before I started carving my own path, one that didn't include Viv. This is going to sound crazy, but . . . before that, I held on to this thought . . . this hope that she might return."

"I kept thinking the same thing—expecting that Gerard was going to walk through that door and tell me it was all a bad dream. That was, until I received his ashes by courier the other day." She motioned toward the box resting on the mantel.

"Damn. That's heavy. How you doing?" His eyes held a genuine, deep concern.

"I'm fine." She gave him a light smile.

"Once I let that go—realized it wasn't going to happen—that she wasn't going to walk through the door . . . that's when I was able to move on. It freed me, in a sense."

Remi grabbed Leo's hand and rested it on her knee, observed his well-manicured nails.

He had piano fingers. She'd heard her grandmother Lorraine say that about people who had long, skinny fingers. He pulled her hand to his lips, kissed the back of it. "I'm here for as long as you need me, until you get to that place where you can move on."

"I appreciate that," she whispered. Her eyes met his. Her palm found his cheek. With a faint smile, she said, "Now, help me finish going through these files."

"Let's get to work, then." Leo chuckled.

Remi came across a worn, leather-bound journal. She hesitated before opening it. Inside, Gerard's neat script filled the pages—business notes, scattered thoughts. She even saw ideas for the winery scribbled on notebook paper. *He was making his own plans for* Joie, she thought with a subtle smile. Tucked between two pages, a photograph caught her attention. A candid shot of the two of them—Remi's stomach the size of a watermelon. Both of them young, smiling like they had the world in their hands. Her throat tightened.

Leo seemed to notice the change in her posture. "What's up?"

She held up the photo with a soft, bittersweet smile. "We were so young. Just starting our family. So full of vision. We thought we had forever."

Leo reached over, gently took the journal, and set it aside. "You did start to build something. Something worth continuing. You're building *Joie*."

She blinked back tears. "I don't even know what that looks like without him."

"Maybe it's not about doing it without him," Leo said, "but with the part of him that's still here."

Remi looked at him, her eyes softened. "You always say the right things."

Leo gave a half smile. "I say what I mean. There's a difference."

She touched his arm. "Thank you."

"For what?"

"For being here."

"Anytime." He gave a small nod. "What is it that you're looking for in all of this stuff, anyway?"

She sighed. "Just trying to make sense of everything. I've found bank statements I didn't know existed, stock options, a trust I forgot he set up for Zoe. Another insurance policy. This man had money everywhere."

Leo took a sip of his tea. "He was diversifying." He chuckled.

"He was doing too much and not telling me." Remi giggled.

Leo reached for one of the unopened file folders.

"After reviewing these bank statements, I'm still trying to figure out who he made this five-thousand-dollar payment to. Just an odd payment that stands out."

"Let me see." Leo grabbed it from her. "You have to look at the detailed ledger."

"My eyes are starting to cross," Remi said.

Leo studied the bank statement. "Okay, here's the payment."

"Who's it to?" Remi asked, while taking a long sip of her tea.

"Looks like . . ." He paused for a moment. "Bianca Fuentes Perez."

"What?" She snatched the paper from his grasp. Observed the line item for herself. "Why in the hell would he give Bianca five thousand dollars and not tell me?"

Leo observed the other statements. "It wasn't a one-time thing, Rem. It was a recurring auto payment that spans . . . years, looks like."

Remi froze. Her heart started beating rapidly against her chest. The beating was so loud, it rang in her ears. A silent scream brewed in her belly.

Leo reached for one of the unopened file folders and flipped it open. "This one says 'Private—Personal Correspondence.' You wanna look—or no?"

Remi's mind raced. She didn't know if she was ready for more. She was stuck somewhere between curiosity and not wanting to know what was inside the file folder. The payments to Bianca already had her stomach in knots. "That's the folder that was in the safe."

Leo passed it to her without a word.

She sat there, closed her eyes for a moment, then opened it slowly.

Her thoughts drifted back to a time when a woman named Iris had invaded their lives. She'd been a co-worker at Gerard's firm, long before he started his own business. What started as a fling turned into months of betrayal. Late nights, secret phone calls. Gerard had insisted that Iris meant nothing—she was something to kill time while they were going through a rough patch. *A mistake,* he'd said. But Iris had fallen in love. She'd even called Remi on the phone just to tell her how much *in love* she was with Gerard—to declare that he was going to leave his family for her. He hadn't, of course. He'd apologized, begged her forgiveness. And though it had taken Remi months to forgive him, and even longer to trust him again, they had managed to move forward and start fresh. In time, they found their rhythm again. But now, with Gerard gone, she feared that somewhere in this stuff—in his belongings—Iris would be there, buried in the pages.

Her heart pounded in her chest. She didn't want to relive it again. Didn't want the pain to creep back in. But she braced for it as she reached for the thick bundle of printed emails and handwritten letters, clipped together. The pages didn't seem to scream Iris's name. No. But Bianca's handwriting she recognized immediately. Her hands trembled as she skimmed the pages.

Leo didn't interrupt, just silently watched her as she read.

Some letters were short. Others were rambling and emotional. They spanned several years. One from three years before simply read:

> *Gerard, my marriage is falling apart. Harry has learned the truth, and my relationship with Mila is crumbling. She's wondering why Harry is leaving us. I'm not sure how long I can keep the truth from her.*

She deserves to know you're her father. I'm not asking for anything more—you've been more than generous over the years—but she needs to know the truth. And so does Remi.

Remi's throat tightened. "Oh my God . . ."

"You okay?" Leo asked quietly.

Her breathing was rapid, scattered. She felt like her heart might stop at any moment—it seemed to skip a few times. Leo rested his hand on her shoulder.

"Gerard is Mila's father," Remi whispered in a daze, connecting the dots.

She wasn't sure if he understood the gravity of what she was saying. She said it, not necessarily to him but to herself. Leo gave her a moment. She exhaled slowly, dropped the pages into her lap. Her voice was hollow. "They both lied to me. For years."

Leo reached for her hand. She was grateful he didn't say anything to try to explain or justify Gerard's actions. He didn't ask any questions, either. He was just silent, allowing her to just *be*. She needed to make sense of everything. Remi let the silence settle between them, the fireplace whispering softly, crackling in its own rhythm.

She whispered, "This changes everything."

Leo looked at her steadily. "It only changes what you let it."

She blinked at him, tears threatening to fill her eyes. She got up and started pacing. Anger replaced the shock she'd felt only moments earlier. Then the hurt set in, followed by shock. Anger—shock—hurt, took turns filling her space like a roller coaster. She wanted to scream. "I don't know how to carry this."

"You don't have to. It's not your burden to bear. It's hers, now that Gerard is gone. She owes you some answers. She owes her daughter some answers as well."

She sat back down on the floor next to Leo, leaned into him slowly, her cheek against his chest. For a moment she let herself feel both the devastation and the comfort—grief tangled with betrayal. The pain was softened by his presence, just a little bit. But there was still a sting in her chest, and anger was beginning to develop again where the hurt once was. Outside, the wind rustled through the vineyard, as if the land itself understood the secrets that had just been unraveled.

Chapter Fifteen

Bianca

The flight to New Orleans had been quiet. Headphones in, sunglasses shielding her eyes although the cabin lights were dim, Bianca's thoughts were heavy. The news from her doctor still echoed in her thoughts—*the cancer is back*. Touching down at Louis Armstrong New Orleans International Airport stirred something inside her. It wasn't just the cancer, but thoughts of deception that had haunted her for many years of her life. She wondered if the cancer was the consequence of the betrayal she carried. Bad karma always had a way of striking those who deserved it.

Her Lyft dropped her off in front of her abuelita's old shotgun house in the Seventh Ward. She still owned it but hadn't lived in it for years. The porch sagged slightly, and the bougainvillea along the fence bloomed fiercely. Abuelita Josefina's birds of paradise also thrived in the front yard. Bianca stood on the steps for a few minutes before going inside.

The house was quiet. The staleness of being closed up hit her nose immediately. She dropped her bag near the door, flipped on the ceramic lamp, and walked slowly to the kitchen. Everything was exactly as she'd left it the last time she was there. She made coffee the old way—the way Abuelita made it—percolator on the stove. It was late for coffee, but she needed it. The coffee on the plane hadn't come close to satisfying her caffeine craving. She sat at the table with her phone. She texted Remi: **Landed. I'll call you later. Don't worry the girls. I'm okay.**

The lie came easily. She was far from being okay.

A few minutes later she was at her laptop, signed into her boutique's system, catching up on orders for Chic Threads and scrolling through inventory reports. She was trying to focus on anything that took her mind away from CT scans, lymph nodes, chemo, or the sobering tone of her oncologist's voice. The distraction didn't last long—the silence of the house pressed in.

Her mind drifted to thoughts of Chic Threads. It had been her one good thing. The thing that had given her so much pride, and forgiveness in a sense. She only wished Abuelita could've seen it. She'd have been so proud of the young girl who had given her so much grief. The girl who was complicated and had trouble following her around everywhere she went like a dark shadow. She had found herself in more bad situations than she could count. But Chic Threads was a far cry from the Bianca that Abuelita knew. The Bianca that Abuelita knew stayed woven in her grandmother's prayers.

She still remembered the night the cops had pulled her and Lissette out of a stolen car on Elysian Fields. She hadn't even known it was stolen—just that Lissette said they had a ride. She said her boyfriend had a new car, and Bianca didn't ask questions. The flashing red and blue lights, the cold metal cuffs pressed against her wrist, had her shaking. She was sixteen. That night could've gone a thousand different ways, but Abuelita had shown up at the station, the colorful wrap covering her salt-and-pepper hair. Rosary beads were strung from her neck like armor. She didn't say a word in the taxicab ride home, just held Bianca's trembling hand in silence. That silence, somehow, had said more than any lecture could have. She was disappointed, yes, but she gave her grace. She always did.

Maybe it was because she felt sorry for her. After Bianca's parents walked away, leaving her in Abuelita's capable hands, she had always been left to piece together her own sense of belonging. And although Abuelita was passionate about their Cuban heritage, consistent and unwavering about passing it on to Bianca and Antonio, the lessons never fully sank in—not right away. They were there always, but Bianca just chose to ignore them. She preferred to do her own thing. She was trying to find her way, and always hoping to make sense of the ache that came from being left behind. Her parents' absence had made her vulnerable. And that vulnerability had hardened into defiance. It was the reason she was so secretive about things, why she carried them like a shield. Because if she held them close enough, no one could take them away.

She had chosen to come here instead of her uptown home, to feel closer to Abuelita. This house, tucked away in the older part of their New Orleans community, still carried the essence of her grandmother—her spirit still suspended in the creak of the floorboards, the faint smell of rose water and tobacco, the soft sound of old Spanish lullabies seemed to echo faintly in the quiet of the house. Rosary beads were still looped over the bedpost in Abuelita's room. The curtains that she had sewn by hand still hung on the windows throughout the house. The kitchen drawers were still lined with the same floral paper—hadn't been replaced in decades. She told herself that she might refurbish the house, but she couldn't bring herself to erase Abuelita's memory. Even after her brother Antonio threatened to put it on the market, she'd somehow managed to keep him at bay, at least for now.

Bianca ran her fingers along the edge of the laminate countertop, remembering the mornings she used to sit at this very spot, watching Abuelita brew coffee and warm sweet bread on the stove. Back then life was simpler. Abuelita had been her anchor, the voice that reminded her she came from a family of strong, resilient women. Now, Bianca needed to feel that strength again, to remember that she was stronger than she was feeling. She had to remember who she was before the diagnosis, before the divorce, before the distance she now felt with Mila. She lit a candle in the kitchen to rid the house of the staleness.

Later in the afternoon, she met Dr. St. James in her private office uptown. The woman greeted her with a gentle hand on her arm and warm eyes, and a kindness in her voice that Bianca needed. "I've reviewed your charts, Bianca. We have a few options, and they're aggressive but promising."

Bianca nodded slowly. "What's the best one? I don't care how hard it is."

"I say we start with chemo and see how that works. After that we'll try radiation."

"Okay," Bianca said softly.

"We'll schedule a port placement and get your first round of treatment started as early as next week. Will that work for you?"

"Yes, I'll be here next week to begin treatment."

"Good. Let's kick butt." This time Dr. St. James gave her a smile. One that eased her fears, gave her a little bit of hope.

Walking out of the office, though, Bianca felt detached, like she was watching someone else's life unfold. She pulled out her phone again and there were no messages from Remi—not a single one. She hadn't expected to hear from Mila, but she'd thought Remi would've replied to her text from last night. Nothing. She started a text to Mila, then stopped. Started one to Remi, deleted it. Instead, she typed: **Two weeks, then**

I'm back. Save me a glass of wine. She meant for it to be light, but just as she pressed Send, her throat tightened.

That night, Bianca stood on her abuelita's porch with a glass of red wine she really didn't want and watched the street become dark. A neighbor's music played faintly—zydeco. Crickets buzzed in the night air. It was the kind of New Orleans night she remembered and loved growing up. She and Remi would play hopscotch in the middle of the street in the summer until the streetlights came on, and then they would retreat to their separate houses, only to do it all again the next night.

And now, facing the fight of her life for the second time, she told herself she would love again—and this time she wouldn't take that love for granted. She'd dance again, but to a new rhythm. She'd laugh again, but more heartily. It wasn't over. She had so much more life to live. She just needed to get through these next few weeks.

Chapter Sixteen

Remi

Remi studied Mila closely, taking in the curve of her eyes, the texture of her hair, the small, familiar mannerisms she'd seen a hundred times before, only this time she was observing them with fresh eyes. She searched for traces of Gerard in the girl—the child she had known since birth and had loved and cherished deeply as her own niece. But now everything was different. The truth had cast a shadow over every memory, every moment, and the thought of it made her stomach turn. Their relationship would inevitably shift. She just didn't know how.

Her relationship with Bianca would change too—irreparably. As far as Remi was concerned, their friendship was over. She had questions, yes, but once they were answered, there would be nothing left to say to the woman who had betrayed her in the most unforgivable way.

She sat with the weight of it. Years of shared history, of laughter, secrets, sisterhood—now tarnished beyond repair. Betrayal had silently crept in, slowly unraveling the threads of trust.

Remi thought back to the countless nights she and Bianca

had spent together like sisters—since they were children. Two girls, very different but drawn together in the chaos of middle school. Bianca, the loud one, the wild one, with flaming red streaks in her hair that drove her abuelita crazy and a laugh that carried across courtyards. Remi had been quieter, bookish, observant, cautious in ways most kids weren't. But Bianca saw her when others hadn't.

She remembered the first time Bianca stepped in to defend her. They were twelve years old. A group of girls had cornered Remi in the hallway, teasing her about her *proper* way of speaking. She had frozen, didn't know what to say or how to push back. But Bianca had stormed in like a hurricane, her backpack slung over one shoulder, her voice louder than the bullies'.

She's better than all of you, Bianca had snapped. *And if you've got a problem with her, you've got a problem with me.*

That's all it took. From that day forward they'd been inseparable. And nobody messed with her ever again.

There were many more times when Bianca had come to her defense. Their families were intertwined. She had loved Bianca's abuelita, as if she was her own grandmother. And Remi's grandmother Lorraine had embraced Bianca like family. Remi had confided in her about her fears, her grief, her loneliness after Gerard's passing. And all the while Bianca had been keeping *this* from her. It wasn't just about the betrayal; it was about the deception and the erosion of honesty between them. Remi knew that Bianca was secretive—it was just her way. But this was unacceptable. There was silence where there should have been truth.

Mila shifted in her seat in the chair across the room from Remi. She brushed hair from her face—the part that peeked from beneath her hat, as she flipped through the pages of a *Cosmopolitan* magazine. She was oblivious to the storm brewing behind Remi's composed observation of her. How would

Mila handle the truth when she finally learned it? Would she still see Bianca as the mother who raised her? Their relationship was already strained enough. Mila accused her mother of destroying their family. Would Mila also resent Gerard for what he had kept hidden? Would she still consider Harry her father after learning the truth? How would Zoe handle this after all she'd been through with Bas and the baby? Would they all look at Remi and expect her to fix it, as she'd always done? Would she survive this? Would she . . . would she . . . would she?

Remi wasn't sure of anything anymore. But she knew one thing: The truth changed everything. She had purposely ignored Bianca's calls and text messages. She didn't want to discuss this by phone. She wanted her in person, where she could see her face; observe her expressions. She needed her back in Napa, and if she didn't return soon, Remi was willing to fly to New Orleans just to confront her.

She picked up her phone, read Bianca's text, and then breathed deeply before typing the words: **When will you return to Napa? We need to talk.**

She stared at the screen after sending the message, her thumb hovering as if waiting to retract it, to pull the words back in and sit with her silence a little longer. But it was done. The message had been sent. Remi hated the way her heart pounded afterward, like she'd opened a door that she wasn't yet ready to walk through. She wasn't interested in apologies or explanations via text. This conversation needed eyes, breath, and presence. She needed to see Bianca's face when she asked her the question that was burning inside her since she found out the truth: *How could you?*

Not just how Bianca could sleep with Gerard—but how could she sit across from Remi, year after freaking year, pretending like it had never happened. How could she smile at Mila, knowing she had lied and covered up the truth for the child's entire life. How complex of a web she had weaved. It was unforgivable.

She then turned to her own daughter, who sat at the island in the kitchen, hunched over a bowl of cereal, slurping it down as if it was her last meal. Remi tossed her phone onto the couch and stared out the window at the vineyard.

Bianca's reply came quickly: **Sounds serious. I'll call you in a little bit.**

Remi responded without hesitation: **This is a conversation that needs to be had in person.**

She stared at the screen, watching the *typing* . . . bubble appear, disappear, then linger. Was Bianca reading? Thinking? Bracing herself?

Finally, a reply: **The girls okay?**

Remi typed back: **The girls are fine.**

Another pause, then: **I'll try to get a flight back tonight, then, if it's urgent.**

Remi typed: **It's urgent.**

Remi closed her eyes, a mixture of dread and relief washing over her.

She set down the phone again and exhaled, her fingers tapping absently against the phone. Remi wasn't sure what she would say first. The betrayal still burned in her chest like a fresh wound. Part of her wanted to scream, to demand an explanation, to hurl every emotion she'd bottled up since the truth had come to light. But another part of her—the calmer, steadier part—wanted to keep her composure. She deserved answers, but she wouldn't let Bianca see her break.

She walked over to the window, peering out of it. The vines stretched for acres, kissed by early summer sunlight. This place had become her sanctuary, her place of peace. She refused to let the past steal that from her.

Behind her, Zoe's voice called out. "Mom? Everything okay?" she asked softly, spoon paused in midair.

Remi turned to face her daughter, forcing a smile. "Yeah, baby. Just some things I need to take care of."

Zoe watched her for a moment, then nodded slowly and went back to her cereal.

Mila looked up from her magazine. Remi could feel her eyes and knew that her curiosity was pressing.

"Is my mom coming back?" Mila finally asked.

"Yes," Remi said. "Tonight, hopefully."

Zoe came into the living room, slid onto the sofa. "Are you two fighting?"

Remi hesitated before answering. She wanted to be honest with the girls—something Bianca hadn't been. "We're . . . not in a good place."

"Does it have something to do with Daddy?"

Remi took a deep breath. Zoe was more perceptive than she let on.

"Yeah," Remi said, quietly. "It's complicated."

Zoe moved from the sofa, came closer, and hugged her mother. "I'm sorry, Mom."

Remi held her daughter tightly, surprised by how much *she* needed the embrace. "Me too, baby."

The doorbell rang. Both of them froze. Remi looked at the clock on the wall in the kitchen. She moved to the door cautiously, opening it slowly. On the porch stood Leo—holding two takeout bags and wearing a smile.

"I brought lunch," he said. "Didn't think you'd have the energy to cook."

Remi stared at him, stunned at first. Then she softly said, "You really didn't have to."

"I wanted to." He held out the bag. "Thai food."

She took it and stepped aside. "Come in."

As Leo entered, Zoe grinned. "Hey, Leo."

"Hey, superstar," he said, giving her a fist bump.

"Have you met Mila?" Zoe asked. "She's like family."

Remi stepped in and explained, "Mila is Bianca's daughter."

Zoe's words lingered in the air, like a quiet revelation. *She's like family*. She had no idea just how much like family Mila truly was. The sentence struck Remi like a thunder bolt—panic surged through her chest, fast and unforgiving, like a freight train barreling through without brakes. She tried to steady her breathing, but the truth clawed its way up to her throat.

"Pleased to meet you, Mila." Leo gave Mila a nod.

"Same," said Mila.

Remi placed the food on the counter, still shaken by the weight of the evening—Bianca returning and the questions.

Leo reached into the bag. "And before you ask, yes, I brought spring rolls."

Remi gave him a small smile. "You're too thoughtful."

He leaned against the counter and lowered his voice to a whisper, "Pretty sure you needed a friend."

She met his gaze. "I certainly did."

In the quiet that followed, she let herself exhale. She was grateful for his presence. And they ate Thai food in the middle of the afternoon.

All day she'd been rehearsing what she would say to Bianca and imagining every possible outcome of their conversation. She wondered if there would be shouting, silence, tears—maybe all three.

The knock at the front door was more of a light tap. Remi didn't rush to answer it. She stood in the foyer, steadying herself. The sunlight had long retreated and there was only darkness against the windowpanes. When she finally opened the door, Bianca stood there, flight weary and unsure, her luggage at her feet.

Remi said nothing. Bianca's mouth parted—just slightly, as if to speak, but she hesitated. Her hair was pulled back into a sleek bun, and she wore black leggings with an embellished denim jacket. Her eyes were tired, and she suddenly looked older, more fragile. Maybe guilt had a way of aging a person.

"I took a Lyft from San Francisco," Bianca finally said, her voice hoarse. "Longest ride ever."

Remi stepped aside wordlessly, allowing her in. She was grateful that the girls had taken off for Bodega Bay and had planned to have a late dinner somewhere along the way back. That way she and Bianca could talk privately—or fight—whichever it ended up being. They walked to the kitchen without speaking, the air thick with years of friendship and betrayal. Bianca turned to face Remi, her posture stiff.

"Before you say anything," Bianca started, "I just want to say I'm sorry. I feared that when you started talking about going through Gerard's things—"

Remi leaned against the counter, arms folded. "You're sorry," she repeated, tasting the words, trying to feel something from them.

"I never meant for it to happen," Bianca continued. "It was a mistake, a moment of weakness—"

"No," Remi cut in, her voice calm but firm. "Stop calling it that. A moment is a kiss you regret. This was much more. Don't minimize it."

Bianca flinched as if the words slapped her. "You're right. It wasn't just a moment. But it *was* just a one-time thing, though—many, many years ago. It was a bad decision on both our parts. Alcohol played a huge role."

Remi looked down at the kitchen island. "You sat in my home. You ate my food. We laughed together, cried together. You played auntie to my daughter. All the while—"

"I didn't plan to sleep with Gerard."

Remi stared at her. There it was—the confession. Heart pounding raw truth.

"Yet you did." Remi's voice cracked, just slightly, and she hated the way it made her feel vulnerable. "You did."

Bianca's eyes brimmed with tears. "It was early in my marriage with Harry, and I was going through a tough period in my life. And Gerard . . . Rem, I didn't mean for it to happen. But it did. And I hate myself for it every day."

Remi was silent and just let her ramble on.

Bianca looked at her. "I didn't mean to betray—"

She was grateful for self-control because in her mind she wanted to drag her across the hardwood flooring, by her hair, no less. But what good would that do?

Remi interrupted. Her voice raised. "You absolutely *did* mean to betray me. You both did! You had every opportunity, nineteen years' worth of opportunities to tell me the truth, but you both held onto this secret for-fucking-ever. And the only reason you're telling me now is because you know that I know—"

"I wanted to tell you, Remi, I did. I begged Gerard . . . wanted us to come clean."

Remi hated the sound of her using the word *us* when referring to her and Gerard. It was difficult enough ridding her thoughts of them sleeping together, wondering when it was that it happened. Where it was and, moreover, where *she* was when it took place. She didn't want to know, not really. But then again, she did. It might've eased the anxiety she was feeling, and the tightness in her chest, or maybe it would intensify it.

"Gerard was terrified of losing you. You were his world," Bianca continued.

"And you?" Remi spat. "Were you his world too?"

"I was his very big mistake, and he never let me forget it."

"You had an obligation to me, an allegiance to me. You owed *me* loyalty, not Gerard."

"I, too, was afraid of losing you, Remi," Bianca admitted.

Remi paused for a moment, then she turned away from Bianca's watery eyes. She couldn't remember ever seeing her cry, even when her abuelita died. She'd held it together, refusing to let her guard down even then. She may have cried in private, but never in front of Remi. Still, Remi couldn't let the tears distract her from unleashing all her hurt and pain onto Bianca.

"And now, because you both were these selfish . . . fucking . . . individuals, we all have to suffer the consequences . . . because you couldn't abstain. And because of your secret, all of our lives are forever changed."

"You're right." Bianca dropped her eyes to the floor.

"Was it good for you? The intimacy with my husband?"

"I barely even remember it, Rem. It was so many years ago. And I was drunk."

"Like you were drunk the other night when you were pushing up on Leo? You wanted to screw him too?"

Bianca dropped her head in shame. And Remi regretted the words, but it was too late to take them back.

"I thought I knew you," Remi said softly. "You were one of the only people I trusted."

"I never stopped loving you, Remi. As my friend. As my sister." Bianca's voice cracked. "I messed up."

Remi exhaled long and slow, then turned away, gripping the edge of the countertop to steady herself. "I don't know what to do with this," she admitted.

"You don't have to do anything today," Bianca said gently. "Or tomorrow. Or ever. I just needed to say it. You deserved that much."

The silence that followed wasn't awkward—it was heavy. Finally, Remi broke the silence. "I need space. I need some time also."

Bianca nodded. "I'll go. I can probably get a flight out as early as morning."

"You can stay until morning." Remi said. "But then you have to go."

Bianca turned to leave the kitchen.

"Bianca."

She turned.

"If you really meant everything you just said," Remi said in a composed but distant voice, "then give me the dignity of rebuilding without you watching."

Bianca nodded, tears falling. "I understand."

Remi stood still, listening to Bianca's slow strides on the staircase.

She thought she would feel healed once she heard the truth, but she didn't. She didn't feel lighter, either.

All she felt was anguish.

Chapter Seventeen

Remi

Remi didn't move from the doorway for a long time. The weight of what happened the night before pressed on her chest like a stone. A part of her wanted to crumble to the floor and cry. Another part—the stronger one—stood upright, steady. She had survived the truth. The kitchen clock ticked loudly. A pot of coffee she'd brewed earlier sat on the counter, untouched. She poured herself a cup anyway, hands trembling slightly. She walked out to the sunporch. The sun was brighter now.

She pulled the afghan tighter around her arms and sat down in one of the wicker chairs, legs tucked beneath her. This porch had been her refuge throughout a few summers but had somehow managed to bear witness to several stages of her life—joy, grief, hope, now betrayal. She had shared wine and dreams with Gerard on this same porch. Now, as she sat here alone, what she felt was anger toward him. He had been her everything. She knew him better than she knew her own self—loved him with every fiber of her being. He was the yin to her yang, and even when he'd messed up with Iris, she'd forgiven him.

In the distance she could see Leo making long strides toward her house. She tried with all her might to still her heart—which seemed as if it were going to burst out of her chest. She tried to get herself together before Leo saw her falling apart.

He stepped onto the porch. "Good morning." His smile was bright like sunshine, which was what she needed.

"Good morning to you," Remi said, attempting to make her voice smile, though her face wasn't smiling at all.

"You better?"

Remi nodded. "I don't know. I think so. I will be."

He sat in the wicker chair beside hers, a cup filled with coffee gripped in his hand. "She's gone?"

"Yes."

Leo didn't push. He just sipped his coffee.

After a while Remi asked, "Do you think you can forgive someone for something like that? Something that rips the floor out from under you?"

Leo looked out toward the hills. "I think forgiveness is less about them and more about you, Remi. It's about whether you want to carry that weight for the rest of your life."

Remi absorbed his words in silence. She knew she wasn't ready to forgive, not yet. Maybe she never would be. But she also didn't want to carry someone else's burden, nor live in bitterness for the rest of her life.

"I just want to focus on *Joie*," she finally said. "This winery was supposed to be a new chapter. Supposed to bring me joy."

"And it will be, Remi," Leo said. "It's going to be everything you dreamed of and more."

She smiled faintly. They sat for a while longer in comfortable silence. Her phone buzzed and she picked it up. It was a message from Paloma: **Your bottling equipment is set to arrive this week! Let's talk about marketing and social media, okay? Everything's moving forward. So proud of you, amiga. Joie is happening.**

Remi stared at the message, her heart swelling with hope. She needed hope at that moment. It was like a rainbow after a storm.

"Let's do something today," Leo suggested with a beaming smile. "I know just the thing, if you're game."

"I'm game," Remi replied.

The wind was playful along the Sonoma Coast, teasing Remi's curls as Leo maneuvered his drop-top white Mercedes up the winding route of Highway 1. The sky was perfectly blue—not a cloud in sight. A cooler sat on the red leather back seat of his car, filled with vegetables from the farmers market, aged cheese, prosciutto, and a bottle of white wine. The sound of Kirk Whalum's saxophone belted from the speakers and serenaded them. Remi enjoyed the drive; she felt a sense of peace, solace, a temporary escape from reality. The farther they drove along those cliffs, the more she almost forgot about the truths she'd uncovered and the confrontation that had taken place just last night. *Almost.*

Leo found a perfect spot for a picnic. He spread a handwoven blanket out on the ground—a deep navy one that he'd packed into his trunk.

"Cheers," he said, pouring wine into the stemless glasses and passing one on to her.

"To beginnings," she added. The glass was cool in her hand. The wine crisp, floral, citrusy.

Seagulls passed overhead. Down the slope, a family with two children chased each other through the sand, their laughter carrying over the waves that crashed against the shore. Her mind drifted to Gerard and Bianca, but she tried not to let the thoughts consume her—tried not to visualize them together.

The waves were steady, relentless, and she liked that about them. No matter the storm, no matter the change, the sea always returned itself.

"I'm not ready to forgive either one of them," she whispered.

Leo passed her a bundle of green grapes. "Then don't. Until you're ready," he said. "You deserve to move at your own pace."

They ate in the kind of silence that didn't require filling, the kind that healed. Around them, the coast pulsed with life, seagulls cried, the scent of salt from the ocean danced in the wind, the sea whispered. And she found herself listening intently to all of it.

"At least I have Zoe," Remi said out of the blue. "She's the one good thing in all of this. He gave me Zoe."

"That is a good thing. Vivian and I didn't have any children together, and my son—my son before Vivian . . . our relationship is a little strained."

"I didn't know you had a son. Is he here . . . in Napa?"

"No, he's in Virginia. Stationed there. He's a Marine," Leo said. "He followed in my footsteps."

"You were a Marine?"

"Once a Marine, always a Marine. Always faithful. Semper fi." Leo reached into his wallet and pulled out a worn photo, its edges curled.

Remi took it and studied the face of a young man in full dress uniform, decorated with gold buttons down the front and medals pinned on the lapel, a white hat perched proudly on his head. "Look at you." She smiled widely. "Looking all serious."

"It was a serious time in my life." Leo smiled broadly.

She handed him the photo back. "Why is your relationship with your son strained?"

Leo sighed. "After I divorced his mother . . . he pretty much divorced me too."

"That's tough," she said softly. She felt the ache behind his words.

"Yeah." He nodded. "Hopefully one day we'll figure it all out. But until then, I have to keep on living."

"Understood," she said, her voice gentle.

As the sun began to set, they packed up the picnic basket. The sun softened as they drove from the coast. The temperature was much cooler now too.

Remi looked over at Leo. "I had a good time today. Thank you for the daycation. It was nice just to *be*—without having to feel. Or explain."

Remi looked down at her hands, resting on her knees. Her wedding ring still on her finger. She hadn't taken it off. Not because she didn't want to, but because she didn't know what to replace it with. That ring had become a part of who she was—a wife. Even though he was gone, and even though he'd betrayed her—she was still his wife.

After a moment she continued. "You are one of the few people who understands me. Understands what I lost. What I'm carrying."

She caught Leo studying her. He seemed to be looking at the soft edges of her profile against the window of his car. "You've always been carrying something, Remi," he said. "I always saw past your polite smile. There has always been a heaviness about you."

Remi blinked, the weight of his words settling against her chest. "What do you mean?"

"I mean . . . you give so much to everyone else, Remi. To Gerard. To Zoe. And from what you told me, to Bianca. You seem to have a need to take care of everyone. But you rarely give anything to yourself."

She was quiet, her lips pressed together. The fact he saw all of that mystified her. She knew it was true, though. She had, in fact, buried her wants behind everyone else's needs for so long. But now stepping into her own life again felt both thrilling and terrifying.

"You being here—it means more than you probably realize," she said.

Leo reached for her hand but didn't take it. He only let his fingers brush against hers.

Remi looked down at their hands. That simple touch sent a wave through her. Not a dramatic wave—just . . . human. She exhaled, slow and long.

"I think I forgot how to hold myself up, instead of everyone else."

"You did what you needed to," Leo said. "That's not a crime. But now? Now maybe it's time to live."

For a long moment neither of them spoke. The sky over Napa was beautiful with twilight approaching—lavender blue with specks of gold where the sun had already started disappearing. He reached for her hand—fully this time. She didn't flinch, nor retreat. She let her hand rest in his, palm to palm, fingers curled together. Remi allowed herself to feel—not like someone's wife. Or someone's mother. Or someone's anchor—but to just feel like herself.

Chapter Eighteen

Bianca

Bianca's decision not to return to New Orleans hadn't come easily. It gnawed at her all night at Remi's. As much as she wanted to be at Abuelita's home during this time when she felt so broken, the truth was, she was exhausted. She was tired of pretending to be strong and in control, when clearly she wasn't. The cancer treatments would cause her to feel weak and vulnerable. The fact that she'd hurt her best friend in the entire world, well, that caused her the most angst.

As much as she wanted Dr. St. James to administer her care and treatment, her body said otherwise and made the call for her. The idea of another flight was more than she could bear.

So she stayed.

Staying meant compromise—going to someone new, someone local, who could continue her treatment plan. Someone she didn't know, and who knew nothing about her. A stranger who hadn't known her history, nor what she went through during her first bout with cancer. Dr. St. James promised to coordinate everything, to connect her with a local oncologist in Napa, someone with the same treatment protocol. It made sense medically, but emotionally . . . not so much. But Bianca, exhausted, let herself say yes.

She couldn't stay in Napa, not near Remi, who had warned her to stay away. There was so much that remained unresolved between them. There were too many words between them, some spoken in anger, others never said at all. And Bianca didn't have the strength to hold her own pain while carrying the weight of someone else's disappointment—not right now.

So she rented a beach house on Bodega Bay, at least an hour away, something modest, tucked above the dunes. It was a place where the ocean could speak for her when she didn't have the strength to talk. A place far enough from everything to give her room to breathe.

When she arrived there were no grand entrances, no flurry of text messages, just a Lyft from Napa to Bodega Bay. A pair of dark sunglasses barely hid the dark circles beneath her eyes. She touched the keypad on the door, stepped into the house with her suitcase in tow, and looked around the space. The smell of saltwater drifted through the open patio door, the sheer white curtains blowing in the wind to a rhythm of their own. She made her way through the house, taking note of how much thought had gone into bringing the beach inside to this space, and how comfortable it was. The two bedrooms in the back each opened to small decks—perfect for early morning coffee or late-night glasses of wine. She took note of the kitchen. It was small, but open and airy. It would work, and besides, she wasn't sure how many meals she'd be preparing—maybe a cup of broth here or there, something to help settle her stomach after the chemo. Her treatments would make her feel fatigued and sick most days.

She was thinner, paler. Her signature lipstick was absent, and her hair pulled back into a haphazard knot. After settling in, she placed the teakettle on the stove, made herself a cup of hibiscus tea with honey the way she liked it. She collapsed onto the couch with a quiet sigh. With the television muted, she watched from the large window as the waves crashed against the shore.

The house was eerily quiet. It pressed down on her chest like a weight. Bianca lay on the sofa, her hands curled around the mug of tea. Her head ached from the kind of pain that broken relationships brought with it. The truth was that cancer hadn't broken her. It was the guilt that had done her in. The stillness gave her no place to hide, at least not from the memories or the choices she'd made. And especially not from the face she couldn't stop seeing when she shut her eyes—Remi's, the moment Bianca realized she knew the truth.

Remi had always been the anchor in their friendship—practical, grounded, fiercely loyal. Bianca had often been the messier one—impulsive, prone to tangents and making risky decisions. Remi had loved her through it all. She had supported her when Harry left, not realizing the real reason behind his leaving. He knew the truth. He had overheard a conversation between Bianca and Gerard, an argument about whether their spouses should know the truth.

It had taken all her physical strength to keep Harry from rushing over to Remi's and Gerard's home in the middle of the night to not only confront Gerard *but to beat the living shit out of him*, as he put it. He deserved it, in Harry's opinion. And Remi could *do better*, as far as he was concerned.

Harry cried when he learned that the beautiful girl who had called him Daddy for the past sixteen years of her life was not his biological child. "She's mine anyway," he said angrily, voice raised in a way that Bianca had never heard.

"You two won't take that away from me. I will fight you with everything in me."

Bianca didn't dare challenge him. She had too much to lose. Her mind drifted to the night that had haunted her for so many years. Remi and Gerard had thrown one of their holiday parties. Gerard had cooked up a feast as usual, his specialty—a spread of Creole classics that filled the house with warm, spiced aromas. Shrimp and grits with just enough heat to make your eyes water, gumbo thick and dark like the bayou, sweet potato pies, and bread pudding. The fireplace crackled. Guests spilled out onto the wraparound porch, glasses of wine in hand, laughing and dancing under the strings of white lights.

It had been a perfect night. New Orleans–style Christmas songs played on the stereo. Remi had drunk too much for a woman who was with child—though she didn't know she was pregnant at the time. It was what made her sick. Zoe was already growing in her belly, and she didn't even know it. Remi had gone upstairs to lie down, completely oblivious to the moment that was about to unfold.

They'd all been drinking that night. There wasn't a sober soul in the house. Bianca and Gerard had been left to wish their guests a peaceful night, to clean the kitchen and put food away. Gerard had been blowing out candles in the kitchen when Bianca walked in and placed the silver ice bucket on the kitchen counter. She paused, watching him. The one-too-many glasses of Merlot had caused her head to spin. The top two buttons of his shirt were undone, sleeves rolled up to his elbows. They both reached for a glass at the same time, the touch lingering a lot longer than it should have. He caught her eye and smiled faintly, a quiet kind of smile that said *thank you for being here*, and something else.

Bianca could still smell his cologne, even now—something

woodsy and expensive. The silk of her hunter-green dress brushed against her thighs. She still remembered the taste of cognac on his tongue. The way his hands explored her body. The way he pushed himself inside her, with no thought of the consequences that would follow.

The shame burned through her chest the moment it was over. And it burned even now. The truth was, she could've stopped it. She should have, but something in her wanted to feel wanted, to taste what Remi had. Bianca wanted to win, even if it meant losing everything.

Remi had looked radiant that night, glowing in a deep burgundy dress that she had chosen with great care. She was proud of their beautifully decorated home, the people they'd invited. Bianca had betrayed her that very night. She had cracked the foundation of everything—destroyed their friendship and so much more. And now she was trying to patch together the ruins of it, while her body waged war on itself.

Bianca placed the cup on the coffee table and buried her face in her hands. She needed music. Music had always been her healer. It lifted her spirits when she was low, cradled her. Even as a child, when life felt uncertain, music had soothed her soul.

And nobody did it for her like Prince Rogers Nelson.

She had fallen in love with him at a young age, had every album he ever released. Prince was her guy. She saw herself in his story, in his music. In a way his unstable childhood mirrored hers. His parents had separated when he was ten, sending his world spinning. Bianca had been twelve years old when her own parents left. The abandonment still burned deep within her. Like Prince, she had found comfort in melodies when words weren't enough.

She smiled, remembering the night she dragged Remi to

one of his concerts at the Saenger Theatre in downtown New Orleans. Dressed in purple and sequins—Bianca's hair in a spiky twist with purple streaks and Remi's golden tresses pulled up into a '90s hip-hop style, with two Afro puffs on each side of her head. They'd climbed into the back seat of Grandma Lorraine's Caprice Classic, sliding against the white leather seats as she pulled out of the driveway.

"I don't know what y'all find so fascinating about this Prince fellow," Grandma Lorraine said in her thick New Orleans drawl, and peered at them in the rearview mirror. "He wears tight pants and high-heel shoes."

The girls had burst into laughter.

The truth was, Remi hadn't found him fascinating at all. She was just along for the ride because Bianca had insisted. Bianca, on the other hand, had kept every vinyl, every CD. And when Prince died, she'd mourned like she'd lost family. It was personal for her.

Now, as "Let's Go Crazy" rang out from her Bluetooth speaker, she danced like she had back then—younger, free, and more alive. She let the music push back the heaviness she was feeling.

She unpacked her suitcase, placing neatly folded underwear into drawers, hanging dresses and slacks in the closet, lining up shoes along the wall. Then she found herself at Whole Foods, gathering what she needed to nourish herself: fresh vegetables, meats, juices, freshly ground coffee beans. All the essentials. The treatments would last for weeks. She was preparing her space and her spirit for what lay ahead.

As the sun began to set over the bay, casting soft orange streaks across the water, Bianca settled into a wicker chair on the deck. She watched as the waves crashed gently against the shore. The sliding glass door cracked just a little, for the music inside to drift out. She held a glass of store-bought wine in her hand—not the kind Remi would've approved of, not something worthy of celebration. But it reminded her of her friend all the same. And with that thought came the ache in her heart, that hurt in the pit of her stomach. She wouldn't get to see *Joie* come to life. She wouldn't walk through its doors or sip from its first vintage, like they'd talked about doing.

She took a sip of the wine, letting it rest on her tongue for a moment. Remi would've teased her for drinking something so ordinary. And they would laugh about it. They laughed about all sorts of things—their families, their children, about life. Always dancing. Remi had a way of making everything feel like art, even the everyday things. *Especially* the everyday things. Remi was laid-back and cautious, but she always thought outside the box. She moved through the world with care, but her ideas were bold, untamed, and full of vision. She had helped in the early stages of Chic Threads. Part of it was her vision.

Bianca remembered that afternoon on Remi's porch in New Orleans, a pitcher of sweet tea resting on the table. They were supposed to be sketching out a business plan, with budgets, timelines, and vendor lists. Bianca had even brought a notebook over. But then, Remi came out of the house with a vision board and a pack of scented markers.

Bianca had rolled her eyes. "Seriously? We're not building a bank."

Remi just grinned. "No, we're building your dream, sweetheart. Watch and learn."

And then she'd taken over the porch floor, cutting out pictures of women wearing the latest fashions—bold jewelry, shoes, cosmetics. She'd scribbled words in big, loopy handwriting: *power, beauty, own your space.* At the time, Bianca thought it was ridiculous. But now that board lived in the back room at her boutique, proudly displayed—creased at the corners, edges curled, but still holding every ounce of Remi's spirit with it.

She sat there for a bit longer, sipping her ordinary wine, lost in memories of moments that would never come again.

Chapter Nineteen

Remi

Remi stood in the center of the space, at the heart of *Joie*. The winery wasn't just about wine. It was about rebuilding, repurposing, reclaiming something of her own. Over the past few weeks, her mornings had begun before dawn, coordinating with contractors, purchasing new equipment—a fermentation tank, crushers, filtration equipment, and even bottling equipment. Afternoons were blurred with design meetings and endless paperwork. And it was time she considered hiring some experienced staff.

This evening, though, as Remi balanced herself atop a wine barrel where the tasting room would soon take shape, sifting through a stack of invoices, Paloma appeared with two glasses and a chilled bottle of rosé.

"Ignore all that for an hour," she said. "We're drinking this one because we made it. Remember that barrel I told you we didn't think had aged well? Turns out, it aged perfectly."

Remi accepted the glass, and Paloma poured wine into it. She gave it a gentle swirl and inhaled. "Mmm. Smells nice." She took a sip and closed her eyes. It was tart, crisp, and laced with sunshine.

"Good, huh?"

"So good."

Paloma hopped up onto the neighboring barrel, settling beside her. The two women shared laughter and the bottle. Amid all the hustle, they hadn't made time for the talk that needed to be had between mothers.

Paloma had survived the death of a husband, for much longer than Remi had. Her husband, Pedro, had passed on when Bas was three. She had raised her son on her own. She was a single mother, who worked hard and who had insisted her son grow into a man of integrity. And he had. Her values ran deep in him.

"I assume Bas talked to you about . . ." Remi began.

"He did," Paloma said softly, exhaling. "I'm so sorry they had to go through that, experiencing grown-up things neither of them was prepared for."

"I wish I had known. I could've at least been there."

"Same."

"I didn't even know they were involved like that. I thought they were just friends—summer friends."

"Mi amiga," Paloma chuckled gently. "You missed all the signs. I suspected it a couple of summers ago. I saw the way he looked at her—with real love, real care. He was infatuated even then."

"Really?"

"Yes. She breathes life into him," Paloma said. "He doesn't look at Sage that way."

"She seemed to come out of nowhere. And Zoe wasn't exactly thrilled. Not at first."

"I don't think Sage is anything serious. More of a pastime than anything else. I guess that's why she left a couple of days ago."

"Oh, she did?"

"She didn't fit. Cut from a different cloth, that one."

The women laughed.

Remi swirled the last of the rosé in her glass, watching the pale pink liquid catch the fading light. "It scares me a little," she admitted. "Zoe and Bas. Everything between them—it wasn't just teenage love. It was real. And real things leave marks."

Paloma nodded. "They carry each other, though. Even now."

"She was never quite the same after she lost the baby," Remi said. "I knew something was happening because she was quiet in a way that made me nervous."

Paloma leaned back on her hands, sighing. "I knew Bas was heartbroken about something, too. Something deep and serious. I remember walking into his room when he was home for Thanksgiving and finding him staring at the ceiling, not even pretending to study. And Bas is always doing something. That stillness—I know now that it was grief."

"I never knew," Remi whispered.

"They tried to do the right thing," Paloma said. "They were young, but so sure of each other. And when things got too hard, they didn't ask for help. Those kids just tried to handle it on their own."

"We did the same thing as kids." Remi's voice turned gentle. "Do you think they still love each other?"

Paloma didn't answer right away. She gazed outside at the vineyard, where the rows of vines stretched like a quilt across the earth. "Love like that? It doesn't disappear. It might quiet down, change shape, but it doesn't vanish. I think they're both still trying to figure out how to carry it."

Remi nodded slowly, her chest heavy with the weight of what happened between her and Bianca. "Maybe this place," she said, gesturing around them, "can be healing for all of us."

Paloma reached out for Remi's hand. She took it—held tightly. "Then let's make it a place where healing can happen."

They sat in silence—sipped rosé, the evening wrapping around them. Somewhere beyond the fields, the sun shone brightly, and then a breeze swept gently through the open window and brought with it a certain freshness that was full of possibility.

The scent of fried chicken hit Remi the minute she stepped through the door. Sade's smooth voice floated through the house, wrapping around her like an old friend. In the kitchen she found Mila at the stove, nervously flipping chicken, jumping each time the grease popped. Zoe was beside her, stirring something in a large bowl.

"What in the world is going on in here?" Remi froze, taking in the scene—flour all over the counters and some on the floor, and dishes stacked high in the sink.

"We're making you dinner." Mila made the announcement cheerfully.

Zoe looked up from whatever she was mixing. "We wanted to surprise you, Mom. You deserve it."

"Yeah," Mila chimed in. "So just go in there and relax, put your feet up. We got you."

"That's very sweet of you both, but—"

"Mom," Zoe cut in, firm but loving. "Let us take care of you, like you always take care of us."

"Do you want to hear something else—something a little more upbeat?" Zoe nodded toward the Bluetooth speaker. "I mean, Sade can be depressing sometimes."

"Music's fine." She raised an eyebrow at her daughter and said, "And Sade is not depressing. She's . . . passionate."

Zoe giggled. "If you say so."

Remi smiled and did as she was told. She sank onto the living room couch as the fire swayed to the music from the fireplace. She slipped off her shoes and stretched out her legs. From the kitchen she could hear the clatter of utensils and the girls' laughter in between the sizzle of frying chicken.

She closed her eyes for a moment, taking it all in—the music, the smells, the unexpected care from the girls. She smiled. When she opened her eyes Mila called from the kitchen, "Do you like garlic mashed potatoes or roasted ones?"

Remi smiled. "Either. I trust the chefs."

Mila grinned and disappeared back into the kitchen.

Watching Mila move around in the kitchen the way Gerard used to unnerved Remi—just a little. Her thoughts moved to an uncomfortable place, but she willed them back. She didn't want to ruin the girls' surprise with thoughts of Bianca and Gerard—and their betrayal. And she certainly did not want their betrayal to change the way she thought of Mila—the girl she'd loved since the day she was born. The child she had watched take her first steps. The teenager she'd talked to about her menstrual cycle because she started it while spending the weekend at her house. She loved her, and that wouldn't change—but she couldn't control these thoughts that constantly clouded her brain.

A few minutes later Zoe appeared with a glass of wine. "Your favorite," she said, offering it.

Remi took it. She was touched. "I don't know what I'm going to do with you two."

Zoe nodded, cocked her head to the side playfully. "Just love us."

"I do love you," Remi said. "I've been really busy with the winery lately. It's nice to relax."

Zoe flopped onto the couch beside her, curling her legs under her. "That's why we're doing it. Tonight, no emails. No calls. No vineyard stuff."

"*Vineyard stuff?*" Remi laughed. "Okay, okay. I surrender."

Just then, a loud pop came from the kitchen, followed by Mila's yelp.

"I'm okay!" she called out. "Just some aggressive grease."

Remi and Zoe exchanged a look, then burst into laughter.

The music shifted to another Sade classic—slow, sultry, and familiar. The house was full of noise, full of mess and full of love. It was exactly what she needed.

They decided to eat in the formal dining room and pulled out the good china, which the girls appreciated, making them feel as if their meal was special. The room was filled with lively conversation and laughter. The girls knew that something was amiss between Remi and Bianca, but they didn't bring it up—didn't ask any questions—not yet.

"Mom . . . question," Zoe began.

Remi froze. *Here it was*, she thought. The questions about Remi's and Bianca's fight.

"I'm listening," said Remi.

"Say you have this friend—" Zoe said.

Remi's heart pounded. She wasn't ready to divulge what was going on with Bianca, or reveal truths that would change their lives forever. Matter of fact, it wasn't her place to tell them. She wouldn't bear that burden. Not now. Not ever.

"Say your friend went to this frat party, and someone slipped something in her drink."

Mila gave Zoe a sideways glance. Zoe gave her a look that said *it's okay.*

Remi's eyes moved quickly between the girls, from Zoe to Mila, and then back to Zoe.

Zoe continued with her hypothetical statement. "What if she passed out, and when she came to, she was in one of the bedrooms of the house, completely naked? And she didn't know what took place. She just grabbed her clothes and ran out of there as fast as she could."

"Did this friend of yours go to the police?"

"No," said Zoe. "But she went to the clinic, where she found out she was raped."

"She should've filed charges."

"What if she doesn't know who to file charges against—doesn't know who did this to her?"

"Has this friend talked to her parents—her mother?"

"She doesn't have a good relationship with her mother. It's not like you and me, Mom. I can talk to you about anything, just about. She can't talk to her mom like that."

At that moment, Remi knew.

She looked at Mila—straight in the face. "When did this happen?"

Mila didn't say anything at first. She just dropped her head and stared at her plate for a moment. When she looked up tears began to flood her eyes. Her voice cracked. "Before Christmas break."

Remi understood. The anger, the distance, the toboggan on her head—*all the time*.

"Remove the hat. Let me see your hair."

Mila slowly removed the hat from her head, her face drenched in tears. A bald spot sat at the crown, jarring Remi. Remi's heart ached. She stood, walked over, and reached out instinctively but stopped herself, afraid to make Mila feel worse.

"Oh, baby . . ." she whispered. "Why didn't you tell someone?"

Mila just shook her head, shoulders curling inward as though trying to disappear.

Remi wrapped her arms around her, held her tight.

"Do you want to do something about it? Go to the police? Get a lawyer?" Remi asked. "You might want to talk to someone who can help you through the trauma of it, sweetheart. Because clearly, it's taken a toll on you."

"No, I want to forget it ever happened—erase it permanently from my brain," Mila whispered. "I want my hair to stop falling out."

"Sweetheart, your hair won't stop falling out until you find peace, until there's a resolution."

"I wish I could transfer to a different school. I couldn't wait for summer break because I don't want to go back there."

Remi smoothed Mila's hair gently, her hand pausing at the rawness of the bald spot.

"Then I will advocate for you not going back." Remi wasn't sure how she would do that, considering she wasn't speaking to Bianca—and wasn't sure if she would again. "We'll figure something out."

Mila looked at her, eyes wide. "Promise?"

"I promise to do what I can, sweetheart."

Fresh tears slid down Mila's cheeks.

"We'll deal with it," Remi said. "There are other schools. Other paths. What matters is you. Your safety, your mind, your heart."

Mila bit her lip. "What if I'm never okay again?"

"You will be," Remi said softly. "Maybe not all at once. But you will in time. We'll take it one step at a time."

"Thanks, Aunt Remi."

Remi held her until she stopped trembling.

Zoe mouthed the words *thank you*.

"I guess I should tell my mom, huh?" Mila asked softly.

"I really think you should." Even through her anger, Remi found herself on Bianca's side, fighting for her as a mother. "She loves you and wants so desperately to repair what's broken between you. This would be a good start."

Mila didn't respond; she just dropped her head.

"Give her a chance," Remi whispered.

Mila nodded. "Daddy's sending for me. I'm going to New Orleans in a few days. I guess I can do it then."

"Okay, sweetheart. Talk to your mother. Let her help you to navigate this."

"Okay," Mila whispered. "I love you, Aunt Remi."

"I love you more."

And she meant it—with everything in her.

Chapter Twenty

Bianca

The sterile smell of the treatment room was familiar. She sat in the vinyl chair, arm outstretched, skin cold beneath the alcohol swab, and waited for the nurse to hook her up to the IV. The port beneath her collarbone ached every time the needle went in, but she didn't flinch. She had already prepared herself for the pain. A tote bag full of books rested at her feet and a Yeti filled with ginger tea sat on the table nearby.

The treatments before had stripped everything from her—her hair, her appetite, her energy, her dignity. She remembered the day she stood in front of the mirror and saw the first bald patch. She'd stared at her reflection, stunned by how hollow her eyes had become, how foreign her body looked. That night, she had shaved her head for the first time, not for control or vanity—but because she couldn't bear to watch herself disappear piece by piece.

"Let me help," Remi had said gently. She had taken the clippers and trimmed Bianca's head almost bald.

They'd done it together in the quiet of Bianca's bathroom. There were no tears, no music, just silence except for the buzz from the clippers. When it was over, Remi had touched Bianca's bare scalp and kissed her forehead.

"You're still you," Remi had whispered.

The mastectomy came after the third round of chemo, when the tumor hadn't shrunk enough. It felt like a punishment—another part of herself gone. Her femininity, her sensuality, everything she'd held close reduced to scars and skin she didn't recognize. And though she'd had her breast reconstructed, it was nothing like having her own.

Harry was already gone by then, but Remi was there through it all. She'd held Bianca's hand after the surgery. She sat beside her during the nights Bianca woke up in a cold sweat, unsure if she was alive or dreaming. She answered the calls when no one else did. The times that Bianca had cried, Remi never told her to be strong. She just let her fall apart. And that—more than any chemo or other treatment—was what helped her survive.

This time would be different, though. This time she'd be alone. Remi wouldn't be there to hold her hand, to help shave her head, to be her support, to play Prince's "Kiss" over and over again. Now, three years after her first fight with cancer, the scars remained, but so did she. Bianca had made it through the first time, not whole—but alive. And she only hoped she'd make it through unscathed this time too.

She returned to her place on Bodega Bay, with its beauty and untamed quietness. The sun was light and warming, but the wind still carried a chill with it at night. Bianca reclined on the sofa with a woven blanket draped over her legs to shield her from the cool air. The chemo had left her drained, nauseous, fatigued, and brittle. Her skin was pale, and not even the summer sun could change that.

The television was low and unintelligible. A mug of tea sat cooling on the coffee table, half full and long forgotten. She had drifted off to sleep sometime around noon. Her bones ached. When she awoke the sun gave light into the room. She reached for her phone on the end table. It was five thirty.

There was one unread message: **Mom, I'm flying into New Orleans tomorrow. Can you pick me up at the airport? My flight gets in at three o'clock.**

And below it, ten minutes later: **Never mind. I called Dad. Should've known you were too busy.**

Bianca sat up slowly, the weight of the words heavier than the blanket on her legs. Her thumb hovered over the screen. *Too busy*. She stared at the phone, willing herself to call, to text, to explain. But the feeling didn't come, only the quiet crash of the waves against the shore from the open patio door.

She leaned forward, pressing her elbows to her knees, head in her hands. Everything ached—her body, her pride, her motherhood. She contemplated informing Mila where she was, letting her know that she had not gone back to New Orleans as planned but was still in California. Bianca didn't want anyone to know she was still close by. She blinked away the burn in her eyes, then pushed herself up. She made her way to the kitchen, poured out the cold tea, and started a fresh cup.

Bianca stood at the counter, watching the kettle begin to steam. She thought of Mila in high school—how fiercely independent she'd been, how easily she had let that independence excuse the growing distance between them. *She's strong*, she'd told herself. *She doesn't need me like that*. But the truth was, Mila always needed her, just not in ways Bianca knew how to give. And so Mila had leaned on Harry. They had bonded in a way Bianca had never managed to replicate. He understood her humor, her moods, her silences. He showed up at recitals, parent-teacher conferences, all of it. He saw her. Bianca hadn't been jealous of their relationship—not exactly, but she noticed. The way Mila lit up around him. The way she trusted him. And then came the divorce, and that was the quiet death of everything.

Bianca reached for the kettle and poured the water slowly into her cup. She sat down at the kitchen table and dialed Mila's number. There was no answer. She opened her messages again and scrolled to Mila's last text. She stared at it for a moment, then typed: **I'm sorry I missed your message. You're right . . . I haven't shown up when it matters, but I want to change that. I'm trying. Please don't give up on me.**

She sat with the message, debating whether to send it or not. Then she hit Send. There was no immediate reply. She had lost her. *Again.*

Bianca reached for her phone again, her thumb hovering over Mila's message thread. There was no reply yet, just the blue check marks confirming the message had been read. She sighed, then stepped out onto the deck. A cool breeze brushed against her face, and the sun was low now. She needed to see Mila and talk to her, but she didn't want anyone to know where she was. A part of her wanted to fight the cancer alone this time, but another wanted to hash things out with her daughter, or at least give it a try.

She sat with the phone on her lap, watching light fade across the floorboards of the porch. The sun was going down. She unlocked her phone again, opening the message thread. Still no response. Her thumb hovered, then slowly typed: **I'm at this address. If you are free, maybe you can come here instead of going to New Orleans. Maybe we can talk, yell, or sit in silence. I'm here. Please don't share my location with anyone. I'll explain when . . . if you come.**

Bianca hit Send and then set down the phone. She exhaled through the tightness in her chest and leaned back against the chair. No reply came right away, and she didn't expect one. The longer she sat, the more the air cooled as dusk approached. Her body was heavy, the ache in her bones more prevalent now. She stood slowly and stepped back inside, leaving on the porch light—just in case. In the living room, she stretched her body along the couch, pulled the blanket over her legs, and let her eyes close. Sleep came for her quickly.

The sound of a car door slamming jolted her upright. Bianca blinked, disoriented, her heart thudding in her chest. She glanced toward the window. A shadow moved across the porch. And then there was a light tap on the screen door. It wasn't loud, but enough to shake her fully awake. She pushed aside the blanket and stood up slowly.

Bianca opened the door, just in time to see the black Toyota pull away from the curb.

"Mila."

"You told me to come," she said softly.

Bianca stood frozen for a moment, as if moving might make her daughter vanish before her very sleepy eyes. Her heart smiled.

She stepped aside. "Come in, baby."

Mila slowly stepped inside, her eyes scanning the place. "This is nice."

Bianca smiled. "I like it. It's very peaceful and calming here."

Mila set down her bag and turned to her mother, brow furrowed. "Mom, why are you here and not at home? What's going on?"

"Let's sit." Bianca gestured toward the couch. Mila did as she was instructed.

Bianca took a seat next to her, close but not touching. "The cancer is back. And now it's moved to my lymph nodes." She admitted that quickly. She wanted to put it out there.

"What? Why didn't you say something?"

"I didn't want anyone to know. I wanted to tackle it on my own," she said. "I'm doing chemo. It's hard and takes everything I've got most days. Which is why I couldn't—"

"Go back to New Orleans," Mila finished quietly.

Bianca nodded.

Mila exhaled, her eyes glassy now. "Is that why you left Napa . . . Aunt Remi's so suddenly?"

Bianca hesitated. "For the most part—yes."

"And you and Aunt Remi . . . you're not speaking?"

"She told you that?"

"She didn't have to. She hinted at it. But Zoe and I—we could tell."

Bianca sighed. "We'll work it out. We've been through worse," she lied. Nothing was worse than what she was currently going through with Remi.

"Hope so," Mila said. "You've been friends for like . . . forever." Mila paused. "Does she know? About the cancer?"

"No," Bianca said quickly. "No one does. And no one knows where I am, and I'd like to keep it that way."

"Mom—"

"Mila, please." Bianca's voice wavered, but she held Mila's gaze. "Let's just keep this between us. For now. Please?"

Mila breathed deeply. "Okay."

They sat in silence for a while, the weight of the conversation lingering between them. The room was dim, lit only by the porch light shining through the window and the soft glow of a nearby lamp. Bianca shifted slightly, adjusted her position.

"You hurting?" Mila asked gently.

Bianca gave her a light smile. "Mostly just tired."

"Do you have meds?"

"Something for the nausea." Bianca exhaled. "In the kitchen."

Mila stood. "I'll get them."

She walked into the kitchen. Bianca heard her opening cabinets, then running water. She returned with Bianca's orange prescription bottle and a glass filled with water.

"Here you go," she said softly.

Bianca took a pill and drank slowly. "Thank you."

Mila sat back down, gently reached for the blanket, and pulled it over her mother's legs.

"You want to lie down?" she asked.

Bianca nodded.

Mila helped her ease back onto the couch. She adjusted the pillows, tucking one behind Bianca's back. Mila sat beside her again, not speaking—just resting her hand lightly on her mother's forearm.

"I'm glad you came," Bianca whispered.

"I am too," Mila said. "I didn't know how much I needed to."

Bianca closed her eyes, the tension slowly leaving. Her heart was full.

And for the first time in a long time, they sat—not in grief or anger—but in something that felt more like love.

Daylight poured in through the kitchen window. Bianca slid a pan of bacon into the oven, scrambled some eggs in a bowl, and dropped a few slices of bread into the toaster. The smell of coffee filled the space as it began to brew.

Mila walked into the kitchen, rubbing her eyes, her hair tousled.

"How was the bed?" Bianca asked without turning.

"Super comfy." Mila leaned against the counter.

"Good." Bianca moved around the kitchen while Mila watched.

"I need to tell you something," Mila began. "Something happened during Christmas break."

Bianca poured coffee into a mug. Then she stopped and tensed up. "What kind of something?"

"I was at a frat party during Christmas. My friend Keisha and I. Somebody slipped something into my drink—I think. Next thing I knew, I was passed out, naked, alone. I didn't know what happened. Still don't."

Bianca froze. Tears brimmed her eyes, but she fought them.

Mila kept going. "I went to the clinic. They confirmed that I was raped."

A sound escaped Bianca's mouth—sharp and involuntary. Her body became tense immediately. The pain in her chest was sharp. She wanted to scream as she listened to her daughter's words. *Had she really heard them correctly?* She set down her coffee mug. "Oh my God, Mila . . ."

"I didn't tell you because, well . . . we don't really talk like that. Not about real stuff. Not really. And I couldn't tell Dad."

Bianca's eyes filled with tears this time. Her words choked. "That's my fault. That's completely my fault." She reached for Mila's hand, her voice trembling.

She prayed she didn't pull away. She didn't. "That's the reason for the head coverings." Bianca nodded toward Mila's head. A silk scarf had replaced the toboggan. "Can I see?"

Mila looked at her, breathing deeply. She trembled, and it looked as if she might cry. Slowly, she reached up to remove the scarf. Bianca blinked rapidly, her eyes fixed on the bald spot at the crown of her daughter's head. She closed her eyes. Her fingers shook as she touched Mila's scalp.

"I want to transfer to another school. I can't go back there next year."

"Then you won't," Bianca said instantly. Her heart ached, but she was on the verge of anger. Her eyes narrowed. She blew wind from her mouth. "Whatever it takes."

"And my hair is falling out from the stress of holding it in."

Bianca gathered her into her arms and hugged her fiercely. "You don't have to hold anything in anymore, not with me."

Mila clung to her, not completely trusting but not fighting it, either.

Later that night they sat on the deck listening to the cicadas humming loudly in the distance. The air was much cooler than it had been earlier in the day. Bianca played music on the stereo—soft Spanish melodies. The slow, gentle strum of an acoustic guitar filled the house and spilled out onto the porch. Mila curled her knees to her chest on the old wicker love seat. Bianca sat nearby, barefoot, the blanket around her shoulders and a mug of ginger tea in her hands.

Neither of them spoke for a while. They just relaxed against the whisper of music and the faint scent of the ocean. Bianca was just grateful for Mila's presence.

"I didn't think you'd believe me," Mila said eventually, her voice barely above a whisper.

Bianca looked over at her, startled. "Why would you think that?"

"Because . . ." Mila hesitated. "You always told me to be smart and careful. To not ever put myself in sticky situations."

A flicker of pain crossed Bianca's face. "Mila, telling you to be careful doesn't mean I would blame you. That wasn't your fault. None of it."

Mila nodded slowly, her eyes fixed on the dark sky. "I guess a part of me thought you'd be disappointed that I had ended up in such a stupid situation."

Bianca reached over and took her daughter's hand. "I am furious someone hurt you. If I knew who it was, I'd probably—" She blew air from her mouth, feeling the heat in her face. Her lips pursed. "It's probably good I don't know who it is right now." Bianca leaned back in her chair. "I'm ashamed that we weren't close enough for you to tell me sooner. But disappointed in you? Never, baby."

Mila's throat seemed to tighten. She looked down, trying to blink the tears away before they could fall. "I didn't know how to talk to you."

"That's my fault too. I thought if I raised you to be strong like me, you'd never feel broken. I didn't realize I was teaching you to hide from me. It forced you to run to your father. You two were closer, I get it—he's a great father—but it was hurtful watching you slip away from me."

Mila looked at her.

Bianca sighed, then leaned in closer. "I want to fix this, Mila. Not just what happened at the party, but us too. I want us to be okay."

Mila's lip trembled. "I want that too."

Bianca reached for her hand. "Then let's start here. Let's just . . . take care of each other for a while."

Mila took her mother's hand, and for the first time in a long while the silence between them felt safe.

When Bianca finally spoke, her voice was calm but firm. "I've been thinking about what you said, about wanting to forget. I get it. I do," Bianca continued. "But baby . . . forgetting and healing aren't the same."

Mila sighed. "It hurts just to think about it. I don't even remember the faces, just the feeling. The fear of waking up and finding out you've been violated—in the worst way."

"He shouldn't be allowed to get away with it," Bianca said. "The fact that he's walking the same earth as you and allowed to still breathe."

"I don't think he should either," Mila admitted. "But what can I do? I don't know who it was. I don't even know who to blame."

"You don't need to have all the answers today," Bianca said. "But there are people who can help you figure it out. People who deal with this all the time—investigators, advocates, attorneys who specialize in cases like this."

Mila hesitated. "What if it doesn't go anywhere? What if it only makes it worse?"

Bianca nodded gently. "That's the risk. But doing nothing—carrying it alone—that's what's already making it worse."

Mila's shoulders sank. "I don't want it to consume my mind—control my life anymore."

Bianca looked at Mila, her eyes gentle. "Then let's take your control back. On your terms."

Mila looked at her mother for a long moment. Bianca hoped that she knew there was no judgment—only fierce love.

"What's the first step?" she asked.

"Well . . . we can talk to a victim's advocate. I'm sure there's a center here in Sonoma County who works with survivors. They'll know how to handle it gently, so you don't feel any more traumatized than you already are. No pressure. Just options."

"Should I tell Dad?"

"Only if you want to, baby."

"I don't." Mila took a deep breath. "I don't want him sharing it with Jen. I don't like her."

"You mentioned that before, that you don't like her. What has she done to make you feel that way?"

Mila sighed heavily. "I heard her on the phone once with one of her girlfriends. She said something about you—that she thinks Dad is still in love with you, even though he's mad. And she said that she was tired of living in your shadow. Tired of being compared to you."

"She said that?" Bianca's posture straightened, her interest piqued. Something stirred inside her, a flicker of satisfaction she tried to hide. A subtle smile crept into the corner of her mouth. She hoped Mila hadn't noticed. *Still in love with her?* Even if it wasn't true, the possibility sparked something inside her.

"Yes that, and she wished you would just go away already."

Bianca froze. The words hit hard. A lump swelled in her throat, and for a moment she couldn't speak. Her mind raced, her thoughts scattered, then gathered around a single idea—the texts. The ones from that unknown number. *Could it be her?* Bianca didn't know. But the possibility was there, and she couldn't dismiss it.

"We won't involve your dad just yet. We'll do this together—you and me."

Mila nodded. "Okay."

Bianca felt something steadying inside her. If she didn't know any better, she'd say it was hope.

Chapter Twenty-one

Remi

The interior of the tasting room had begun to transform as contractors moved around, measuring and planning. The place was finally coming together after weeks of work. The vision was slowly taking shape. Sunlight beamed through the floor-to-ceiling windows, warming the polished concrete floors. The scent of fresh paint was still in the air.

Remi walked the space slowly, running her hand along the edge of the custom walnut bar—a design she and Paloma had dreamed up, after a long evening of tasting wine blends. She wanted something that would cause people to linger for hours, and this bar was it. She passed by the shelves, where bottles would soon stand, the wall where a mural would be painted by a local artist, and at the far end of the room, where tastings would occur.

Remi exhaled and stopped in the center of the room. She reflected on how she had poured everything into this place—her money, her energy, and all her hope. She turned as the foreman entered with a clipboard. He gave her a few updates on the plumbing. Remi nodded, but her thoughts had drifted. She thought of Mila. It was a few days since that brief text:

"Made it, Aunt Remi. I'm okay." But there had been no follow-up.

She wondered if Mila had seen her mother yet. If they'd sat down and talked. If she'd told Bianca about what she'd gone through over Christmas break. Remi tried not to worry, and she certainly didn't want to intrude. She wanted to be a part of Mila's next steps, to help her through it, but it wasn't her place to interfere. It was up to Bianca to help navigate her daughter's healing, and she hoped that she would.

She sent her a text: **I hope you're okay, sweetheart. Just checking on you.**

She turned away from the window and headed toward the storage area in the back. She picked up the stack of mail and sorted through it. A colorful postcard inviting her to a winery networking mixer was the first to capture her attention. The words, "*wine tasting, light eats, and an opportunity to connect with other industry professionals*," were sprawled across the front of it.

She took a picture of it and sent it to Paloma, with a simple text: **Let's go!**

Her response was swift: **Got the same invitation. We're there!**

Remi smiled to herself. Working with Paloma came naturally. Their partnership was built on trust, mutual respect, and open communication—qualities Remi deeply valued. She'd learned so much from her. And they jived. They always seemed to be on the same page about things.

As she tossed the postcard aside and reached for a roll of blueprints, her phone buzzed again. It was a reply from Mila: **Everything's fine, Aunt Remi. I saw her. We talked. I'll tell you more later.**

Remi exhaled, relieved. When she looked up, Leo was peering into the window. She waved him in.

He stepped fully inside, the door closing behind him. "Thought I might find you here," he said.

"This has become my home of sorts. So much needs to be done." Remi gave him a warm smile.

He looked around, taking in the space—the bar nearly finished, the walls freshly painted. "It's really starting to look like something," he said, walking slowly. "Like you."

Remi let out a small laugh. "A little unfinished, you mean?"

Leo smiled with warmth in his eyes. "No. I mean beautiful in a way that doesn't try too hard."

She raised an eyebrow. "That was dangerously close to a compliment."

"I live on the edge," he said, his smile like sunshine as he paused near the wall where the mural would go. "That mural is going to be a nice touch."

"Incredibly nice. I can't wait for it."

"I know you're busy here, but I was wondering if you'd like to take a drive with me," he said.

"Where to?"

"San Francisco. I have a stakeholder meeting there in a few hours."

Remi looked around the winery. There was nothing pressing that needed her attention.

"Sure. Why not?" She shrugged. "Let me freshen up and let Zoe know where I'm going."

"Cool. I'll meet you at your house in thirty?"

"Perfect."

Leo's car moved slowly down Highway 29, the vineyards blurring past in shades of green and gold. It was early enough that the sun was just starting to spill across the valley. Remi sat in the passenger seat, her elbow resting on the window ledge, fingers tapping against her knee in an absent rhythm. Her thoughts were a million miles away. The quietness of the drive took her to a place that made her tense—the conversation between her and Bianca the night before she left for New Orleans. The betrayal. The confrontation that had pretty much ended their friendship. The truth was, she missed her. She hated to admit it. Not Bianca per se—but the friendship. The camaraderie. The peace of having someone who was a constant in her life. It depressed her in a way that she couldn't quite explain, even to herself.

Leo drove in comfortable silence, one hand on the wheel, the other resting loosely on the gearshift. The stereo played soft jazz, something mellow and contemporary. As they merged onto I-80, the vineyards gave way to rolling hills. Remi watched as the scenery changed, and she felt the shift. Her thoughts were still caught between the winery and Bianca, between what was unfinished and what had already been undone.

Leo glanced at her. "You hungry? We can stop before we hit the city."

She shook her head. "Not yet. Maybe later."

He nodded and kept driving. They passed the familiar markers—Vallejo and Berkeley, and then the curve of the Bay Bridge rose ahead. The San Francisco skyline loomed in the distance.

As the car crossed the bridge, Remi finally spoke. "I keep thinking about Bianca, and everything that went down."

Leo didn't look away from the road, but his voice was soft. "Has to be pretty devastating."

She stared out the window. "It's like . . . I don't recognize my life anymore."

"Understandable. Grief happens in many forms. Not only are you grieving Gerard's death, but now you're also grieving your friendship with Bianca. Whether you fix it or not, it's still painful."

Remi gave him a look. "There's no fixing this."

Leo shrugged, as if he didn't believe her words, as if they had no meaning.

Remi nodded slowly. "It's overwhelming."

Leo reached for her hand, gave it a tight squeeze. They were quiet again as the bridge carried them into the city. San Francisco welcomed them—the hills, the noise, the hustle and bustle. As they exited the Bay Bridge and merged into the city streets, Leo leaned forward, scanning for the next turn.

"My meeting is in SoMa," he said referring to San Francisco's South of Market neighborhood and glancing at his watch. "Not until noon, but I figured we'd get here early."

Remi nodded and watched the city come alive around them. Cafés opening for lunch, cyclists weaving between parked cars, people in business suits walking briskly down busy sidewalks, coffee cups in hand.

He glanced at her. "You can come with me or hang out nearby. There's a bookstore around the corner."

"I'll take the bookstore," Remi said with a faint smile. "I don't feel like being charming today."

Leo laughed. "Fair enough."

They drove a few more blocks before pulling into a small garage. As they exited the car, the city's noise wrapped around them with car horns and voices.

Leo slipped the strap of his laptop bag over his shoulder. He looked at her with care. "You okay to kill an hour on your own?"

"I'm good," Remi said. "I'll find some coffee and a good book."

They walked together down the block, Leo pointing out the café where he would meet his contacts. He paused outside the quiet bookstore with a faded awning and a small window display of local authors and new releases.

"I'll text you when I'm done," he said.

Remi nodded. "Go be brilliant."

Leo smirked. "I'll try."

She stepped inside as he walked away, the bell above the door chiming. She wandered past fiction, then poetry, her fingers trailing along spines of books until she reached a quiet corner near the window. Somewhere between the rows of books and the city moving outside, she found peace. She sat with a cup of coffee that she'd picked up at a nearby café.

An hour and a half later, the early afternoon rush was forming. Remi waited outside the bookstore, a small paper bag of books in one hand, her phone in the other. A minute later Leo rounded the corner, sunglasses on his face, his jacket flung over his shoulder.

"Hey," he said. "How was the bookstore?"

"Quiet but dangerous," Remi replied, holding the bag of books in the air. She fell into step with him. "How was your meeting?"

"Good. Very productive," he said, then nudged her with his elbow. "Now I'm starving."

"I could eat," Remi admitted. "I saw a place a couple of blocks back. A tiny spot with a handwritten menu. Looked like a hole-in-the-wall."

"Those are the best ones."

Ten minutes later they were seated at a small table on the patio of a taqueria. The waitress brought over chips, salsa, and a pitcher of margaritas with tajin-dusted rims.

"This is what I needed," Remi said, squeezing lime onto her taco. "Something simple as tacos and margaritas."

Leo raised his glass. "To simplicity."

They clinked glasses and took a sip. Before long, the table was littered with lime wedges and crumpled napkins. They had laughed heartily all afternoon, talked about everything, and finished off two pitchers of margaritas. Leo was easy to be with.

"Want to walk a bit before we head back?" Leo asked. "I think we've both had a few too many."

Remi said, "Let's walk."

And they did, side by side through the noise of the city—

neither one saying much, but both feeling just a little lighter than before.

The drive home was quiet. The music was soothing, maybe a little too much. She slipped her sandals from her feet and reclined in the passenger's seat. The sun beaming down on the windshield made her drowsy, so she dozed off. When she awakened, Leo was pulling the Mercedes in front of her house. He looked over at her.

"We're here," he said.

She straightened in her seat. "Wow, I was out of there."

"Thanks for the company."

"Thank you for getting me out of the city, taking my mind off things."

"Anytime."

He jumped out and rushed to her side of the car. Ever the gentleman, he opened her door. She stepped out and gathered her bag from the bookstore and the sandals in her hand. She walked to the door barefoot. He shut the door and leaned against the car.

She turned back. "What?" she asked.

With a wide, beautiful grin, he said, "Nothing. Just watching you walk."

Chapter Twenty-two

Bianca

Bianca squeezed Mila's hand as they attended their meeting via phone with the Victims' Resource Center.

"We're just going to talk," Bianca said. "You don't have to commit to anything today."

Mila nodded, but her shoulders were tight, her jaw locked. She kept her eyes on the hardwood floors of the beach house.

"Hi, Mila," a woman said softly as she joined them on the phone. "I'm Kathleen."

Mila looked up at Bianca, then spoke into the phone. "Hi."

The woman's voice was calm. "I'm one of the advocates here at the Victims' Resource Center in Los Angeles County," Kathleen said. "Would you like to talk with me for a bit?"

"Yes," Mila said softly, just above a whisper.

"I understand your mom is on the line as well. Would you like for her to stay on?"

Mila looked at Bianca, then replied to Kathleen. "Yes, I want her to stay on the line."

"You attend UCLA, right?"

"Yes."

"Can you tell me what happened the night you were violated, Mila?" said Kathleen. "Did it take place on or off campus?"

Finally, Mila spoke. "It was off campus. I was at a party with my friend Keisha—a frat party."

"And what happened at the party? Were you drinking or using drugs?"

Mila looked at Bianca, then cautiously answered, "We were drinking. I left my cup to go dance. When I came back, someone had to have spiked it with something, because I don't remember anything after that," Mila said. "I didn't want to believe it, but I was tested, and I really was raped."

Kathleen's voice was steady. "I'm so sorry, Mila. You didn't deserve that. I'm glad you are willing to talk about it."

Mila's hands trembled slightly in her lap. "I don't know who it was. I don't even remember how I got in that room."

"That's more common than you'd think," Kathleen said. "Memory loss can happen when drugs are involved, or trauma. But we can still take steps without you having all the details. You don't have to remember everything for us to help you."

Mila glanced at Bianca, then turned her attention back to the phone. "What steps?"

"Well," Kathleen began, "the first is to make sure you feel safe—emotionally and physically. Do you?"

"Yes."

"Then, if you're open to it, we can help you file a report, even if it's delayed. We can walk you through a forensic interview with professionals trained to work with survivors. No pressure. Just support."

Mila swallowed hard. "But what if it doesn't lead anywhere?"

Kathleen nodded. "It might not. But sometimes even just telling your story—getting it out—is a kind of justice. And in some cases, others may come forward. Maybe you're not the only one."

Bianca reached over and rested a hand on Mila's back.

Mila took a deep breath. "Okay. I want to try. I don't want to carry this anymore."

Kathleen's voice seemed to smile. "That's a beginning, Mila. A brave one."

Later that night the house was still. The television was off, and no music was playing. The only sounds that could be heard were the rhythms of the ceiling fan and the splash of the ocean against the shore outside. Bianca sat in the armchair by the window, her legs curled under her, flipping slowly through a magazine she wasn't reading. Mila walked into the room, barefoot, wrapped in a bathrobe.

"You okay?" Bianca asked, closing the magazine.

Mila didn't answer right away. She sat on the couch, pulling her knees up, hugging them close.

I didn't think it would be that hard," she said quietly. "Just talking to someone."

Bianca nodded slowly. "You did something incredibly brave today."

"It felt like I was saying it out loud for the first time. Like really saying it. Not just whispering it in my head."

Bianca stood and crossed the room. She sat beside Mila and gently pulled her close, their bodies angled into each other.

Mila rested her head on her mother's shoulder. "Kathleen said it helps. Putting words to it."

"She's right," Bianca said softly. "I know it doesn't fix everything, but it's a start."

"I still feel . . . broken."

Bianca swallowed hard. Pain shot through her chest. "You're not broken, Mila. You're grieving. You're hurting. But you're still whole."

Mila closed her eyes. "I was so afraid to tell anyone, to . . . tell you."

"I was so afraid I'd already lost you." Bianca brushed a

hand gently over her daughter's hair. She had removed the toboggan and the scarf. "But today . . . I saw you. I really saw you."

Mila didn't speak for a long while. Then, in a voice so soft it barely reached the air, she whispered, "I don't want to be angry at you anymore, Mom. Don't want to blame you for Dad leaving, not anymore."

Bianca was silent. Guilt sat in her chest. She could barely speak but managed to murmur, "I don't want to give you reasons to be angry."

They sat there until the silence turned warm again—until Mila's breathing slowed and her shoulders relaxed, her body leaning fully into the comfort she hadn't allowed herself in years.

And for a change, Bianca didn't try to fix anything. She knew she would have to tell Mila the truth—someday, about Gerard—but not today. Not when her daughter was giving her grace, as unwarranted as it may have been. She needed it.

Chapter Twenty-three

Bianca

After several weeks of Bianca's treatments, Mila hadn't missed a single one. Bianca watched now as she sat quietly in the chair next to her, earbuds in one ear, studying her mother—eyes bulged, watching intently. She'd started bringing a soft blanket for Bianca after the second round, after she'd noticed her mother shivering beneath the hospital's paper-thin sheets. She brought snacks, too, packed in her denim tote, along with warm socks and coconut water, although Bianca could barely keep anything down most days. Her presence was a welcome surprise.

Mila didn't say much. They both lived in the quietness of the moment—the reality of it. Bianca was sick, and there wasn't a thing either of them could do about it except trust the process of tackling it through treatment. She couldn't undo the time she'd lost with her daughter. There was no way to get back those moments when Mila had needed her most and she hadn't shown up. The times she'd failed her. But maybe this was a beginning. In that cold infusion room, a connection was happening. Intimacy was being born in spite of their painful past. She hated that the cancer was back, but in a way it gave them a reason to fix what had broken a long time ago.

Mila began reading aloud from a book, something she'd found on the hospital bookshelf. Bianca, nauseous and dazed, listened without protest. The sound of Mila's voice soothed her. Sometimes Mila would just watch her, glassy-eyed. Bianca could tell she was trying to be strong, trying not to show that she was worried, but her emotions seemed to defy her. It was hard seeing her child so vulnerable and not being able to help her.

Mila had been angry for so long. She was angry about Harry, the divorce, and Bianca never being there for those important moments of her life. The girl had a lot of pent-up anger about things. But now, as medicine dripped into Bianca's veins, none of it seemed to matter.

"You okay, baby?" Bianca whispered.

Mila nodded. "Yeah. Are you?"

Bianca didn't answer right away. Then, "As well as can be expected."

"Do you think the treatments will help? Will they get rid of the cancer?"

"That's what we're hoping for."

Bianca wasn't sure if the treatments would cure her, but there was no way she was ready to say that out loud, not to Mila. She asked herself the exact same question every day. *Will the treatments get rid of the cancer?* She'd asked her oncologist that question too. She didn't have the answer, either. But the silver lining in all of this was that she did have her daughter back, for now. And that was something to hold on to, at least until the truth managed to find its way to the surface.

After they returned to Bodega Bay Bianca insisted upon going to the beach. Even though the California temperature wasn't all that warm, and the water was likely colder, something in her ached for it. The ocean always held a kind of healing effect for her, in a sense. It was quiet and calming, like it knew things that people had forgotten.

She sat in the water submerged just above her waist. The sun was shining, casting golden shadows across the waves. Today they were slow and steady, not like the day before, when they'd crashed heavily against the cliffs. The water was still cool against her skin, but she didn't care. She wanted to feel it—the earth, the salt, the quiet.

She closed her eyes while her fingers drifted just beneath the surface, stirring tiny ripples in the water. Each breath she took was deep and deliberate. Here, in this water, there were no doctors, no chemo, no hushed conversations about outcomes, just a steady rhythm of the tide. A seagull called out in the distance, causing her to open her eyes.

Mila stood nearby, jeans rolled up to her calves, an afghan wrapped around her shoulders. She shivered from the chill. "I can't believe you're out here, Mom. It's cold," Mila said.

"It's not cold," Bianca replied with a soft giggle. "Just a bit chilly."

She closed her eyes, letting the breeze brush across her face, the sun warming her shoulders. The ocean moved gently around her. She inhaled deeply and let her fingers skim the water as Mila stood next to her in silence.

Pretty soon Bianca stood, the water sliding down her body. She took her time wading back toward the house. Mila met her with the afghan, wrapping it gently around her mother's shoulders. Bianca offered a faint smile in thanks as they began the slow walk back up the beach, side by side.

Inside the house Bianca lit the fireplace.

"Gonna get out of these wet clothes. Last thing I need is to catch a cold," Bianca said. "Find us some music."

Mila nodded and connected to the Bluetooth speaker. A

soft, soulful track filled the space as Bianca disappeared into the bathroom. She stepped into the shower, letting the hot water wash over her chilled skin. Afterward she pulled on a pair of sweatpants and an old, wrinkled Jimi Hendrix T-shirt. Her pale face stared back at her in the mirror. Her hair was thinning in patches now. She'd noticed it days ago but kept pretending not to. She couldn't anymore. She opened the drawer, pulled out her clippers, and clicked them on. It was time. The buzz filled the quiet. Carefully, slowly, she began to shave her head, one strip at a time.

Mila appeared in the doorway. Without saying a word, she stepped forward, gently took the clippers from her mother's hand, and finished the job. When Bianca's head was finally smooth and her hair was gathered on the floor at their feet, Mila handed her back the clippers.

"I want you to cut mine too."

Bianca looked at her, startled. "Really?"

"Even out the part where it's thinning," she said. "It'll grow back."

Bianca searched her daughter's face, as if trying to read something behind her calmness. Mila's hair had always been her pride and joy—her crown. Long, beautiful brown hair framed her face. From the time she was little, she'd loved sitting between Bianca's knees as she styled it, demanding the way she wanted it done. So, watching her now, saying she wanted it shaved, caused Bianca some pause, not in a bad way, but she was in awe of Mila.

"You sure, baby?" she asked.

"Yes, Mom. I want to do this with you."

Bianca hesitated, clippers in hand. She wasn't sure but knew this wasn't just about hair. It was about letting go. Choosing strength. Choosing herself.

She, herself, had done it before—shaved her head during her last round of chemo. Back then, it had felt like a loss, but also a healing of sorts. With time, she'd grown less vain, less worried about appearances. But for Mila—this was different. She was still young, still vain in some ways, still beautiful. Her hair had been her identity for so long. Bianca feared the loss would hit harder than expected, and maybe afterward she would regret it.

"I have scarves," Bianca added, still trying to read Mila. She was trying to feel her out, to see if this was what she really wanted. "Beautiful ones."

Mila shook her head affirmatively, stood tall, eyes clear, face calm. There seemed to be no trace of doubt. "I don't want to cover it up anymore. I want it to breathe. I want to be free."

Bianca blinked, emotion welling in her eyes. The words struck something deep inside her. In that moment she realized, this wasn't just about solidarity, it was about taking her power back. Her throat tightened with emotion. She smiled through the sting . . . lightening the mood. "Well, okay, girlfriend."

She took the clippers and began trimming Mila's hair in the same slow, loving manner in which she'd started with her own. The moment was fragile. The music played on. The fire whispered in the living room.

When she was done, Bianca gently placed the clippers on the sink and took a step back. She looked at Mila in the dimly lit bathroom. And there she was, still radiant. Her beauty shone through boldly, as if nothing had been taken away, only revealed.

She grabbed her daughter's face in her hands and smiled. "You are so . . . damn . . . beautiful."

Mila smiled too, her eyes glossy. "Thank you. I get it from my mother."

"Yes indeed you do." Bianca grabbed Mila by the hand. "Now come on, let's go bake some fish. Hopefully I can keep it down."

They danced into the kitchen, unchoreographed movements. Mila kept up with her mother's rhythm. Bianca pulled the fish from the fridge, seasoned it with butter, rosemary, and lemon juice, and slid it into the oven.

"Why don't you make us a nice salad?" she told Mila.

"I can do that." Mila reached for the head of lettuce and a mixing bowl, began slicing lettuce, cucumber, and tomatoes. She looked up at Bianca. "Mom, I know we talked to that victims' advocate lady the other day . . . Kathleen. And she was really nice and so helpful, but—"

"But what, sweetie?" Bianca braced herself.

"I don't think I want to start a case. I don't want to file charges. I just want to forget it all happened."

Bianca's heart clenched. "You sure? You thought about it?"

"I have. Quite a bit," Mila said quietly. "I just want to be okay. I don't want to relive it over and over. I just . . . I just want peace, without all the drama of a case."

Bianca swallowed hard. Her instincts were to protect, fight, to raise hell. But this wasn't about her. It was about Mila. *Her* healing. *Her* choice.

Hesitantly she said, "if that's what you want—"

"It is," Mila said quickly, so sure of herself. "Maybe I can look at another school in the fall, like LSU or Xavier. That way I can be closer to you and Dad, and . . ."

Bianca interrupted. "I can talk to Harry. See what he says."

The thought of talking to her ex-husband unnerved her. They hadn't communicated much since Mila was old enough to speak for herself. Their exchanges had become rare, transactional—an occasional text here and there or a forwarded email. The emotional residue of their past still clung to her, making the idea of reaching out to him feel heavy.

"I don't want him to know about this," Mila said quickly.

"I won't tell him about *this*. I'll just tell him you want to be closer to home—to us. I think he would appreciate having you closer."

"Really, Mom? You'll do that, talk to him?"

"Yes," Bianca said softly.

Mila rushed across the kitchen, threw her arms around Bianca's neck, and hugged her. Bianca's heart became full in an instant. She'd longed for hugs like this so many times. And in that moment, everything she'd longed for—the closeness, the connection, the trust—was finally there.

And that was everything.

They ate fish and salad and settled in to watch the series that Mila had been raving about. The one that had her completely entangled. Soon, Bianca was hooked too. It gave them something to do together, a new shared obsession, a reason to sit close and talk between episodes, to laugh at the ridiculous plot twists.

She stole a glance at her daughter, the flickering from the fire casting a warm glow on her face. Her features had matured. They were stronger, more defined, but there was still a certain softness on her face. Bianca's chest tightened. How had she let moments like this slip away from her in the past? All the time she'd been too busy, too distracted, too consumed. Now, with nothing but time on her hands and nothing but healing on her agenda, she realized this was everything she wanted. It was simply the best.

Chapter Twenty-four

Remi

Oxbow Market was unusually crowded for a Thursday afternoon, but Remi pressed through anyway. She needed a few essentials for the house. She picked up a couple of artisan pizzas, salads, and a box of cupcakes for dessert.

The house had been quiet with just the two of them—she and Zoe. The silence felt heavier these days. It was weeks since the confrontation with Bianca, and the absence of her once best friend lingered. This new space between them seemed strange. Going from talking to someone every single day since the age of twelve to not speaking at all felt like losing a limb or, worse, death. Her emotions in a whirl, grief was mixed with anger, but she refused to give in. Bianca had betrayed her in the most unforgivable way, and nothing could change that their lives—all their lives—would never be the same.

She wheeled the SUV down Trancas Street and stopped at the light, the late-afternoon sun beaming down on her. She pulled the visor down to block it. With a sigh, she turned up the stereo. Dinah Washington's voice spilled through the speakers, "You Don't Know What Love Is," one of Grandma

Lorraine's favorites. She missed her grandmother and would call her when she returned home. If she were back in Louisiana, she would've spent a few days tucked away at Grandma Lorraine's house, her head resting against her bosom. They'd sit in the kitchen eating bowls of gumbo, listening to some of the old greats on the record player. She would tell her about the fight with Bianca, and she'd know exactly what to say. Grandma Lorraine always gave the best advice, and she needed it right now. But she hadn't wanted to tell anyone yet. Because when you said it aloud, that always made it real.

Her eyes shifted to the right, drawn to a young girl with short hair helping a frail woman into the back seat of a waiting sedan. Something about them caught her attention, a familiarity she couldn't immediately place. But then she looked again. The woman's posture, her profile, even the way she pulled her sweater tighter—

It was Bianca. She was sure of it.

Remi's breath slowed as the light turned green. She eased the SUV forward, glancing through the window once more to confirm. The woman didn't look back, but Remi didn't need her to. She knew the frame and the face. Despite the sunglasses, the weight loss, and the scarf covering her head, there was no mistaking the woman's identity.

Bianca was back in Napa. And she hadn't told a soul.

The thought of Bianca's return unsettled Remi all evening. She picked at her pizza and barely touched her salad. Her appetite had vanished and was replaced by a gnawing in her chest.

"Are you okay, Mom?" Zoe asked, pausing midbite.

Remi looked up, not even realizing her daughter was observing her. Her mind raced. "When's the last time you talked to Mila?"

Zoe raised an eyebrow. "Not since she left for New Orleans." Zoe poured more ranch dressing over her salad. "Why? What's going on?"

Remi hesitated before answering. "Nothing. I just . . . I thought I saw Bianca today."

"In Napa?" Zoe blinked. "

Remi gave a slow uncertain nod. "I think so."

Zoe tilted her head. "She wouldn't be here and not tell us. Right? She'd stay with us . . . here at the house."

"Right," Remi replied softly. Her voice said one thing, but her gut whispered something else entirely.

After dinner, she sat with a glass of Merlot. Soft music played to soothe her soul as she relaxed on the sunporch.

"Mind if I join you?" Zoe asked softly, peeking her head out the door.

"Not at all, sweetheart. Come on out."

Zoe took a seat in the chair adjacent to Remi's. "Mom, you know how you told me that if you had known what I was going through, you could've helped me?"

Remi nodded hesitantly. "Yes."

"Well, if I don't know what's going on with you, then I can't help you." Zoe grinned. Her frazzled cornrows had been replaced by two thick braids on each side of her head. "I know that something happened between you and Aunt B. And you haven't been the same since."

"You're so observant." Remi smiled at her daughter.

"I'm not a kid anymore. You can tell me what's going on, and we'll work through it together," she said. "Isn't that how it's done?"

Remi sighed long and hard. "This is really heavy, even for you."

"I'm tougher than you think," Zoe shot back.

Remi smiled. "Let's just say, it's something that I can probably never forgive her for."

"Well, I know this—" Zoe began. "There has never been a time in *my* life that Aunt B wasn't around. She's been a present figure since the time I was born. She's family. So, whatever it is, I'm sure she didn't mean to hurt you."

Remi looked down at her wineglass, turning it slowly in her hand. The silence hung thick. Crickets chirped just outside the screened window. Zoe didn't push. She waited patiently.

"It was more than just a falling out," Remi said finally. Her voice low, barely audible over the music. "It was betrayal. The kind you don't come back from. The kind I hope you never have to endure with any of your friends."

Zoe sat up straighter but still quiet.

"There are things I believed were sacred in my life. My marriage. My friendships. My sense of whom I could trust. Bianca and I—we were more than best friends. We were sisters. She knew everything about me. Everything about our family."

She sighed, then paused to steady her breath.

"She crossed a line that can't be uncrossed. One that broke something in me. Something I'm still trying to figure out how to live with."

Zoe frowned, her eyes narrowing. "Did it have to do with Dad?"

Remi hesitated. She knew the truth was out there now. There was no turning back. "Yes. But not just him, though. My whole world. Imagine learning that one of the people you've trusted most in the world helped tear your life apart. That's the kind of pain I'm talking about."

Zoe's face shifted. Concern softened into sadness. "Why didn't you tell me sooner?"

"Because I didn't want you to carry it too," Remi said. "It's not for you to worry your pretty little head about."

"But I am carrying it, Mom. I've been carrying it in your silence."

Remi blinked hard, caught off guard by her daughter's words.

"I just want to understand. That's all. Not to fix it. Just to know what it is that broke us."

Remi leaned back in her chair, watched as the sun went down. Zoe's words pierced her heart. *Broke us.* They were gentle words but sharp, like the edge of truth often was. Her little girl had grown in wisdom, and Remi found herself trying to pinpoint the exact moment that it happened. Somewhere between grief and heartbreak, her daughter had evolved into someone who could sit in silence, ever observant, ask the hard questions, and listen for the answers. And not just any answers but demanding the real ones.

"I'm still figuring it out, baby. But thank you for seeing me."

"You're welcome, Mom. I do see you." Zoe looked at her mother with wide, bright eyes. "When you figure it out, will you let me know? So that I can help."

Remi hesitated. "Yes. I will."

Zoe reached for her mother's hand. Remi took it and held it tightly. There was no more pretending, just two women, mother and daughter, sitting with the truth between them. For a moment anyway.

"I'm going up to take a shower," Zoe announced as she stood up. "Do you need for me to sit with you a little longer?"

"No, baby. I'll be okay. Go on up."

Zoe kissed Remi's cheek. "I love you, Mom."

"I love you more."

Remi's phone dinged and lit up in the darkness. She grabbed it and read the text:

Aunt Remi. I have to tell you something. My mom is not doing well. The cancer is back, and it is running rampant.

Remi's heart sank as she read the words on her screen. Her breath caught in her throat. She sat upright, the wine in her hand forgotten, her chest tightening as she reread the message. *The cancer is back.*

"Oh no," she whispered. Her voice cracked in the darkness of the porch.

She stood and walked toward the screened window, holding the phone like it might fall apart in her hand. Her mind raced with images of Bianca hooked up to IVs. Fragile, the way she had once been, years ago. The nights Remi had stayed with her, sat with her during her treatments. All those silent prayers.

She thought they'd beaten it. She believed, despite everything, that Bianca was in the clear. Remi sank into the chair again, thumb trembling as she typed:

How bad is it? Is she in the hospital?

She stared at the screen, waiting for the typing bubbles. None came.

A lump rose in her throat as the heaviness settled in. The unresolved history, love, and betrayal all collided with the one thing that had always made her pause when it came to Bianca: She was still family.

A tear slid down her cheek, followed by another. And before she knew it, she was crying uncontrollably. "Damn you, B," she whispered. "Damn you for doing what you did . . . and damn you for being someone who I still love."

Mila texted back: **She's at the hospital. Providence Queen of the Valley. Please come.**

"I knew that was her I saw earlier," Remi whispered to herself, remembering the fragile woman she'd seen on the street.

She stepped into the house and placed the wineglass in the sink. Her hands were already moving—gathering keys, her sweater, her bag.

"Zoe!" she called.

The betrayal could wait, she thought. The pain could wait. But Bianca might not be able to.

Chapter Twenty-five

Remi

The road ahead was blurred as tears trickled down her cheeks. She blinked them away. She didn't have time to fall apart. She glanced over at Zoe in the passenger seat, her face solemn as she stared straight ahead. The drive to the hospital was quiet. Remi didn't play any music. And she was thankful that Zoe didn't want to talk either. She didn't want the noise or conversation to distract her from her thoughts.

When they walked into the cold hospital lobby, she spotted Mila right away—though she almost didn't recognize her. Her head was shaved. Her frame, much like her mother's, leaned against a brick wall, arms crossed tightly over her chest, earbuds in. She looked exhausted. Remi stood for a moment, just watching her.

Mila looked up, eyes locking with hers. She didn't smile or wave. She just walked slowly toward her. When they reached one another, she didn't say anything. Mila opened her arms and hugged Remi tight. Then she hugged Zoe.

Remi touched Mila's hair. "This is different. I almost didn't recognize you."

"Yes," she said, almost in a whisper. "It was something I did on a whim. I wanted it gone."

"I understand, honey," Remi said. She hoped that Mila was able to heal. "It really brings out your features . . . your beauty."

"Thanks, Aunt Remi."

Remi grabbed her hand and squeezed it.

"She's upstairs," Mila said, her voice hoarse. "She had a rough night."

Remi swallowed. "Thank you for texting me."

Mila gave a slight nod. "She didn't want me to. Didn't want anyone to know, but I couldn't keep it to myself anymore."

"How bad is it?"

Mila hesitated. "Worse than she lets on. She got an infection from the chemo. And when they ran some tests, the doctors realized the cancer has now moved to her chest wall."

Fear caught in Remi's throat as she followed Mila down the long hallway with buffed floors, until they reached the shiny silver elevators. She didn't say anything—couldn't. She was stuck in a daze. Her hands trembled slightly as she adjusted her purse strap on her shoulder. She wasn't ready.

Upstairs, nurses moved quietly from room to room. Others gathered and chatted amongst one another at desks while answering phone calls. Remi followed Mila through the corridor until they reached Bianca's room. Her heart pounded beneath her chest.

Mila pushed the door open. Remi and Zoe followed her inside. Bianca lay curled in the bed, a colorful silk head wrap covering her head, a hospital gown swallowing her small frame. Her eyes were closed. An IV dripped quietly at her side. Machines in the room hummed.

She looked nothing like the vibrant woman Remi once called her best friend. The beautiful Cuban girl with generous hips and an ample bosom. The knockout body that Remi had wished was hers. The girl who was the life of the party.

The one who was ready to fight anyone who looked at her wrong or who gave Remi any grief. She had been her protector.

Remi stepped inside, careful not to let the door creak. For a moment she just stood there with her heart heavy.

Then Bianca began to stir. Slowly, her eyes fluttered open. When she saw Remi, her expression didn't change.

"You came."

Remi's throat tightened. "Of course I did."

Bianca blinked slowly, shifting in the bed. "I told Mila not to tell anyone."

"I know, but she was worried. Don't blame her."

Bianca shook her head slowly. "I don't. But I didn't think you would come, even if you knew."

"I didn't think I would either." Remi's voice cracked. "But I'm here."

Bianca reached for the cup of water beside her bedside, her hand trembling too much to hold it. Remi crossed the room and caught the cup before it spilled. She held it to Bianca's lips. Bianca drank, and when she leaned back against the pillows, her voice was nothing more than a whisper. "I'm so sorry, Remi. For all of it."

Remi gently reached for Bianca's hand. "We don't have to talk about that right now. Let's focus on getting you healed and out of here."

They didn't say anything else, just held on to each other.

As the sun crept into the window and cast a shadow across Remi's face, she squinted. She tried to remember where she was. The uncomfortable orange chair in the corner of the room was a quick reminder. She scanned the room, and then looked at Bianca, who was bright-eyed and watching her.

She smiled lightly. "The girls went downstairs to get breakfast."

Remi straightened up in the chair. "Okay."

"I'm glad you came, Remi."

Remi gave a nod and then a slight smile. "How are you doing with all of this? Mentally?"

"I have my affairs in order."

The words struck Remi like a dart to the chest. She blinked from the pain. It meant that Bianca was thinking she might not get better.

"That's good," she said, forcing composure. "Have to make sure your daughter is covered in case something happens."

"I listened." Bianca smiled.

Remi remembered those days during Bianca's first bout with cancer, how she'd practically lectured her on wills, powers of attorney, and life insurance, making sure Mila would be okay.

"They're letting me go tomorrow," Bianca said.

"What are the next steps?" Remi asked.

"Surgery is an option, but it's pretty invasive." Bianca lifted her bed. "They're going to try radiation first. But there are no guarantees that they will shrink it. The chest area is difficult."

"Okay," Remi took it all in. She was solemn. Seeing Bianca here again felt like déjà vu. "Where are you staying?"

"I've been renting a little house in Bodega Bay. It's kinda secluded. I was there to heal." She paused. "And to stay out of your way."

"I would come there and stay with you, but *Joie* is really taking off and I need to be there to oversee things. Equipment is being delivered in a few days . . . filtration system is installed next week."

"Mila will be there to help, at least until I'm done with radiation. She doesn't go back to school for a few more weeks," Bianca said. "Then I'm going back to New Orleans."

Remi turned toward the window, watching an elderly couple slowly shuffle through the hospital's glass doors.

"Why don't you come back to the house . . . in Napa?" she said finally. "Just until . . . you know . . . you're done with radiation, and you're stronger. Or ready to go back to New Orleans."

Bianca blinked. "You sure about that, Rem?"

Remi wasn't sure, not entirely. But she threw caution to the wind. It was something she'd learned from Bianca.

She said it anyway. "I'm sure."

The words hung in the air like a peace offering of sorts. Though she wasn't necessarily offering forgiveness or suggesting that she had forgotten what happened between them, it was out there now, irreversible. And good, bad, or somewhere in between, Bianca was coming home with her.

She freshened the sheets and linens in the room that Bianca had occupied before. A vase of fresh wild irises was placed on the bedside table, their violet petals vibrant like her. Remi opened the windows, letting the early afternoon breeze flow through, carrying with it the scents from the garden below. This would be Bianca's place of healing, and Remi did what she could to make the room comfortable for her.

She made her way downstairs and started a pot of chicken soup on the stove—a single chicken breast, wide egg noodles, chopped onions, celery, and sweet carrots. The aroma slowly filled the kitchen. She brewed a pitcher of lavender iced tea, let it cool, then placed it into the fridge.

When the doorbell rang, it startled her. The girls had gone to pick up Bianca from the hospital and she wasn't expecting them back so soon, nor anyone else.

Leo stood on her doorstep, holding a bag of green tomatoes in one hand and a bottle of Pinot Grigio in the other.

"For you," he said, handing over the wine. He lifted the tomatoes with a proud grin. "From my garden."

"Well, hello." Remi took the bag and stepped aside for him to come in. "You have a green thumb, I see."

"I do indeed. I didn't always have one. Something I picked up after . . . you know, after Viv was gone."

Remi nodded.

He flashed a smile full of perfect white teeth. "Thought I'd fry them up for us in a nice lunch . . . if that's okay."

"Be my guest."

Leo headed straight for the kitchen like he knew his way around. "Smells like something's already going on in here. What's in the pot?"

"Chicken noodle soup," she replied. "For Bianca."

He paused, turning to face her—wide-eyed. "For Bianca? Okay."

"A lot has happened since we last spoke," Remi said. "I found her in the hospital. The cancer's back."

"Wow, I didn't know there was a first round of cancer."

"Yes. This is her second bout. And now it has spread. The doctors are just managing the pain at this point."

Leo's face softened. "I see."

"Don't judge me."

He shook his head gently. "I would never judge you, Remi. I think you're incredible. And Bianca? She's lucky to have a friend like you—a real one. Most people wouldn't do what you're doing. Choosing friendship over pride."

"Thank you for that," she whispered. "Because lately I've felt like the stupidest person on earth."

"On the contrary," he said, pulling a skillet from the cabinet. "You don't even know what a rare jewel you are."

He caught her eyes as he set the pan on the stove, started the fire beneath it. His eyes lingered on her for moment, steady as he poured the oil into the pan and got to work.

Remi rolled up her sleeves and joined him at the counter, pulling out a cutting board and knife. "I'll slice. You season."

"Yes, ma'am." Leo washed the tomatoes in the sink, then handed them to her one by one as he dried them with a paper towel. She worked quietly, slicing each one into thick rounds.

"Cornmeal's in the second cabinet," she said, nodding in its direction.

Leo found it easily and poured some into a shallow dish, then added salt and other seasoning. "Got any cayenne pepper?"

"You know I do." She reached for the spice rack and tossed him the small bottle. "Not too spicy, though."

He chuckled. "I got you."

As he prepped the cornmeal, she beat an egg in a bowl beside him, then leaned back and watched him work. His movements were rhythmic and calm. They cooked together, Leo dipping and dredging tomatoes, Remi dropping them into the hot skillet. The oil sizzled as the tomatoes browned. The scent of vibrant seasonings filled the kitchen.

"This takes me back," she said.

Leo looked over. "To what?"

"Louisiana. My grandmother Lorraine's house. She used to fry green tomatoes in the summertime. She, too, had a thriving garden. I'd sit at the table and watch her. Music on. Big glass of lavender tea."

"What music would she play?"

"She loved Dinah Washington. She liked Ella too." Remi's eyes were dreamy, like nostalgia was resting behind them.

Leo grabbed his phone, scrolled quickly, and soon Dinah Washington's sultry voice filled the kitchen.

Remi closed her eyes for a moment. "Yep, that's it."

They stood shoulder to shoulder, flipping tomatoes as they browned. She glanced up at him—took in the sight of the man who stood in her kitchen, frying green tomatoes. They talked and laughed.

"You always come through right on time," she said softly.

Leo looked at her, then reached for a plate from the shelf, lined it with paper towels. "I'm glad I could be here. You heal me too," he said softly.

She smiled up at him and breathed in his scent. "I'm glad," she whispered.

He leaned down—slow, hesitant, his tall frame towering over her. Their lips met in a kiss, so gentle it felt as if they had kissed before. She closed her eyes. Rational thought told her to pull away, but she didn't—couldn't. His kiss didn't feel like temptation or wrong. It felt like comfort and stillness.

When he pulled away, his voice cracked as he whispered, "I'm sorry, Rem. I had no right—"

"It's okay," she said softly, her fingers still brushing his cheek. "It's okay."

She let her hand linger for just a moment longer before gently pulling it away. They stood in silence for a moment. Remi leaned back, breathed in slowly. She could still feel the touch of his lips on hers. His presence beside her grounded her like she hadn't felt in weeks.

"You just caught me off guard," she said finally. Her voice was calm, but with an edge of truth.

Leo nodded and chuckled nervously. "I caught myself off guard."

She sighed. "This . . . whatever this is—we should tread carefully. There's a lot going on in my life right now."

"I know," he replied. "And I'm not trying to complicate anything for you."

"It already is," she said softly. "You're Vivian's. And Gerard—he's only been gone . . ."

"I *was* Vivian's. And in some ways, I always will be," Leo said, choosing his words carefully, "but that part of my life ended long ago. And Gerard . . . he was your husband. I would never try to take his place."

Remi looked at him. She saw the pain behind his eyes—the patience in his voice.

"I don't need anyone to take his place," she said with a steady voice. "But maybe I need someone who understands what it's like to lose everything and still wake up the next day."

Leo nodded. "Then maybe we just be that—for now—two people helping each other breathe again."

Remi let out a deep breath. "Okay," she whispered.

They stood at the stove in stillness—as two people with wounded hearts, and tentative hope, wrapped in shared grief and something new that neither of them recognized. They dared not give it a name.

"I don't want to be another thing you carry," he said. "If there's a space for me, I want it to be one you choose—not one you feel obligated to fill. I'm your friend. Your confidant. Your peace."

Remi's throat tightened. The air between them was full of unspoken things.

And even after he was gone—after they'd eaten green tomatoes in her kitchen and sipped white wine—Leo's kiss lingered in her mind. It wasn't just the kiss itself, soft and unexpected, but everything it carried with it: comfort, curiosity, the quiet promise of something new—though she had no idea what that *something new* was. She touched her lips absent-mindedly, as if trying to hold onto it a moment longer. It had been so long since someone had looked at her—really seen her and taken her needs into consideration. And that made her chest ache in the most dangerous way.

Chapter Twenty-six

Bianca

Bianca sat on the edge of the bed, her hands resting in her lap. The wild irises beside her gave off a familiar scent, one that took her back to childhood summers in Louisiana. It was a time when Abuelita would place fresh-cut lavender flowers in chipped mason jars all over the house, insisting they would keep the bad spirits away. Bianca never believed in that kind of thing, but right now, she desperately needed something to believe in.

The room was bright and filled with Remi's care. She could feel it in the clean linens, the open windows to let in fresh air, the soft lavender sachet tucked beneath her pillow. It unsettled her more than it comforted her. Remi's kindness always had a way of touching her heart, but right now she didn't feel deserving of it.

She lay back easily, her bones aching. The pain meds dulled it some, but the deeper aches—the emotional ones—no prescription could heal. She stared at the ceiling and tried to settle her thoughts. But some of the worst ones entered her mind anyway.

She didn't want to die here; not in Napa Valley, and certainly not in Remi's house with everything between them still unresolved. After all, Remi had said that she wanted the *dignity of rebuilding without her watching*. She wanted to give her that dignity, that space to heal. But she also didn't want to die alone. Hell, she didn't want to die at all. She still had so much to live for. She knew she had to die someday—everyone did—but she wasn't ready right now. There were so many things that she wanted to do.

Her eyes drifted to the corner of the room, where her suitcase sat unopened. Her life had been reduced to luggage, a few outfits, and some medications. She hadn't expected Remi to offer her a place to stay, or come to the hospital, or to look her in the eye and still call her *friend*. She'd been anything but, and the guilt of it tore her apart. She hadn't even forgiven herself. How could she expect Remi to forgive her?

She reached for her phone. There were no new messages, no more threatening texts—for now. She had buried that secret deep. Though she hadn't done as she'd promised Remi, that she would call the police and report it. Right after she made that promise, her life had begun to unravel and take a different turn. And now the texts seemed to have ceased, so she wouldn't worry about it. It was something that she would keep buried.

Outside the window, the vineyard looked peaceful, still. It reminded her that life kept moving forward whether you were ready or not. Life just kept on *going*. She closed her eyes for a moment, just for a little bit of meditation and gratefulness.

"I'm sorry, Remi," she whispered to herself. "For everything."

After a brief nap, she made her way downstairs. She was tired of lying down and wanted to be where life was. Remi, Mila, and Zoe sat around the island in the kitchen, laughing and discussing—well, she wasn't sure what. She hated that she felt like an intruder, though.

"Sorry, I didn't mean to . . . interrupt," she said.

"It's okay," Remi said. "Would you like some tea?"

"I would love some," Bianca said, making her way into the living room. She collapsed on the couch, breathing heavily. Some days it took every ounce of energy just to walk a few steps. "Thank you."

She watched them for a moment, listened to their voices and laughter, but then her mind drifted somewhere far from the sunlit kitchen in Napa—this place that offered peace—to her home in New Orleans and her boutique. What would happen to it all if she didn't get better? Who would manage things if she couldn't return? The idea of letting go, of surrendering control of those things that she'd built, simply made her stomach turn and feel unsettled. She hadn't let herself really think about it until now. But the truth was staring her in the face. She needed to start putting things in order. She needed to contact Daphne, her realtor, consider selling the house, maybe even the boutique. Both had been her pride and joy for so long. The house where she'd built a family with Harry, raised Mila. She now needed to say goodbye to it. Saying farewell to the boutique, well, that would be the worst of it all. It was something that she had worked so hard for, but now she didn't know if she had the energy to keep on fighting for it.

She swallowed hard, with her eyes fixed on the window now as she looked out upon the patio and the pool, but not really seeing any of it. Bianca had always been the one who handled everything in her life, making the hard decisions. Even when married to Harry, they constantly bumped heads about how things should be run, both in the home and their marriage. She had her own mind, her own way of doing things, and sometimes she tried to wear the pants in the house. That infuriated him. He wanted to lead, be in control, and have the final word. But Bianca had never been one to fall in line easily. She didn't know how to be quiet when something felt wrong. She flat-out refused to shrink herself just to keep the peace. And that was their constant battle—his need to be obeyed, her need to be heard.

Now, she felt as if she was losing control, like the things she held dear were quietly slipping away from her. Her home, her health, her business, her daughter's trust—once she discovered the truth. She was even losing her sense of self. The steadiness she once prided herself on had been replaced by uncertainty, and no matter how hard she tried to tighten the grip, life was moving fast, and without her permission.

"Earth to Bianca," Remi said, leaning on the edge of the kitchen island.

Bianca looked up, caught off guard. "Hmm?"

"You disappeared for a second." Remi's tone wasn't judgmental but aware. She walked over, brought the mug to her. "Here you go."

Bianca reached for the cup. "Thanks."

"You okay?" Remi asked, her voice quiet enough so the girls wouldn't hear.

Bianca managed a smile, "I'm fine."

"You don't look fine."

Bianca was tired of lying and being secretive about things. It was secrets that had her in conflict with Remi, and she didn't want to be in that place anymore.

She looked down at her tea and then at Remi. "I was just thinking . . . about everything. The house in New Orleans. The boutique. All those things that need to be handled."

Remi sat next to her on the couch. "Well, they don't need to be handled today. You should focus on healing, on getting well. Nothing is final."

"I'm just so used to handling things."

"I know you're trying to make peace with the idea of not being here anymore, but B, the truth is, you're still here," Remi said. "And all that stuff that you're stressing about will work itself out."

Bianca's voice trembled. "You're right. I just don't want things to fall through the cracks."

"If you don't get yourself healed, you won't have to worry about any of those things. You, yourself, will fall through the cracks." Remi touched her hand. "Just allow yourself to relax for once."

She swallowed, her voice soft. "I don't know how to do that."

"You'll figure it out, because at this point you don't have a choice."

Remi was right.

There was one thing that she needed to take care of right away. Slipping outside to the patio, Bianca tucked her cell phone into the pocket of her bathrobe. She sat in one of the patio chairs, soaking up the evening sun for a moment before pulling out her phone. Her fingers hovered, then dialed a number that she hadn't dialed in a long time—Harry's.

He answered on the second ring. "Hello, Bianca."

"Hello, Harry. Is this a good time? I'd like to talk."

"I'm in traffic on the I-10. Looks like there's been an accident, so I'm not going anywhere fast. Go ahead."

"I wanted to talk to you about Mila. She's thinking about switching schools in the fall, and I think it's a good idea. She'd be closer to home—closer to you—"

"She mentioned it already," he said, cutting her off.

"Oh." A bit of silence followed. Bianca wished Mila had told her that. It would've spared her this awkward phone call.

"I also know you're sick again," Harry said. "That the cancer's back."

A lump formed in Bianca's throat. She braced herself, for judgment, for blame. She waited for him to say that it was karma. That this was the price she was paying for all her wrongs.

Instead, he said, "I just wanted to say . . . I hope you find your way back to good health."

Her voice cracked. "Thank you," she said softly. "And I know I've said it before, more times than I can count, but I'm sorry, Harry. For everything I put you through."

"I'm not angry anymore," he said quietly. "What happened . . . it was a terrible betrayal, yeah. But it didn't change my relationship with my daughter. I'm still her father. I always will be." He paused, then added, "Besides, forgiving you was really for me. My blood pressure was out of control."

Bianca let out a soft laugh. "Have to watch that blood pressure. It's no joke."

"Trust me, I know it." He chuckled. "But I've got it under control now."

"I'm glad to hear that," she said softly.

"I'll send for Mila soon, so we can start looking at schools. Maybe LSU."

"That sounds good."

Her heart smiled. They'd had a real, rational conversation, and it felt good. She didn't want to ruin it. She wanted to end it on a note of peace.

"Well, I hope traffic lets up soon."

As if he didn't want the moment to pass just yet, he said, "Take care of yourself, Bianca. Mila needs you."

Her voice broke. "I know."

After she hung up, she sighed deeply, then smiled.

Chapter Twenty-seven

Remi

By now, Remi could check several things off her list. The contractors had finished their renovations—walls painted, floors done. The tasting room was nearly complete, with its walnut bar top that had already been installed with pendant lights. The fermentation tanks stood in neat rows, joined by crushers, and a newly installed bottling system. Filtration systems were scheduled for installation in the coming week.

The past two weeks had been a blur of movement and momentum. Remi had immersed herself in Napa's bustling wine scene, attending industry events downtown, shaking hands, exchanging cards, asking questions, listening closely, and soaking up all the insight she could. But tonight's industry event was different. It wasn't just another networking opportunity; it was a chance to begin carving out *Joie*'s identity among the valley's most respected names.

The stakes felt higher. She wasn't just going to be there as an observer anymore. She was stepping into the room as a peer, a new name in the world of winemakers. Every detail mattered—the tone of her voice, the conviction in her pitch, her confidence. This was where *Joie*'s story would begin to resonate outside of the winery walls.

She stood in front of the mirror and smoothed the dress over her hips, pausing to turn slightly, checking every single angle to be sure it fell just right. The fabric hugged her frame in all the right places. She slipped a pair of silver hoops into her ears and colored her lips with mahogany, the color adding just the right amount of drama. Finally, she slipped into her black strappy heels. Tonight she needed to look like the woman behind *Joie*. The one who had earned her place at the table.

Downstairs the girls were gathered around the kitchen island, deep in conversation; their laughter could be heard before Remi reached the bottom step. Bianca relaxed on the sofa, her eyes lightly closed. She opened them when Remi entered the room.

"Woo-hoo. Look at you," Zoe whistled.

"Do I look okay?" she asked nervously. "Is this dress too much? Maybe I should wear slacks."

"You look fabulous," Mila said. "And you are working that dress."

Remi hesitated, then smiled. "Okay, I'm trusting you two."

She reached for the small brown pill bottle on the island, shook two into her palm, then grabbed a bottle of water from the fridge.

"Here you go," she said, handing the pills and water to Bianca.

"Thanks." Bianca smiled. "You look good, Rem."

When the doorbell rang, Remi instinctively smoothed her dress once more before heading to answer it. She pulled the door open to find Leo standing there in tan khakis and a crisp blue blazer, hands tucked casually into his pockets.

"Ready?" he asked, not crossing the threshold, but sticking his head inside. "Hello, ladies."

"Hey, Leo," Zoe called from the kitchen.

"Hey, superstar," he said with a grin.

"Hello," Bianca and Mila both said in unison.

"Wish me luck," Remi said to them.

"You'll be fine, Mom. You got this."

The winery hosting the event sat nestled in the hills just north of downtown Napa, it's glass-paneled tasting room glowing against the twilight. Rows of parked cars lined the gravel path leading to the entrance. Inside the room buzzed with a crowd of vintners, sommeliers, and marketing professionals. The voices intermingled with the sound of live jazz coming from a trio in the corner of the room.

Remi stepped inside, arm lightly hooked through Leo's. She scanned the room, her eyes settling on a few familiar faces from previous mixers. A server passed by with a tray of sparkling rosé. She took a glass, the stem of it resting between her fingertips.

She locked eyes with Paloma, who quickly made her way across the room, wearing a blue linen two-piece suit.

"You made it," she smiled and nudged Remi.

"Yes. I wouldn't have missed it for the world."

"Hello, Leo," Paloma said. "You both look great."

"Thanks, Paloma. So do you," Leo said, and then tapped Remi's elbow. "I see someone I know. I'll be right back."

Leo disappeared. Paloma raised an eyebrow but didn't say anything.

She linked her arm with Remi's. "There, across the room . . . gray slacks, green shirt. That's Christian Carter. He owns a marketing firm in the Bay Area, Pinnacle Strategies. It's a small firm, but very influential. I think Pinnacle would be a great fit for *Joie*. I'll introduce you later."

"Okay."

"Go mingle. We'll link up later." Paloma slipped away and caught up with someone she knew.

Across the room a few women gathered around a well-dressed man from one of Napa's most respected vineyards. A younger couple stood by the cheese spread, talking distribution. Remi took a deep breath and approached a group gathered near the fireplace, easing herself into the conversation.

They were discussing trends in sustainable winemaking, and she found herself contributing easily. She talked about her plans for *Joie*, and the contemporary trends she'd already adopted. A few people nodded, intrigued. As the evening wore on, Remi moved from conversation to conversation, her nerves settling a bit more. She glanced across the room at Leo. He was watching her with quiet admiration—watching her shine. A smile crept into the corner of his mouth.

Later, as Remi and Leo stood near the exit and the crowd began to thin, someone tapped her on the shoulder. She turned to find a man she'd met briefly at another mixer, John Gabriel, who ran a midsized distribution in Sonoma.

"You're building something that people are talking about," he said. "I'd love to come by and visit *Joie* sometime. See what you're doing over there."

John Gabriel wanted to visit Joie? Her heart beat rapidly in her chest.

"I'd be happy to give you a tour once it's up and running," Remi said, attempting to keep her voice steady.

"I'll look for the invitation," he said and then slipped out the door, waving goodbye to a few of his colleagues.

As they stepped back into the night, Remi exhaled. Leo held the passenger door of his Mercedes open for her and she climbed inside. She didn't have all the answers yet, but she was gaining her footing. *Joie* was becoming a name in the valley, and she was ready for whatever came next.

* * *

She found Bianca on the sunporch, a silk scarf on her head, an afghan wrapped around her shoulders. Soulful music drifted from a Bluetooth speaker.

The door creaked as she stepped outside.

"How did it go?" Bianca asked.

"Very well," Remi said with a smile. "I made some great connections tonight. Think I might've also found a marketing company. And guess what? People are raving about Mila's design. Her logo was the talk of the evening."

"That's cool. She'll be happy to hear that."

"A couple of people are interested in seeing more of her work. She needs to think about putting together a portfolio."

"I'm sure you'll have her a business plan worked up by morning—a whole presentation with scented markers and all." Bianca laughed and then went into a coughing spell. She took a sip of mineral water.

Remi laughed too. "Ha ha."

"I had to say it." She regained her composure, sat up straight. "She'll be a business owner before she's twenty-one."

"If she sticks with me, she just might," Remi said. "I've already written her a check for the work she put in."

"It's really coming together for you, Rem. Congratulations. I had no doubt that it would," Bianca said.

Remi took a seat in the chair adjacent to Bianca. There was a relaxed silence between them for a moment, only the sound of cicadas humming loudly.

"Did you have dinner?" Remi asked her.

"Mila whipped up a pot of homemade soup for me. Used some ingredients from the garden. She's getting pretty good in the kitchen."

Remi had noticed that too, and usually the thought of it unnerved her, but not tonight. She was still reeling from her evening.

"I'm not surprised. She's a chip off the old block. Or should I say *blocks*." She said it casually, masking her true feelings about it. Then she changed the tone of the conversation. "You know that little vintage candy shop you love so much . . . downtown?"

"The one with the wine-tasting bar?" Bianca asked and closed her eyes for a moment, appearing to be savoring the thought of it. "Oh my God, those darn wine truffles. They are to die for."

"I had Leo stop by there, right before they closed their doors for the night." Remi grinned. "I got you some of those truffles."

"You didn't."

"I did. They're in the kitchen," Remi said. "And if I were you, I'd hide them. Because if they're still there in the morning, they're fair game."

"Well, I'd better hide them right away," Bianca teased.

"You'd better."

Bianca settled into the wicker love seat. "Not that it's any of my business, but you and Leo seem to be getting kinda close lately."

"You're right. It's not your business," Remi replied with a small smile. "But if you must know, we're just two friends—one helping the other through a difficult time. That's it."

Bianca nodded slowly. "That's good. But if it ever turned into something more . . . I just want you to know you deserve all the happiness in the world, Rem. And fuck any judgment from anyone."

Remi let the words sink in. They were comforting. Her thoughts moved to the kiss she had shared with Leo. There should've been guilt that followed, but there wasn't.

She didn't reply, just stood and headed toward the door. "You need anything before I head up?"

"No, I'm fine. Thank you," Bianca said. "I'll be going up soon too. Got an early morning."

"Radiation tomorrow?"

"Yes."

"Okay, we're doing it together."

Bianca nodded a yes. "Good night, Rem."

"Good night," Remi said softly.

Chapter Twenty-eight

Bianca

She stood in front of the mirror, eyes fixed on her chest—the spot that was marked during her simulation appointment. The ink—this vivid tattoo—would remain, long after the radiation was over, a permanent reminder of what she'd been through. It would stay etched in her skin forever.

The oncologist was precise, gently mapping out where the cancer had spread to and where the radiation would strike. The mark was a guide for the radiologist—a road map of sorts. She reached up and gently touched the spot, her fingers lingering over it.

Today was the day.

She sat in the waiting room, her knee bouncing up and down at a fast pace. She bit her bottom lip, while chill bumps rushed up and down her arms. Her heart raced.

Remi placed her hand on Bianca's knee, stopped it from bouncing. She grabbed her hand and gently held on to it. "Relax. It's going to be okay," she whispered.

Bianca nodded slowly, blinked rapidly. "I just hope they get it all."

"Prayerfully so," Remi said. She gave her a reassuring smile.

Bianca had slipped Abuelita's rosary beads into her luggage the last time she was there. Now they were wrapped around her fingers like a vine. She held on to them tightly. She closed her eyes and whispered a prayer—a brief but sincere one. Tears threatened to fill her eyes, but then she heard the nurse call her by name.

"Bianca Fuentes Perez." She said it almost too softly, too gently.

Bianca stood.

"I'll be right here when you're done." Remi smiled.

She lay on her back, stretched out on the treatment table, the cold surface pressing against her. In her ears, Prince's "Purple Rain" played softly—his voice and the guitar wrapping around her, easing her fear. When the machine started, it made a steady, whirring noise. A myriad of thoughts raced through her mind. She focused on staying still, willing her body not to move, even though her emotions were all over the place.

She trembled from the thought that this might not work, that the radiation might not remove the disease from her body. Or that the cancer would spread to other parts also crossed her mind. It seemed as though her options were slowly trickling away. If this didn't work, where would she go from here? The thought of surgery unnerved her. Her abuelita's rosary beads lay wrapped up in her clothing across the room. She wished they were in her hands, wrapped around her fingertips, quieting the noise in her head.

Thirty long minutes later, it was over. And now the process of waiting would soon begin—to see if the cells died. Then there would be the follow-ups and side effects. The part where hope was all that was left. She dressed quietly, solemnly; wrapped the rosary beads around her wrist.

The drive home was quiet, somber.

She wanted nothing more than to get home, curl up in the

center of the bed, wrap herself up in a blanket, and sleep the rest of the day away. And that's exactly what she did.

The next few days were spent in that same spot, sleeping and barely eating. As dark circles formed around her eyes, depression began to set up camp in the dark corners of her mind. A part of her wanted to give up—fighting was too hard, and she was losing strength.

That morning, like every other for the past week, as daylight made its usual intrusion into the room, she covered her head with the blanket. She just wanted to sleep and so that became her fight—a fight to keep still, to sleep the days away, to disappear. In a nutshell, to keep everyone at bay. They wanted her to eat, come out of the room, to engage, but she didn't want any of that. No, today she only wanted to sleep. But that was short-lived.

She was awakened abruptly by Mila.

"Mom!" She nearly screamed it. "Mom, wake up."

Mila stood in the shadows of the room, arms folded tightly over her chest. Her face completely covered in tears, her eyes red and swollen. Her breathing was off as her chest heaved up and down.

Bianca stirred and struggled to open her eyes. She slowly pulled herself upright in bed. When her gaze found her daughter, she winced. "Baby, what's wrong?" she asked, searching Mila's eyes. Her gaze drifted to the hills of dark curls on her head that were beginning to grow back.

"Is it true?" Mila's voice cracked, her teeth clenched. Her brows narrowed into a frown.

Bianca's heart pounded rapidly. "Is what true?" she asked but already knew even before Mila spoke the words. She knew her past had come to haunt her in the worst way, and before she was ready.

"That Uncle Gerard is really my dad."

Bianca sat frozen for a moment. The words pierced her heart. Reality was in her face, and she had to deal with it. She had always been the girl who would fight like hell at the drop of a hat. She was strong, the kind that wouldn't back down. But Mila standing in front of her now, heartbroken and furious . . . that shook her and made her want to run for the hills.

Almost in a whisper, she said, "Sweetheart, I was going to tell you. I just didn't know—"

"So, it's true, then."

"Many years ago, I made a mistake . . ."

"You slept with your best friend's husband? How disgusting." She sighed heavily and dropped her arms to her sides, loosening her stance a bit. "It's why you and Aunt Remi have been at odds lately."

"Who told you this?" Bianca asked.

Mila shook her head. "I can't even believe you. And I can't believe my dad didn't tell me, either. You both deserve each other."

"Who told you this?" Bianca asked again. Her voice firmer now.

"The only person brave enough to tell me the truth. Her eyes bulged as she said, "Jen."

Everything in her stood still. How dare she—this woman who wasn't even family, who was barely a fiancée, had the audacity to tell her daughter something so deeply personal.

"It wasn't her place," Bianca said, anger rising in her chest.

"No," Mila snapped, her voice breaking. "It was your place. Or my dad's. And neither of you said a damn word." She was crying hard now, her chest heaving as if she might have an anxiety attack.

"Come here, baby." Bianca stretched out her arms.

"I can't be with you right now." Mila stormed out of the room.

"Mila," Bianca called her as she forced herself out of bed and hurried to the door.

Just outside, Zoe stood frozen against the wall, arms folded against her chest, her shoulders heaving up and down, tears streaming down her face.

Bianca stopped short. "I'm so sorry," she whispered.

Zoe didn't speak. She just looked at Bianca with eyes full of contempt. She turned and walked swiftly down the hallway, then slammed her bedroom door shut.

Chapter Twenty-nine

Remi

She'd taken Paloma's advice and hired Pinnacle Strategies, a marketing team that was small but sharp. One that understood her vision and would help shape the story behind the brand. She'd also hired a software company to implement a full wine management system, one that would streamline everything from inventory tracking to tasting notes, shipments, and wine memberships.

Next on her list was hiring the right staff, people who believed in *Joie*. She planned to start small, with the objective of building a tight-knit team. A few of Paloma's relatives, who had worked at the Ortiz winery before it closed, had already expressed interest. They were familiar with the land, and they respected the kind of place Remi was building. She would interview them first.

Joie's business side was finally taking shape, and she couldn't be prouder. What began as a dream at the beginning of the summer was evolving—quickly—into something real, structured and promising. The foundation was becoming solid. Licenses were in place. Distribution discussions had moved beyond preliminary talks, and a few boutique shops in the Bay Area were already on board. The branding, which was Mila's hand-sketched design of a grapevine curling into the shape of a heart, had been adopted. And what was more, it was gaining attention for its elegance.

Remi spent the morning with her newly hired marketing team, shaping the campaign that would introduce *Joie* to the world. By noon they had begun laying the foundation for a strong social media presence and strategizing distribution. Piece by piece the vision was taking form. *Joie* was becoming a brand.

Remi stood at the head of the wooden table in the winery's converted office. The office space still held the smell of fresh paint, still was unfinished. She hadn't gotten around to decorating, at least not yet. Aside from the table, nothing else had arrived. A few furniture pieces were on back order, and she was still browsing for artwork that captured the spirit of Napa and the soul of *Joie*.

But today wasn't about all that.

Tablet in hand, she glanced up at the mounted screen behind her. The *Joie* logo illuminated there. The afternoon sun filtered through the tall windows. When her phone rang, she silenced it. Seeing it was Zoe calling, she made a mental note to call her back when she got a free moment.

"So, the story is just as important as the wine," Remi said, scanning the faces seated around the table. "We're not just selling a product, we're offering people a sense of place, of renewal. Of joy, really."

The room was still for a moment before Camille, the lead strategist, a sharp woman, nodded. "That's exactly the angle we want to lead with. Authenticity. Storytelling. Napa has a lot of wineries, but few are owned by women of color with real histories of perseverance and personal transformation."

Remi nodded, grateful that someone else could see the heartbeat of *Joie*.

"Distribution," Camille's colleague Marcus chimed in. "We're in touch with regional outlets and boutique shops in the Bay Area. They want small-batch, narrative-driven wines. *Joie* fits that."

"What about events?" Remi asked.

"We suggest soft-opening weekend tastings. By invitation only," Camille said. "Media, influencers, local sommeliers. And then slowly expand. Word of mouth will be key."

Remi leaned back in her chair, processing it all. The winery she'd dreamed of in the quiet of grief and uncertainty was materializing before her eyes. And though the journey had been hard-won, she felt something she hadn't in a long time—deeply rooted pride.

"Let's move forward," she said, her voice firm but warm. "I want the first bottles out by end of summer, early fall. And I want a big event, a wine tasting with all the influencers there, to introduce *Joie* to the world."

Applause followed. It was happening and fast.

Paloma gave her a wink, followed by a light, warm smile.

Her phone buzzed again with a text message from Zoe: **Mom, I need to talk to you right away!**

Before Remi could reach the house, she spotted Zoe running toward her, meeting her halfway between the house and the winery. Tears were streaming down her face, her expression stricken with panic.

"Baby, what's going on? Are you hurt?" Remi asked, grabbing her daughter and holding her.

Zoe shook her head, gasping for breath. "Mila's gone and I don't know where she is!" Her voice cracked. "She just found out that Aunt B slept with Dad . . . and . . . that he's her father." She looked up at Remi, eyes wide with confusion. "Mom . . . is that true?"

Remi sighed. Panic rushed through her. This was not how

she'd planned to tell her daughter the truth. This chaotic clumsiness had not been part of her plan.

"Where's Bianca?"

Zoe shrugged. "She's in the house."

Remi grabbed Zoe's hand and walked with her to the house.

Bianca sat on the sofa, hands covering her head. She looked up with red, tired eyes as Remi entered.

"What happened?" Remi asked Bianca.

"Harry's freaking girlfriend . . . fiancée . . . whatever the hell she is, took it upon herself to tell my daughter something so personal . . ."

"What? What gave her the right?" Fury raced through Remi's veins.

"So, it's true?" Zoe asked. "Mom?"

"Zoe, sit," Remi demanded.

"Mom, is all of this true?"

"Zoe, please sit down."

She needed to get herself together—gain control of her own emotions, take hold of the moment and all it brought with it.

Zoe sat in the chair adjacent to Bianca.

Remi softened her voice. "It is true. Yes."

Bianca turned to Remi. "This is my fuckup. So let me explain."

Remi nodded.

Bianca turned to Zoe. "Yes, Zoe, it is true. Many years ago . . . I messed up. I made a horrible mistake. I betrayed your mother and I've regretted it every day since. Yes, your dad is Mila's biological father."

"So, she's my sister, then."

Bianca shook her head. "We didn't plan for either of you to find out this way."

Zoe stood up and paced the floor. "This is just so weird. So messed up. I don't even know what to say or think."

"This is certainly not your burden to carry, Zoe. It's mine. All mine," Bianca said.

"We have to find Mila," Remi said softly, interrupting. She looked at Zoe. "Where do you think she went?"

Zoe looked up at her mother, eyes wet with tears. "She called a Lyft."

Bianca pulled her cell phone out of the pocket of her pajamas and went to the kitchen. "Harry has a GPS tracker on her phone. I tried calling him earlier, but he didn't answer. Let me try calling again," she said, shaking her head. "I've made such a big mess of all this."

Remi sank onto the sofa, letting her body ease into the cushions. She held out an arm to Zoe and gently said, "Come here, sweetheart."

Zoe sat beside her mother, eyes still damp, releasing the tension of her shoulders just a little bit. Remi wrapped her arms tightly around her, holding her close.

She wanted to bask in the joy of the meeting she'd just come from—the sense of accomplishment still lingering. But all of that faded now. Her need to protect her daughter took center stage.

Chapter Thirty

Bianca

Her phone only rang halfway before she picked up.

"Bianca what's going on? Is everything okay?" Harry's voice carried with it a touch of panic.

"I need you to find Mila's location. She's gone missing."

"What do you mean? What happened?"

"Your girlfriend, or fiancée, or whoever she is . . . she told Mila about Gerard being her father."

Harry went silent for a long moment. "Jen did?"

"It wasn't her fucking place," Bianca shouted. "And I think she's been sending me text messages. Stalking me like a psychopath."

"What kind of text messages?" he asked.

"Sinister, creepy ones. Why don't you ask her about it," Bianca said. "In the meantime, can you find my daughter, please? I need to try to fix this."

She'd always been careful about not referring to Mila as *my daughter* but always said *our daughter*, in order to keep the peace. But today she didn't care about being considerate of his feelings or thoughtful. At this moment Mila was *her* daughter, and that was it.

"I'll find her location," he said calmly.

Bianca ended the call. Pain rested heavily on her chest.

Remi pulled the SUV into the beach parking lot at Bodega Bay and shut off the engine. Without uttering a single word, Bianca stepped out and walked slowly toward the water, the wind tugging at her dress. The waves were aggressive as they crashed against the shore. Mila sat alone in the sand, knees pulled tightly to her chest, staring out into the ocean as if she was waiting for it to speak to her—to give her the answers she so desperately needed. To help her make sense of the chaos that had just unraveled in her life.

Bianca sat next to Mila, not close but a short distance.

For a moment neither of them spoke, only the sound of waves filled the space between them. Finally, Bianca broke the silence. Her voice was soft and laced with regret.

"I know you hate me now. And I don't blame you. I can't even begin to tell you how sorry I am. If I could change what happened, I would. If I could change how I kept it all a secret, buried for years, I don't know, I still might."

Mila didn't respond. She just kept her gaze fixed on the water.

Bianca continued, choosing her words carefully. "Your dad and I made the decision that it was better for you not to know. Not until we were ready to tell you. We didn't want to complicate your life. You were Harry's daughter in every way that mattered, and he didn't want that to change. Neither did I." She paused. "Harry loves you more than life itself, Mila. That's never been a lie."

Mila's voice was barely above a whisper. "Who does that to their best friend, though?" she asked.

Bianca inhaled. "Someone very young and stupid."

Remi and Zoe joined them, forming a circle in the sand. Remi settled between Mila and Zoe and took each of their hands in hers.

She looked at Mila, then turned to her daughter. "Zoe, you and Mila were already sisters...have been since before you could walk."

Zoe nodded slowly in agreement.

"And Mila, you and your mother . . . you were building something, healing what was broken between you. You were really starting to bond. You shaved your head. Not just because your hair was falling out, but in solidarity. Against cancer. Against rape."

"That was before—"

"Before you found out the truth. I know," Remi said gently. "And you have every right to be upset. We all do." Her eyes drifted to Bianca. "This has disrupted all our lives, for sure." She turned back to Mila. "And your feelings are valid. *Our* feelings are valid. We're hurt. We're mad as hell. But maybe . . . just maybe we don't have to let it destroy us. Maybe we can still find a path forward."

They all sat in silence.

"What if we can't recover?" Mila asked softly. "This is so much."

Remi gently squeezed her hand. "We will, sweetheart. I truly believe that we will. Certainly not today, and maybe not even tomorrow, but we will."

Mila stared straight ahead, her face still holding on to the pain. Bianca could see she wasn't ready to let go.

They all clung to Remi's words.

Zoe rested her head on her mother's shoulder.

The weight of it all still hung in the balance, but a glimmer of hope hung there too. And for that, Bianca was grateful.

At the house, Bianca made herself a cup of ginger tea and carried it to the sunporch along with her laptop. She needed to decompress after the day's events. She was fatigued, but not just from the radiation treatment she'd endured a few days earlier, from the emotional toll of everything that had transpired. She was exhausted.

She sat on the wicker love seat and gazed into the evening sky, letting herself sink into the cushions. Her body surrendered, but her mind was on a million different things. She tried to make sense of what healing might look like now, and whether it was even a possibility. What would her abuelita think of her now, all wrapped up in this mess? Could those rosary beads and prayers get her through this?

She pulled the laptop into her lap and logged into the Chic Threads inventory system and did some work. She needed a distraction. Fourth of July sales were good with so much traffic in the city for the Essence Festival. April, May and July were her best months, when the city hosted festivals and foot traffic was booming in the French Quarter. She loved being in the mix of it all, meeting people from all over the globe. It was the reason she loved Chic Threads so much—the people. And the joy of making them look and feel good.

Amelia was holding it down for her—running the boutique seamlessly. Bianca was grateful for her. On impulse, she opened a new tab and ordered a gift certificate for an entire afternoon of pampering and tranquility at Amelia's favorite day spa in the French Quarter. She sent it to her with a simple note: *"Thank you for everything."*

She closed the laptop and sipped her ginger tea. Her mind drifted back to the day's events—Mila shouting at her, calling her out for betraying her best friend. She'd certainly felt as if she'd hit rock bottom.

When she heard the door creak open, she knew who it was.

"So much drama today," Remi said, cradling the stem of a wineglass, the bottle in her other hand.

"To say the least," Bianca murmured.

"I think Mila will be okay. She just needs time," Remi said, taking a seat in the chair opposite Bianca. "None of us knows what tomorrow will bring."

"Yeah. But I'm not sure how many more tomorrows I really have," Bianca said, her voice flat. With her gaze fixed, she sipped her tea.

"Let's just hope you have many more. That the radiation treatment was successful."

"If not, my options are starting to dwindle." Bianca shook her head, reality hitting her hard.

Remi took a sip from her wine; her eyes fixed on Bianca. "The Bianca I know wouldn't let any of this defeat her. She would fight like hell—until there's no fight left in her."

"I'm softening, Rem. Tired." She breathed deeply and closed her eyes for a moment. "I have fought my whole life."

"Giving up is not an option. That would be too easy."

Bianca nodded faintly but didn't speak. The truth was, her will to fight was slowly slipping away.

Finally, she said, "I have a daughter who hates me, a best friend I pushed away, and a disease that's trying to kill me. What exactly am I fighting for?"

Remi didn't blink. "All of those things. That's exactly why you fight."

Bianca shrugged. Her silence was saying what her voice couldn't—that she didn't believe that anymore.

Chapter Thirty-one

Remi

Remi gazed out the window as Zoe, Bas, and Mila sat at the edge of the pool, their feet dangling in the water, soaking up the final days of summer. Soon they'd all be heading back to school.

Sundays were usually easygoing and peaceful, but today she worked. She was busy preparing for *Joie*'s big tasting event. A notebook lay open on the island in the kitchen as she jotted down some notes. There was still so much to do: prepare the space, select the wines, finalize the menu. She needed to hire caterers. Her marketing team was hard at work designing artwork and promotional materials for distribution. Personal invitations would be mailed to a select number of guests.

The local artist Remi had commissioned to paint the mural in the tasting room had already begun work on the piece and had promised to finish it before the event. Furniture was scheduled to arrive in the coming week, and interviews for staff had already begun.

Things were falling into place.

She sat at the island as soft music played on the Bluetooth

speaker. She closed the notebook and exhaled, letting her gaze drift back to the sunlit backyard and the laughter that echoed through the screened patio door. Then she opened the Pinterest app and began scrolling through images on her iPad. The decorations needed to reflect *Joie*'s essence—warm, sophisticated, and inviting. They needed to blend in with the tasting room's soft lighting and the earth-toned, soft peach walls.

The winery's outdoor space was just as beautiful as the inside. In the garden flowers and vegetation were in full bloom—lupine, poppies, and wild irises. Even a few California fuchsias were beginning to pop up. She envisioned decorating the garden area with high-top tables draped in flowing white tablecloths, soft candlelight, and strings of white lights overhead. Every detail mattered.

She imagined how the evening would come together. The late-afternoon sun would stretch across the garden. Guests would move from table to table, wineglasses in hand, laughter rising. Each station would offer something different—a crisp Sauvignon Blanc, a velvety Pinot Noir, and of course *Joie*'s signature wine—the sparkling rosé with notes of strawberry and citrus—would be the centerpiece of the tasting. The wine would be paired with small bites. Not just a tasting but an experience. An introduction to the world.

Her phone buzzed. It was a message from Camille, her marketing lead: **Final draft of the invitation is ready. Want to review before we print?**

Remi typed a quick response: **Yes, email it to me.**

When her phone buzzed again, she thought it was Camille texting back. Instead, it was Leo, sending a photo that he'd snapped of her during their daycation at the beach. In the photo, she was looking away—somewhere in deep thought. She smiled and typed: **When did you sneak this one in?**

He replied: **While you were far, far away.**

Remi smiled.

Bianca quietly walked into the kitchen, fully dressed. She'd been closed up in her room for days—tiptoeing on the edge of depression. When Remi saw her appear, a flicker of relief softened in her chest, grateful for the small sign that she hadn't given up. She had started to worry.

"Glad to see you." Remi gave her a smile.

"Thought I might cook something. Cooking always lifts my mood." Her voice was soft but steady.

"Well, by all means, cook," Remi said with a small laugh.

"Mind if I borrow the car? I want to pick up a few ingredients. Seafood and fresh vegetables."

"Of course. You feel okay to drive?"

"I think so."

Remi paused, then said, "Maybe I'll tag along. Give you a hand."

Bianca glanced at her, the faintest trace of a smile forming. "I'd like that."

The drive was quiet at first, but not in a heavy way—just comfortable. The windows were down, letting in a breeze. Remi allowed her to drive. She wanted Bianca to feel as if she could do normal things again. She warned that if she felt fatigued, she would take the wheel. Bianca kept one hand on the wheel, the other resting in her lap. Remi watched the way her expression softened when the wind caught her hair, how the sunlight danced across her face. Her hair was beginning to fill in again—just a little bit.

Remi's heart saddened at the thought of how they'd gotten to this place. How their friendship had evolved into such a bad awkwardness. How betrayal had torn them apart. Their sisterhood had been such an important part of her life, and now she didn't even recognize Bianca, or her own life for that matter. Things were so different now. It was as if they were becoming reacquainted when they'd known each other so intimately their entire lives. Had Bianca not gotten sick, they would not be in this car together, nor the same house. They wouldn't be in the same space at all. It was as if the universe had other plans, though.

At the market they grabbed a cart and wandered into the produce section. Bianca moved with more purpose than Remi expected, scanning the bins for heirloom tomatoes and bright bundles of herbs.

"These look good," Bianca said, holding up a bunch of asparagus.

Remi nodded. "What are you thinking?"

"Grilled asparagus. Maybe some seared scallops, and a citrus salad if I can find good oranges."

"That sounds amazing," Remi said, picking up a bunch of basil and holding it up to her nose. "You feel like doing this? Cooking?"

Bianca shrugged lightly. "Figured it's better than lying in bed."

They continued down the aisles, grabbing lemons, garlic, crusty bread from the bakery, and a chilled bottle of sparkling water for the ride home.

As they walked toward the checkout, Remi nudged her gently. "Glad you got out today."

Bianca didn't look at her, just smiled a little and said, "Me too."

Remi watched as Bianca moved around in the kitchen as she'd done so many times before. She watched her rhythm—chopping, slicing, arranging. Bianca didn't speak much, but her silence wasn't withdrawn; it was focused. She zested a lemon.

"You're in your zone now, I see."

"It's like therapy," Bianca replied, squeezing the juice into a small bowl.

The scallops sizzled in the pan, the scent of garlic and butter blooming into the room. Remi decided to help. She began tearing basil leaves, laying them gently over the plate of sliced oranges, berries, avocado, arugula, and feta cheese. She moved beside Bianca, close enough to feel the warmth from the stove, to let the silence between them feel like something shared, rather than avoided.

The girls walked into the house after sunbathing by the pool all afternoon.

"Something smells good," Zoe said, a thick towel wrapped around her waist. She took a seat at the island. "Glad to see you up and about, Aunt B."

"Thank you, sweetheart," Bianca said with a soft smile, wiping her hand on a dish towel. "I'm glad to be up and about."

Mila trailed in behind her and climbed onto the stool next to her. She didn't look at her mother—not out of anger or resentment, just . . . restraint. Her silence still hung in the air, but it didn't feel sharp or hostile. It was the kind of quiet that comes with sorting through too many feelings at once. She was still trying to find her way through the pain of it all. Remi could see that she still felt unsure about things, and she was keeping her words tucked safely inside until she was ready to release them again.

Bianca glanced over at her, then back to the stove, saying nothing. She was giving her the space she needed to heal.

"Zoe, can you grab us a bottle of Chardonnay from the cellar?" Remi asked.

Zoe grinned widely. "Us, as in all of us?"

Remi raised an eyebrow. "You're not quite legal drinking age."

"There are exceptions, Mom," Zoe said. "In the privacy of our home, under parental supervision, it's totally allowed."

Remi turned to Bianca for help. "What do you think, B?"

"The girl has a point." Bianca gave Zoe a wink. "Can't hurt."

The ever-observant Mila sat by, watched her mother with careful eyes but said nothing.

"Fine," Remi said with a sigh of resignation. "Grab us a bottle. Actually, bring two."

As Zoe returned and placed the bottles on the counter, Remi reached up for wineglasses.

Her eyes flicked toward Mila, reading her face. "You don't have to have wine if you don't want to, sweetie."

Mila gave a small smile. "I want some," she said.

Remi narrowed her eyes playfully. "So now I'm skeptical. How often are you two drinking when we're not around?" She shot a look at Zoe and then Mila.

"Almost never," Zoe replied, attempting a straight face, but a grin broke through before she could hold it.

Their laughter filled the room—light, unforced. For the first time in what felt like ages, it sounded like home again, and Remi smiled.

Chapter Thirty-two

Bianca

Jane Lee was an Asian radiation oncologist with a good bedside manner. She had good communication skills, explaining things in a way that Bianca understood and appreciated. Bianca could ask all the questions she needed answered without being rushed. And she was empathetic. All the things that Bianca loved about Dr. St. James.

"Hello, Bianca." The petite woman gave her a warm, gentle smile. "Why don't you have a seat."

Bianca slid into the leather chair. Remi and Zoe took seats next to her. Mila stood in the shadows of the room, arms folded over her chest. The fact that she had asked to come along was a surprise.

"I have a bit of good news," Dr. Lee said, her smile brightening. "I have the results of your tumor marker test. It suggests that the cancer is responding to the treatment. And your imaging shows that some of the tumors have shrunk."

Bianca exhaled and released a breath. Tears welled in her eyes, and she let them fall.

"Oh my God," she breathed. "Thank you. Thank you so much."

"Now, of course, we'll need to continue monitoring with more tests," Dr. Lee said gently. "But I'm happy with what I'm seeing so far."

Remi reached for Bianca's hand and held it tightly. Zoe covered her mouth, her eyes wide with excitement. Mila slowly unfolded her arms and let them fall to her sides. She released a breath of relief.

"How are you feeling? Are you getting back to some of your normal activities?"

"Yes. Cooking. And I've been going on walks."

"Eating a healthy diet?"

"Yes."

"Good. Keep it up," said Dr. Lee. "Do you have any questions for me?"

"Yes," Bianca jumped right in. "Do you think the radiation will get all the cancerous cells?"

Dr. Lee didn't hesitate. "I can't say for sure. We'll continue to monitor and see. Let's just keep fighting."

"Fighting is what I know," Bianca said, her voice steady now.

In the car, Bianca let out a loud scream. It wasn't to scare anyone. It was the release of pent-up anxiety, uncertainty, fear—all those things that had been holding her captive. Remi screamed with her, just as loud. Then Zoe. When Mila screamed, something inside Bianca broke. She didn't turn around, didn't speak. She just stared out the windshield with eyes full of tears. She kept her eyes steady—and a gentle smile crept into the corner of her mouth.

Bianca found Mila in the living room, curled up on the couch with a book in her lap, though she wasn't reading it. She looked up when her mother entered but didn't speak. Bianca sat down beside her, close. For a while, neither of them said anything.

Mila looked at her. "I'm glad the treatment is working."

"Me too."

"I'm still trying to figure everything out, but I don't want you to be sick."

"Thank you, baby, that means a lot," Bianca said. "I know you're leaving soon, but I want us to at least check in on each other."

Mila nodded. "Are you going back to New Orleans soon, or will you continue your treatment here."

"I'm still trying to figure that out."

"Dad and I are going to visit LSU next week. Since I missed enrollment for fall, I'll enroll there as a visiting student and then apply for the spring semester in October." Mila gave a light smile.

"That's good. You'll be there with Zoe."

"Yeah, we've been talking about maybe sharing an apartment. She's going to talk to Aunt Remi and see if that's a possibility."

Bianca took a slow breath. The thought of her daughter not staying on campus gave her pause. "Wow, not staying on campus. That's . . . that's something."

Mila smiled faintly. "I think we can handle it. We're mature enough."

Bianca reached out, brushing her fingers gently through Mila's hair. "Your hair is growing back, I see."

"I like it. I think I might wear it short for a while. It gives me courage."

"It's certainly attractive on you."

"Thanks," she whispered.

Later that night the house had settled into stillness. She was the only one awake. She'd gone for a walk earlier in the day. Her breathing was better. She was getting back into her groove. The low hum of the refrigerator was the only sound as Bianca stood at the kitchen sink, staring out into the darkness. Somewhere in the distance, a cricket chirped. She wrapped her hands around a mug of chamomile tea, untouched. She felt and enjoyed the warmth of it for a few moments. Then she closed her eyes for a moment and listened to her own breathing—slow, steady. It was way different from the tight, shallow breaths she'd grown used to since her second diagnosis.

Today had been a good day. The good news, laughter, and a moment of connection with Mila she hadn't dared hope for made all the difference. The fragility of it all pressed softly against her chest. She was grateful.

She walked out onto the sunporch, sat in the cushioned chair, and pulled a throw blanket around her shoulders. The night air was cool. Her gaze lifted to the sky. There was no moon, but the stars were there. They were bright and beautiful, and she started counting them. Then she lifted her head back and whispered into the dark, "Thank you." Not for everything being perfect—because it certainly wasn't—but she was thankful for this moment. This breath. This quiet.

She thought about her home in New Orleans and Chic Threads. During those long, quiet days closed up in her room, waiting on the test results, she'd had plenty of time to think. Time to sift through everything she'd built, everything she wanted to keep, and what she was ready to let go.

Over the summer she'd grown unexpectedly fond of Napa and its surrounding areas. The pace. The space to breathe. The simplicity. She especially liked Bodega Bay and the windswept cliffs, the cry of seagulls below, and the hush of the waves that crashed against the shore.

Later, she'd found herself browsing real estate listings. She felt drawn to the small homes perched above the ocean, like the one she'd rented earlier in the summer. Something with wide windows and space for quiet mornings. A retreat. A new beginning. Maybe she'd move Chic Threads, or open a second location—something more intimate, coastal. Something that felt more like the woman she was becoming and less like the one she planned to leave behind. Bianca wanted to evolve into something else. She wanted to become someone who made the lives of the people she loved better.

Bianca took another sip of tea, and for the first time in weeks her thoughts didn't spiral. They were clear. Tomorrow she would get in touch with her realtor—just to test the waters. See how much her New Orleans property might sell for. And she'd also talk to Amelia about Chic Threads. Maybe she'd want to take it on full time. She was already handling the day-to-day and she was loyal. Bianca trusted her.

There were decisions to be made, real ones. The kind she used to avoid when things felt uncertain. But now something inside of her was shifting. She was ready, not just to decide but to move forward. It was time for her to live.

Chapter Thirty-three

Remi

Remi could hear the crunch of the gravel beneath the crane truck's wheels as it pulled into position. They were earlier than she'd expected, otherwise she would've already been out there to meet them. She made long strides toward *Joie*, heart pounding with anticipation. Zoe and Mila rushed to catch up, and Bianca followed close behind at her own pace.

Paloma was already there, confidently directing the truck driver into place—not that they really needed her help, but she wasn't one to stand still when something big was happening. Leo stood nearby in his athletic shorts and running shoes, hands shoved into his pockets, watching with a relaxed grin.

Leo stepped closer to Remi, smiling. "This is a big moment for you," he said. "I happened to be out for my morning jog and saw the truck pull in."

Remi nodded, her excitement barely contained. "I'm really excited."

Paloma walked over with a wide grin on her face. "This is it, girlfriend. Are you ready to see your name in lights?"

"I'm so ready."

Paloma and Remi held hands as the crane's hoist began to lift, raising the covered sign high off the ground. All eyes turned upward as it was carefully positioned atop the building and secured in place. Then came the unveiling. The cover was removed slowly. Then . . . there it was in bold, elegant lettering: *Joie Winery—Tasting Room. Winery. Vineyard.* In the center, nestled between the words, was Mila's logo. The signage for the winery in full view, for the world to see.

Remi pressed a hand against her chest, overwhelmed. She glanced at Mila, who stood by silently, eyes wide, lips parted in awe.

"That's *your* masterpiece, sweetheart," Remi told her, and pointed at the sign.

Mila covered her mouth with her hands in disbelief. Zoe clapped and let out a cheer, and everyone else followed. Then she wrapped her arm around Mila's shoulder.

"This is so cool," Zoe said.

Bas walked up, wearing sweatpants and an old T-shirt, still rubbing the sleep from his eyes. He looked up at the sign, blinked in amazement, and grinned. Without a word, he gave Mila a high five. The three of them—Bas, Zoe, and Mila—stood huddled in a circle.

Across the gravel, Bianca stood quietly, watching. She didn't say a word, just smiled and looked at Remi with eyes full of pride. It was a look that said *I see you* and *I'm proud of you.* Remi smiled back, soft and warm. Their friendship had changed. That was for certain. It had weathered so many things that should've destroyed them, but the love was still there. It had transcended all that happened. They were still family, whether they wanted to be or not.

Remi felt the fullness of the moment settle around her. As the crane lowered, she stood there, her eyes focused on the signage, taking in every curve of every letter. *Joie Winery*. Every letter leaving an imprint in her heart.

Inside, everyone gathered into the finished tasting room, with its earth-toned, soft peach-colored walls. Paloma held a wine bottle high above her head. The soft light caught the label. *Joie*, printed in elegant script, was wrapped around the slim bottle of blush rosé. "Here's to *Joie*'s first bottle," she announced, her voice full of pride. "It's from our very first batch."

The room quieted for a moment. Remi stepped forward, took the bottle into her hand, ran her fingertips over the label. The moment was surreal. She handed it back to Paloma, who was watching her. Paloma uncorked it with a soft pop. She poured slowly into waiting glasses.

"To growth," Paloma said, lifting her glass in the air.

"To the badass women who built it," Zoe added, raising hers a little higher. She giggled when she caught Remi's eyes. "Sorry, Mom, but you're a badass woman."

Laughter filled the room. Glasses clinked, and Remi gave her daughter a light smile.

Remi watched as Mila held hers close, then touched her glass to Bianca's. She said it in almost a whisper, but Remi heard her, "To the ones who made it through," she said.

Bianca blinked back tears and Remi's smile trembled. Remi raised her glass to her lips, tasting her first batch. The wine tasted like pure, crisp sunlight. Like wonder, excitement, and everything beautiful.

Like joy.

Bianca had started going for walks every evening, just before the sun began to set. A ritual she'd adopted after her visit to the doctor. Tonight Remi decided to join her. They found themselves side by side, making slow strides around the property. Birds rustled in the trees overhead, and then the sprinkler system hissed, watering the rows of vines.

"I've been doing a lot of thinking about my future lately." Bianca breathed heavily as they increased the pace.

"And what did you decide?"

"Decided that I really like the peace and calm that I feel here, in this area," Bianca said. "I called my realtor in New Orleans. She thinks that if I put my home on the market now, she'd have it sold by fall . . . maybe sooner."

"Wow. That's soon."

"And I had a long talk with Amelia. She's totally open to running Chic Threads, at least until I figure out what to do with it."

"Chic Threads would fit really well in downtown Napa."

"Or, even better, in Bodega Bay. It's a cute little area, and I'm quite fond of it. I've been looking at small homes near the beach." Bianca ran her hand through her short curls. "I have my eye on a couple of possibilities. One of them I'm going to see soon."

"Wow. You've done a lot of footwork. Sounds like your mind is made up, then."

Remi felt a bit detached. Normally, these were decisions they would've made together. They would've brainstormed together. Bianca would have asked Remi's advice. They would've also celebrated the fact that she was staying in the area. They would've drunk wine and toasted.

"I don't know how much time I have on this earth, Rem. I want to make sure I spend it being happy. I've done some bad things to the people I love, but still, I have to believe that there's some good out there, even for me."

"There is some good out there for you, B," Remi said.

She looked at Bianca. Color had returned to her skin. She was putting on a little weight. Her mood had lifted. For a while there depression had her bound. But lately, Remi had seen a change.

"I hope so. I was in a very dark place."

"I certainly don't want you in that dark place. I want to see you healthy . . . and happy." Remi paused. "And for the record, I have forgiven you. Not necessarily for you, but for me. You have to forgive for your own self-care."

Bianca choked on her words. "I'm thankful."

Remi reached for Bianca's hand, held it tightly as they walked.

"Maybe I can go with you to see that place in Bodega Bay."

Bianca glanced at her, smiled warmly. "I'd like that."

They rounded the curve in the path, the sign for *Joie* coming up ahead, its letters glowing faintly as dusk began to set in.

Remi looked out over the rows of vines. "Isn't it crazy how something good can grow out of everything bad?"

Bianca followed her gaze. "It's not crazy," she said. "It's what we're made for . . . to grow."

They walked on, side by side. Bianca and Remi were no longer two women carrying grief and old wounds—but survivors moving toward whatever came next, together.

Chapter Thirty-four

Bianca

The house was rustic and tucked into the cliffs, with sweeping views of the ocean and the bay. The kitchen, with its granite countertops and spacious island, was the first thing to draw Bianca in. It opened to a wide, extensive room and the sunporch just off the living area, which was an unexpected bonus. Hardwood floors, which were the original ones, gave the space character.

Bianca and Remi followed the realtor throughout the house, peeking into the two bedrooms, stepping out to breathe in the air and take in the views. It was just the right amount of space for Bianca, and enough for Mila if she decided to visit.

"I'll let you look around. Take it all in," the realtor said. "Let me know if you have questions."

Once she stepped away, Bianca turned to Remi. "What do you think?"

"I think it's gorgeous. Definitely you. You've always loved rustic spaces with killer views."

"I love the kitchen too."

"That's key," Remi said with a grin. "Is it within your

budget? California real estate is a whole different beast compared to Louisiana."

"Tell me about it. Triple the price for the same square footage." Bianca laughed, shaking her head. "But Harry gave me a nice nest egg after the divorce. I invested it well. I could pay cash if I wanted."

Remi nodded. "And your house in New Orleans is on the market. Hopefully it'll go quickly."

They stepped back inside, stood in front of the tall windows that gave light to the entire space, gazing out at the ocean as it crashed against the rugged shore. Bianca walked slowly across the room, letting her fingers trail along the edge of the kitchen island. She paused at the window again, taking it all in—the light, the view, the quietness of the ocean. Then she closed her eyes for a moment.

She could see herself here. Coffee on the sunporch. Prince serenading her while she cooked. She would entertain occasionally, but not much. That was never her thing. It was more Remi's cup of tea. Remi loved to entertain and invite the world into her orbit. Bianca was the opposite. She'd always been a social butterfly by day, mingling with the people who frequented her boutique. She loved being in the mix of things, but once she retreated to her personal space, that was it. She loved the peace and calmness.

"I'm in love with it," Bianca finally said, her smile soft but certain.

"That's what matters . . . that you don't just like it, you love it."

The realtor reentered, her voice bright. "What do you think?" she asked.

Bianca turned, still smiling. "I think I'd like to make an offer."

And just like that, her mind was made up. She was staying.

* * *

They stopped for a late lunch at a well-loved fish market in Bodega Bay, known for its fresh catch and long lines that seemed to be worth the wait. There were plenty of seafood options, but Bianca ordered the seared ahi, charred just enough. Remi couldn't resist the fried prawns.

They took their drinks, crisp local cider, and found a cozy spot outside. The breeze off the bay was cool but not cold. They pulled their sweaters tighter to brace against the wind. Seagulls squealed overhead. Boats rocked gently in the harbor below.

"Lunch here was a good idea," Bianca said, stretching her legs under the picnic table.

"This will soon be your neck of the woods . . . *maybe.*"

Bianca looked out toward the water, her gaze steady. "I love being near the ocean."

"Not much else here. Just fishing and water sports." Remi laughed a little. "But you can always make the drive to Napa whenever you're in the mood for a flea market or antique shopping. Something nonocean-related."

"I could, when I want a change of scenery." She breathed in the scent of the saltwater. "But I love the simplicity of being here."

"Wow, you have changed. Ocean. Quiet. Simplicity. What have you done with Bianca?"

"She's here," Bianca said with a soft smile. "She's just evolved."

"Well . . . it's nice to see the evolution."

"Thank you."

They talked easily, unforced. When the food arrived they savored it slowly. They took their time. Neither of them was in a rush. It was just the two of them, savory food and good conversation—a perfect afternoon.

They took their time driving back to Napa, letting the day unfold slowly. With the windows down and music filling the car, the coastline unraveled beside them as they drove.

Back at the house, Bianca stood in the kitchen, her glass on the counter. She waited for Remi to open the bottle—champagne this time. Zoe stepped into the kitchen.

"What is it that we're celebrating?" she asked.

"Bianca just put an offer on a house," Remi said. "In Bodega Bay."

"Really?" Mila entered behind her, taking a seat at the island. "So, you're staying here?"

Bianca paused, letting the question settle and thinking about her decision. It was one that she'd weighed carefully. She could be impulsive at times, but not this time. During those long, dark days she spent tucked away in her bedroom, she'd faced herself and made some hard decisions about her life.

Now she was ready. She knew what she wanted. She drew in a long breath. "Yes," she said. "I am."

Remi poured champagne into Bianca's glass and then hers. They lifted their glasses in a toast. "Here's to new decisions," Remi said.

"Congratulations," Zoe said. "I'd love to see it."

"Congratulations, Mom," Mila said. "I'm really happy for you."

"Thank you both, but it isn't mine yet. I just made an offer." Bianca smiled broadly, taking a sip of champagne. "Still, I can't wait for you to see it. You're going to love it."

The doorbell interrupted their celebration. Zoe rushed to answer it, and Bas walked in. He wore denim jeans and a faded Lakers T-shirt.

"I just came to say my final goodbyes. I'm headed to the airport."

Mila was the first to reach him, wrapping her arms around his waist. "It's been great hanging out."

"It's been real," he said with a grin. "Great meeting you, Bianca. And always good seeing you, Remi."

Bianca made her way out of the kitchen and gave him a warm hug. Remi followed, embracing him tightly.

Across the room Zoe stood still. She hadn't moved.

Bas glanced at her. "Zoe," he said with a small smile. "I'll see ya later, alligator."

Zoe hesitated for just a moment, then crossed the room and stepped into his arms. She wrapped herself tightly around his waist, her head pressed against his chest. With her eyes closed, she held on, as if letting go might break her.

Bas gently kissed the top of her forehead. "I'll text you."

Her voice trembled. "You'd better."

He nodded but said nothing more. As if saying more might cause him to unravel too. He turned and walked out the door.

Bianca watched Zoe silently, her heart tightening in her chest. She knew too well how complex young love could be, how deeply it could cut, even when it didn't make sense to anyone else. Zoe and Bas had been through so much together, at a young age. It wasn't just puppy love; it was something deeper.

She watched as Zoe stood by the door long after it closed, her arms crossed tightly over her chest, eyes fixed on nothing really. She clenched her jaw tight, but there was some softness too. A tenderness in the way she pressed her lips together, like holding back tears would somehow make her stronger. Remi moved first and wrapped her arms around Zoe and held her tightly.

"You okay, baby?"

Zoe nodded. She crossed the room and headed toward the stairs.

"You want to talk?" Remi asked.

"No, I just want to be alone," Zoe said. "Plus, I need to finish packing."

"Me too." Mila hopped down from the stool in the kitchen.

The girls were leaving in the morning, headed back to school. Soon the house would feel quieter.

In the kitchen Bianca filled the kettle with water. "Tea?" she asked, glancing over at Remi, who was scrolling through emails on her phone.

"Yes," Remi said without looking up. "I'd love some."

Bianca's phone buzzed on the counter. She picked it up and read the message: **The sellers accepted your offer. But they're very motivated . . . looking for a quick closing. They're leaving the country in two weeks. Can you close that soon? Call me.**

"Wow," Bianca whispered.

Remi looked up. "What? What's up?"

Bianca turned the phone toward her. "They accepted my offer. They want to close in two weeks."

"Really? That's fast. Are you ready for that?"

Bianca didn't answer right away. Her lips slowly curled into a smile as the words sank in. A rush of excitement stirred in her chest, her heartbeat quickened.

She met Remi's eyes. "I'm ready."

Chapter Thirty-five

Bianca

Bianca breathed in the fresh morning air, cool against her face. The birds greeted her with soft morning chirps. A gentle breeze blew through her hair. She decided to run today—or rather, slow jog. She wanted to get her heart pumping, but she was careful not to overdo it.

She was feeling good about her future. Not everything had come full circle, but it was getting there. She jogged steadily, the wind pressing against her skin as she picked up the pace toward *Joie*. As she passed the sign, she glanced up, and her heart swelled with pride for Remi, who'd followed her dream and built something meaningful, lasting, in spite of everything. Even when the odds were against her, she beat them. And she felt pride for Mila too—her logo displayed prominently on a winery in Napa Valley. That was no small accomplishment, and one she should be proud of.

She smiled as she rounded the corner near the Ortiz Vineyard, the vines stretching beneath the early morning light. The sun had just started to peek through the clouds. Saying goodbye to the girls would be bittersweet. The summer had held with it so many moments—painful ones, joyful ones—all of them meaningful. All of them were a part of her story now.

She slowed down. Her jog became a brisk walk. Her breath came harder than she'd expected, so she winded down to catch it, get her rhythm back. Her Puma sneakers hit the pavement in a rhythm of their own. In her ears Phillip Lester's acoustic guitar strummed a soft Spanish melody that soothed her. She could feel the muscles in her legs strengthening each day. Her lungs were steadier. She was becoming stronger—physically, mentally, emotionally. She wasn't there yet, but she was well on her way.

By the time Bianca returned to the house the sun had fully risen. She smelled coffee and was grateful. She needed a cup. Mila stood at the stove, barefoot, her curls short but beautiful. She was flipping pancakes in a skillet, and the smell of bacon filled the kitchen. A song was playing low on her phone, something soft.

Bianca smiled, wiping sweat from her brow with her sleeve. "Smells good in here."

Mila looked over her shoulder and grinned. "I figured I'd cook breakfast before Zoe and I got on the road. I made coffee too."

"That's what I'm talking about," Bianca teased, walking over to pour herself a cup.

They moved around the kitchen in a quiet rhythm. Bianca leaned against the counter, took a sip of her coffee, and looked at Mila. "You know, I'm really proud of you."

Mila checked the bacon in the oven. "Yeah?"

Bianca nodded. "What you did with that logo. You showed up. You built something really amazing."

A small smile crept into the corners of Mila's mouth. Her whole face lit up, and Bianca noticed her beauty like never before. "Thanks. I wasn't sure I had it in me."

"Well, you do," Bianca said. "You always have. And there's more where that came from. I'm sure of it."

"I'm gonna miss being here," Mila admitted, glancing around the house that had welcomed them all for the summer—

where memories were made. A place where both pain and joy had coexisted. "But I'm excited about LSU. It'll be sort of a new beginning for me."

"I'm excited for you. This new journey of yours," Bianca said. "You'll have to make new connections . . . new friends."

"I know. But I'm ready."

"You'll be fine. And Zoe will be there."

"Yeah, she will," Mila said. "I'm excited for *you*. I still can't believe you're staying."

Bianca looked toward the window. Her heart warmed every time she thought of that house overlooking the bay. It gave her good vibes. "Neither can I. But it feels right. It really does."

"And I'm glad your health is better. I was really scared when . . ." She paused, took a deep breath. "When I thought I might lose you."

Tears brimmed her eyes when she heard Mila's words. *Thought I might lose you*. It meant she was hers to lose. To hear Mila claiming her as her mother gave her peace.

"I thought it was over for me." Saying those words made her chest hurt and deep, dark thoughts come to the forefront of her mind again. Those thoughts were real. They haunted her in her quiet places. "And I'm not out of the woods yet. Have to keep testing, just to be sure that the cancer is shrinking, and that it hasn't spread anywhere else."

"That's tough."

"Yes, but I'm tougher now," Bianca said.

She watched as Mila pulled the pan of bacon out of the oven and set it on the granite countertop.

Bianca poured more coffee into her cup. "I know things have been hard between us. But if you ever decide to come back—to Bodega Bay—the house has an extra bedroom. It's yours whenever you want it."

Mila poured pancake batter into the skillet. She glanced over at Bianca with a small smile. "I'll come back," she said.

Her words brought joy to Bianca's heart. She needed to hear them. They felt like healing to her soul. Bodega Bay had been where she and Mila had first truly connected, and she hoped it would be the place where they found each other again.

Her phone buzzed in her pocket. She pulled it out, looked at the text in front of her. It was Harry.

I'm supposed to pick Mila up at the airport this afternoon, but she's not answering her phone.

Bianca typed: **She's cooking. I'll have her call you.**

The typing bubble appeared, then disappeared. Then: **How are you doing, Bianca?**

She typed: **I'm doing great. Getting stronger every day.**

Harry replied: **That's great to hear.** He was still typing. Then: **Bianca, you were right about Jen. She was the one stalking you.**

She stood frozen. Her mind jolted back to the very first message she received—the one that had knocked her off course. The feeling of violation; of intrusion that she'd felt. Fear had taken over her entire body, made her restless and uneasy. She had blamed the wrong person for creeping into her dreams, causing her restless nights—when all along it was Harry's girlfriend.

"Wow." She whispered it to herself. Then she typed it: **Wow!**

He replied: **I saw the messages on her phone. I'm sorry that you had to endure that. I confronted her, and we are no longer together. I can't have someone like that around me or my daughter.** Then another message appeared: **If you want to file charges . . .**

Bianca's reply came swiftly, with three simple words: **I'm over it.**

It was true. Bianca really was over it. Sure, she was shocked to find out who was sending the messages, but she'd gotten past all of it. So many things were in the rearview mirror of her life now. She wasn't looking back anymore. She was bracing for whatever came next.

Just as Mila flipped the last three pancakes, she looked up at Bianca. "You okay?"

"Yeah, I'm fine." Bianca slid her phone into the pocket of her leggings.

Remi and Zoe wandered into the kitchen. Remi rubbed sleep from her eyes. "Something smells wonderful. I knew one of you was down here cooking."

Bianca lifted her coffee mug with a grin. "It's all Mila. I'm just an innocent bystander."

Breakfast had been good—hearty. Their last meal before sending the girls off was one for the books. Mila was becoming a great cook. The four of them savored the meal and then talked about the summer and all they'd been through. They laughed and made promises to spend Thanksgiving together.

"I'd like to try my hand at a Butterball turkey," Mila said, fork in midair. "And some Creole mac and cheese."

"Okay," Remi said. "I'm certainly looking forward to that."

"I'll put the rolls in the oven," Zoe said laughing.

"That's all you got?" Remi asked teasingly.

"That's all I got." Zoe grinned. She had refreshed her cornrows the night before.

"Well, I'll bring the wine," Remi said with a smile.

"Of course you will." Bianca smiled and shook her head. "I think we should incorporate some Cuban dishes. Honor our Cuban heritage." She looked at Mila.

"I'd like that," Mila said. "Maybe we can use some of Abuelita's recipes."

"For sure. I have some of them." Bianca smiled. "I'm really excited about Thanksgiving now."

"Maybe we should do it in Bodega Bay," Remi suggested. "Break in your new kitchen."

"That's a great idea," Zoe said.

"Maybe we should," Bianca agreed, smiling widely. She beamed at the thought of her new space. She couldn't wait to make new memories there.

And Thanksgiving was just around the corner.

Bianca and Remi stood shoulder to shoulder, watching as their babies—their girls—slid into the back seat of a waiting Lyft. Luggage packed neatly into the trunk, all the things they'd brought to Napa at the beginning of the summer, and the new things they'd picked up along the way—books, vinyl, little pieces of summer. Their memories were tucked alongside them.

As the Lyft pulled away, moving up the long pathway, past the vineyard and away from the house, they stood still—silently watching.

Just like that, they were gone.

They stood there for a while, long after the car was out of sight, letting the silence settle between them. Bianca took a slow sip of her coffee, which she held in her hand, now lukewarm.

"I think we might be all right. Me and Mila," she said quietly, eyes still on the road from where the car had disappeared.

"I think you will too. She seems to be loosening up a bit."

"I'm glad. I hope we're on an upward trend."

"Zoe didn't seem sad at all," Remi added. "Just waved . . . like it was easy."

Bianca gave a soft laugh. "Maybe it was. For them."

"But for us, not so much." Remi nudged her gently with her shoulder. "We raised strong girls. This is what it's supposed to look like, right?"

Bianca finally turned to her, almost glassy-eyed. "Yeah, it's exactly what it's supposed to look like."

A breeze rustled the trees in the front lawn, as they stood for a moment.

Then Remi said, "So . . . what now?"

Bianca looked back toward the house, the doorway still open, the scent of bacon still lingering in the air.

"I guess we figure out who we are without them around," she said.

They stepped back inside. Now that the girls were gone, quietness filled the space around them. Remi moved around in the kitchen, collecting empty plates and washing dishes in the sink.

Bianca slipped her hand into the pocket of her leggings and pulled out her phone. She scrolled her contacts until she found the number for her realtor in New Orleans. She needed to get that house on the market—and sooner rather than later.

Chapter Thirty-six

Remi

Ripe purple grapes hung heavily on the vines in the foreground of a vineyard. An inviting path leading to white houses off in the distance with red tile roofs—the houses were all nestled on a hillside and overlooking a valley. Remi stood there in awe, eyes tracing every brushstroke. The mural was complete. The piece would be the focal point of the tasting room.

She moved through the space with focus, doing a final walk-through to make sure everything was in order. The tasting was just a week away and every detail had to be perfect. Bottles of wine stood ready, lined neatly along the walnut table. Crisp white linens covered the high-top tables inside. The menu had been finalized. The caterers were prepped. The morning of the event, fresh flowers would be gathered from the garden outside and arranged into simple but elegant centerpieces for each table. Outside, strands of white lights hung like stars in waiting, ready to shine once the sun went down.

Everything was nearly ready. And it was beautiful.

Remi grabbed a chilled bottle of Pinot Grigio from the

cooler and a single wineglass. She uncorked the bottle and then stepped outside to the garden. At the wrought-iron table she eased into a chair and poured herself a glass. She gazed at the vineyard and watched as the sun began to set, beautiful orange streaks painted in the sky. Her heart warmed at how the scene before her mirrored the mural inside. She smiled at the thought. She took a sip of the wine and settled into the chair.

Remi spotted Bianca heading down the path. The evening sun cast a glow against her skin. A sundress clung to her figure and a breeze blew gently through her hair.

"So, this is where you've been hiding," she said with a smile once she reached the winery.

"I came over to see the mural and make sure everything was in order for next Saturday night," Remi said. "Go inside and grab a glass. Join me."

Bianca nodded as she headed inside.

"Check out that mural while you're in there," Remi called.

"Will do."

Remi was lost in her thoughts. So much had happened over the course of the summer—layers shed, truths faced, hearts changed. And here they were nearing the end. They all had become something more than what they were when they first arrived in Napa. Everyone had evolved in one way or another.

Bianca's voice interrupted her thoughts. "That mural is freaking fabulous," she said, stepping back outside. She poured herself a glass of wine. "Do you love it?"

"I absolutely do," Remi said, smiling. She took a sip of her wine. "It was worth every penny."

"She captured all of this so perfectly," Bianca said, sweeping her hand across the view in front of her. "It's uncanny."

"I love how everything is coming together. The winery . . . the first tasting."

"I'm sure it's all pretty exciting," Bianca said. "Wherever

you need me on Saturday I'm there. If you need someone to greet guests, pour wine, or keep the caterers in line. Whatever."

"I appreciate that," Remi replied. "And I'm sure there will be plenty to keep you busy."

There was a comfortable silence between them as they sipped wine and took in the breeze and scenery.

"Have you heard from Mila?" Remi asked.

"Just a quick text. She made it safely to her dad's." Bianca smiled softly. "But I *have* heard from Harry. Quite a bit, actually."

"What? Really?" Remi turned toward her with raised eyebrows.

"Yeah . . . we've just been chatting," Bianca said casually, but Remi detected something more.

"Interesting." Remi grinned. "You've got unresolved history with Harry. Maybe now's the time to finish it."

"Maybe," Bianca said. "But right now my focus is on my health, building a new life, and, hopefully, connecting with my daughter."

"All good things to focus on."

"The house is on the market," Bianca added. "There's already quite a bit of interest. Fingers crossed."

"Fingers crossed." Remi crossed two fingers. "Things are moving fast. Are you sure you're ready?"

"I'm ready," Bianca said, and meant it. "Tomorrow morning I'm going to fly back to New Orleans for a couple of days. I've already hired movers to pack up what I want to transport. Get rid of everything else. Tie up loose ends. Ship my car. I'll be back before your tasting."

"That's sudden. You've got your work cut out for you."

"It's necessary. This is the start of something wonderful."

Remi raised her glass to Bianca's. "To new beginnings, then."

"To new beginnings." Their glasses clinked.

Remi lifted her glass again, smirking. "And to new conversations with ex-husbands."

Bianca laughed, a sparkle in her eyes. "Ha ha."

Their conversation moved easily throughout the evening, as if there had never been a pause in their friendship. Laughter came naturally, the rhythm between them unforced—familiar.

It almost felt like old times, but Remi wasn't ready for it to feel this way—not just yet. There was comfort in the closeness, yes. But also caution.

Some wounds needed more time to breathe.

Chapter Thirty-seven

Bianca

As the Lyft pulled away from the curb and she stepped onto the porch, she was consumed by the Louisiana heat. It was smothering. She used her key to open the door and step inside. She stood in the foyer for a moment—listening. The only sound was that from the central air unit making a whirring noise as it kicked on.

The house smelled stale, and she would light a candle as soon as she was done checking things out. Leaving her luggage at the door, she made her way to the bright yellow kitchen. From the drawer next to the stove she pulled out her pink .45 pistol, cocked it. She made her way through the house peeking into the downstairs bedrooms and then went upstairs to the master bedroom. She looked around. Everything was just as she'd left it when she left for Napa.

She'd always loved her 1920s' Spanish-style home. It exuded character, with its arched doorways and colorful tilework, and exposed beams in the ceiling. She had decorated it with white furniture and plants in huge ceramic and clay pots. Built-in shelving held artifacts that she'd brought back from her trips to Havana and Costa Rica. Huge windows brought sunlight in from the outside.

Downstairs she opened the French glass doors that led out to the patio. She needed to let fresh air flow through, even if just for a moment. Bianca found a candle, something with jasmine and spices. She lit it and let the scent flow through the house. In the family room, she sorted through her albums and found one that she'd taken from her abuelita's collection. Carefully, she placed the vinyl on the turntable. Celia Cruz's voice rang out from the speakers with her Spanish version of "I Will Survive." Her strong, deep voice caused Bianca to dance around the house. She hadn't allowed herself to dance like that in a while, but now she found her rhythm.

In the kitchen she started pulling dishes from the shelves. Even though the movers would arrive in the morning to pack up the house, she felt a need to do something—to busy herself. She placed plates, bowls, and saucers neatly onto the island. Her phone vibrated on the counter and she glanced at the text: **Are you back in New Orleans?**

She smiled to herself and then replied to Harry: **Just got here.**

His text: **Enrolled Mila in school. Now we're picking up her books and going to check out the dorms. She's been talking about sharing an apartment with Zoe. Did she mention that to you?**

Bianca typed: **She did, but I think it's too soon. I didn't want to be the one to tell her no. Be the bad guy.**

Harry's response was swift: **I will tell her no. I'll be the bad guy. Maybe we'll consider it next year.**

Bianca smiled at Harry's subtle protection of her. She had gone through enough with Mila—didn't need for this to be just *one more thing* to draw a wedge between them. It seemed as though they were constantly rebuilding.

Bianca typed a response: **I'd like for her to get a job. Learn what it means to pay her own way. Learn responsibility.**

This is where she often bumped heads with Harry. He

wanted to give Mila the world, while Bianca wanted her to learn strength; to endure things that only life could teach her—like *she* had. Abuelita didn't have much money, so what she got from her were lessons. Things she held dear. Things she didn't know she needed until now.

When Bianca's phone rang she was surprised to see Harry's face on the screen. She picked up and before she could say anything . . .

"I admit, I do spoil her." Harry laughed. His voice was deep, and it made her heart flutter.

"Yes, you do."

"I, too, want her to learn responsibility."

"Where is she right now?" Bianca asked.

Bianca wasn't ready for Mila to learn of her many conversations with Harry in the past weeks—sometimes in the earliest of mornings or in the wee hours of the night. Some days he had simply calmed her fears, or they'd laughed about things from the past. But she didn't want to hear her daughter's judgment about why they should or shouldn't be talking.

"She's in the bookstore, buying her books." He chuckled lightly, understanding Bianca's hesitation. "I'm in the car . . . waiting."

"Good. I don't need her in my business." Bianca laughed.

"You don't want her to know we've been talking?" he asked. "It's the one thing that she's wanted for years, for her parents to stop fighting. To get along."

"Not just yet."

"Your secret is safe with me, then," Harry said. "I won't tell."

It wouldn't be the first time he'd kept her secret, but this time was different.

After a pause, he said, "She can learn a lot from you, Bianca. I didn't want to see it or admit it before, because I was just . . . so mad. But you *are* a strong woman. I think you've made some mistakes, but overall, you're good-hearted."

Her voice trembled. "Thank you," she said softly. "I'm not proud of my past, but I'm really trying to right my wrongs."

"I see that you are. And I'm proud of you."

Those words pulled at her heartstrings. She found herself trying to recover as she pulled glasses from the shelf and stacked them on the counter. Selling the house was a bold move, even for Bianca. She'd built a life behind these walls. She'd fought cancer and grieved a man she loved—behind these walls. She only hoped that the couple who had made her a full cash offer just last night would find the same peace that she'd found here.

She wouldn't take everything to Bodega Bay, just her essentials—clothes, a few dishes, her living room furniture, beds, artifacts. Everything else would go into storage until she could make time for an estate sale of some kind, or purge. If simplicity was what she was really going for, it needed to start now.

"Mila's coming out of the bookstore," Harry said quickly.

"Okay."

"She's hanging out with friends later. I'd like to take you out to dinner if you're free or even up to it. Maybe to your favorite little Cuban spot in Mid-City."

"You hate that place," she said.

"I don't hate it." Harry laughed. "I just got sick of eating there so much. You wanted to eat there every other day."

Her mouth curled into a smile. "I love my favorite little spot in Mid-City. And dinner would be nice."

"Pick you up at seven, then?"

"Yes," she said. "I'll be ready."

In the garage she started her car. It hadn't been driven in a while, so she let the engine roar until it settled into a soft hum. She sat for a moment, hands on the wheel. Then she backed out of the driveway and headed toward the French Quarter. She needed to check up on Chic Threads and see how the shop was holding up, and how Amelia was doing without her.

She merged onto I-10, slipping into the rhythm of the freeway. The city unfolded around her, the skyline beaming with the morning sun, traffic pushing forward the way it always did. It was after rush hour, so there was no stress.

She pulled into a narrow spot just down the block from Chic Threads. The storefront looked the same as when she left it—gold lettering on the windows. The new styles had arrived, and Amelia had done well with dressing the mannequins in the window. They were dressed in bold summer prints. A small OPEN sign hung on the door.

Bianca smiled. She really missed her place. Inside, the familiar jingle of the door chime greeted her, followed by the scent of a woodsy candle. Amelia hadn't seen her coming—not at first. She was engaged with a customer, one of their regulars who was known for being difficult, always looking for a discount. The woman was also always trying to return items to the store—sales tags still attached and reeking of her perfume. There were countless times Bianca had to firmly tell her no, she couldn't return things after she'd worn them. It was a fight that she'd grown tired of having. Bianca wished she could've just banned her from the store altogether. But Amelia handled the woman with her usual style and grace, smiling, although she wanted to scream. She looked up and realized that Bianca was watching. She gave her a warm smile. Bianca winked.

Bianca busied herself by straightening clothes on a rack and refolding clothes on a table.

"Welcome home, stranger." Amelia was finally able to pull herself away once the woman left.

Bianca embraced her. "It's so good to see you."

"Good to see you. You look good. Healthy," Amelia said.

"Thank you. I'm feeling pretty healthy." Bianca smiled. "Everything seems to be in order and running smoothly. But I know it's overwhelming sometimes, doing it by yourself. Maybe we can talk about hiring someone to help out."

Amelia sighed. "Yeah, things have picked up. Those summer tops you ordered are flying off the shelves. I can't keep them on hangers. And there's a long waitlist for the pink ones."

"A shipment's coming. It's just delayed."

Amelia nodded. "So, you're really doing it . . . moving to California?"

"I got an offer on the house last night. We'll see if it pans out. And I'm closing on my home in California in a couple of days."

"Wow, Bianca," Amelia said, a smile on her face. "If you're happy, I'm happy for you. You know I'll hold it down here until you figure things out."

"I appreciate that, more than you know." Bianca headed toward the door. "I'm not going to stay. I just wanted to drop by. Check things out."

"Of course. Take care." Amelia hugged her tightly. "Mila doing okay?"

"Yes. In fact, she's transferred schools. She'll be at LSU now."

"Really? Wow." Amelia laughed and said, "Well, get her over here to work part-time."

"I was thinking the exact same thing," she told Amelia. "A good way to start learning responsibility is with a job."

"I couldn't agree more," Amelia said. "I'll teach her the ropes when she's ready."

Bianca opened the door, and it jingled. "I'll keep that in mind," she said before stepping out into the Louisiana heat.

She walked a few blocks down the street, the air humid

and thick with the scent of fried seafood. Zydeco music spilled out from open doors along the way. She stepped into one of her favorite eateries. She didn't need to look at the menu; in fact the woman behind the counter already knew what she wanted when she walked in. Bianca ordered her usual sandwich with the Italian meats, cheeses, and olive salad soaked into the bread. It was one of the things she would miss about home—a killer muffuletta. The oil was soaked through the paper bag as she left with it and hopped into her car. She couldn't even wait until she got home before ripping the bag open.

Back at home and out of the heat, she relaxed with a glass of lavender iced tea before finally dozing off for a few hours. She was awakened by an anchor on the six o'clock news discussing crime in the city. She pulled herself together. Harry would pick her up soon.

The summer dress she'd chosen to wear was one that hugged her curves in every way. It was off the shoulder and floral, short enough to reveal a set of great legs but not too much. She wore flat sandals with lacy straps that weaved their way up her calves like vines.

When the doorbell rang she gave her neck a quick spritz of perfume and then rushed downstairs to answer it. It had been a while since she'd last seen Harry, but now, standing on her doorstep, wearing khakis and a polo shirt, he was even more handsome than she remembered. The touch of gray in his beard and along his temple. The beard and the gray were something new, hadn't been there the last time she saw him.

"Wow," he said, his eyes giving her a sweep from head to toe. "You look great."

"Thanks." She smiled and grabbed her purse next to the door. She stepped out onto the porch and locked the door behind her. "Let's go."

Bianca sank into the leather seat of Harry's sports car. She slipped a pair of Ray-Bans from her bag and onto her face. He made the short drive from uptown to the Cuban restaurant in Mid-City.

The café was a converted pink house with unmistakable charm. Inside the dining room was a cheerful mix of mismatched chairs in pink, yellow, and turquoise. Caribbean music played from the speakers, and the scent of rich spices—cumin and garlic—drifted from the kitchen and throughout the space.

They started with mojitos and a plate of green plantains to share. She also ordered Caribbean chicken soup. It was her favorite. She wished she could package up an entire batch of it and take it to California with her. She would miss this place after she had relocated to the West Coast. Harry ordered his usual, the lechon amado—Cuban-style slow-roasted pork.

"This is definitely your spot," he said, looking around with a half smile.

She couldn't count the number of times she had dragged him here when they were together.

"I know I used to drive you crazy here in the past," she said with a soft smile, "so thank you for bringing me back."

He smiled. "I admit they have great food."

"The best." She relaxed in her seat and enjoyed the live music being played in the corner of the room.

They spent the evening catching up, laughing, reminiscing, and slipping back into that familiar rhythm that came so easy for them. The hours passed without either of them noticing. Every now and then she caught him watching her across the table.

A few mojitos later Harry drove her home.

He walked her to the door. "I had a great time tonight," he said.

"Me too." She gave him a gentle smile.

"If I'm ever in California—"

She finished the sentence, "Come see me," she said, and kissed his cheek. "In fact Remi's soft opening of her winery is taking place soon . . . in a couple of weeks—a tasting."

"Is that an invitation?" Harry asked.

"Could be." Bianca smiled. "Good night, Harry."

"Good night, Bianca."

She watched as he left her front porch—which was once *their* front porch—and made his way down the flight of stairs and hopped into his car.

She went inside, warmed up her leftover soup in the microwave.

Tomorrow would be the start of something new—something exciting. Her belongings would travel cross-country and meet her in California in a few days. She'd close on her new home in Bodega Bay in just two days, and everything in the universe would be just as it should be.

And she was ready for all of it.

Chapter Thirty-eight

Bianca

Bianca stood in the center of the living room, her furniture situated so that positive energy could flow through the room freely. She opened the sliding glass door to let in fresh air and allow the scent of the ocean to drift in from the outside. She stood in the doorway and watched as the water crashed against the cliffs.

She had closed on the house and received the keys to the place. Boxes were still lined along the wall, not yet unpacked. It would take her days to get settled in and she would take her time—do it at her own pace. Her furniture had arrived as scheduled, and the movers had unloaded everything from their truck and taken the time to assemble beds and other furniture.

Her car hadn't arrived yet, so she'd taken a Lyft to Whole Foods to pick up a few essentials. She was craving grilled fish, so she grabbed a small portable grill and a bag of charcoal along with her groceries.

Now she stood in her kitchen and seasoned the salmon with butter, fresh garlic, and herbs—wrapped it in foil and placed it on the hot grill. She roasted asparagus, squash, and zucchini in the oven.

Music played softly on her Bluetooth speaker. When her phone rang she answered on the second ring.

"Hello, Bianca. This is Autumn from Dr. Lee's office," the young woman said.

"Hello, Autumn."

"I'd like to schedule you for another imaging test," Autumn said. "Dr. Lee would like to see how well the radiation is progressing, to see if it was effective or not," she explained. "I know it's last minute, but we have an opening in the morning. Can we squeeze you in?"

Suddenly her joy faded away. Thoughts of imaging, radiation, and cancer circled in her head when she'd tried so desperately to forget. She felt unsettled again. And the what ifs were back. What if the radiation didn't get it all? What if it had spread to another part of her body? What if . . . what if . . . what if.

"Yes, I think I'm free in the morning," she said reluctantly. A part of her wanted to put it off for as long as she could, but the other part—the logical one—wanted to know if the radiation was working. She wanted to know if the cancer had spread or if she was out of the woods.

"Does nine o'clock work?"

"Nine o'clock works fine."

"Good, I have you down for nine o'clock tomorrow morning. Please fast from all food and drink after midnight tonight, just like you did before," Autumn said, her voice chipper. "Do you have any questions?"

"No."

"Great, then we'll see you in the morning."

She hung up. And then it only took a moment to schedule her Lyft for the morning.

The party was over.

Morning came quickly, and the ride to Napa seemed longer than usual. She lay on her back, the surface of the treatment table cold against her skin. The machine whirred, and Bianca held her breath as she focused on staying still, willing her body not to move. She only hoped the tumors continued to shrink and that the cancer was leaving her body.

When the door opened Dr. Jane Lee stepped in with her usual warmth, her smile bright like the sunshine. "Hello, Bianca, it's good to see you."

"You as well," Bianca said, managing a small smile in return. She wished she didn't have to see the woman as often, but for now, this was a part of her life—scans, treatments, tests. At least for the next year.

"We should have the imaging results in the next day or so," Dr Lee said. "I'll give you a call as soon as we have them."

"Great. Hopefully the cancer is shrinking."

"That's my hope too," Dr. Lee replied gently. "Can I say something?"

"Yes," Bianca said and watched the woman intently, wondering what it was she needed permission to say.

"No matter what the results show, whether the cancer is shrinking or not, try to live every moment of your life. Don't let it stop you." Dr. Lee reached for her hand. "This is from a woman who is also a survivor."

Bianca choked. Barely able to say, "Thank you."

Dr. Lee gave her hand a tight squeeze, then let go. "Any questions for me today?"

Bianca shook her head. "No questions." Her leg bounced beneath the paper gown. She couldn't quite contain her nervous energy.

Dr. Lee reached out, resting her hand gently on Bianca's arm. "Try to relax. We'll take this one day at a time."

And with that she relaxed.

When she called Remi she happened to be downtown picking up a few items from Oxbow Market. She talked her into meeting for brunch. They chose a riverfront restaurant with shaded outdoor seating. A cool breeze drifted off the water and caused Bianca to tremble. By the time she arrived, Remi was there already, seated at a table under a striped umbrella, sunglasses perched on the top of her head and a mimosa in her hand. She waved as Bianca approached.

"Girl, you are looking very California. The golden state agrees with you," Remi said and stood to embrace her.

Bianca smiled and removed her sunglasses. "I'm trying to make my way—ease into it."

They sat, menus in hand, perusing to see what they were in the mood for.

Bianca pointed at Remi's drink and told the server, "I'll have one of those. Pomegranate."

After the server disappeared, Remi sipped her drink and studied Bianca over the rim of her glass. "How was your appointment?"

Bianca hesitated for a moment. "It was fine. Dr. Lee will call with the scan results in a few days. Hopefully there will be good news."

Remi reached across the table and touched Bianca's hand. "It will be. And until then, let's eat up some stuff."

Bianca nodded." Exactly. The French toast is calling my name."

"Think I'm going for an omelet," Remi said.

They laughed and talked like old times, while another round of mimosas appeared without them asking.

"So," Remi said, sipping her drink, "tell me the truth . . . how are you really doing with all of this? You have a lot going on in your life, girl."

Bianca looked down at her lap, then at the river. "I feel better than I have in a long time physically, but having to take these tests . . . this waiting to see the results . . . just really takes me back to a dark place."

"Try not to let it."

"I guess fear just kinda takes over and—"

Remi nodded, her expression softening. "Try not to let fear steal your joy. I've seen you happier than I have in years. When you found your perfect home in Bodega Bay something in you was bursting with life. Live your life, B."

Bianca's eyes welled unexpectedly. "It's like when I take one step forward, I'm always yanked one step back."

"I get it. I know it seems that way," Remi said. "You'll get through it, one step at a time."

Their food arrived, and for a while they ate in silence.

After a few bites Remi leaned in and said, "Do you want to talk about Harry?"

Bianca paused, fork halfway to her mouth. The tears dissipated and a light smile brightened her face.

"Oh wait, what is that smile?" Remi asked.

"There's nothing really to talk about. I think we're just becoming the friends we never were. I'm enjoying the conversation," she said. "We went to dinner while I was in New Orleans."

"Really?" Remi placed a finger underneath her chin.

"It was nothing special, just my favorite little Cuban place in Mid-City."

"Oh my God. Not that place." Remi giggled. "You used to eat there so often."

"It's my fave."

"Don't I know it," Remi said. "You really should broaden your horizons."

The women laughed heartily.

Chapter Thirty-nine

Remi

The tasting room was wrapped in soft, golden light. The huge windows overlooked Paloma's family vineyard, with its rows of sun-warmed lines. It was just before sunset, and light filtered in gently. Doors were open allowing the inside to spill out into the garden. High-top tables, adorned with white tablecloths, were arranged throughout both spaces. Tasting cards with handwritten notes were placed at every setting, along with crisp white napkins and wineglasses with long stems. Small arrangements of wildflowers, freshly cut, sat in small vases.

Guests were greeted with a sparkling rosé, *Joie*'s signature wine, to sip on while mingling. Jazz played softly throughout. Remi moved through the space, chatting with guests. She wore a linen pantsuit with embellished sandals. Bianca worked the room with Paloma, refilling glasses, answering questions. There was laughter and light conversations throughout.

There were several industry professionals in the room, some of them from as far away as the Bay Area. John Gabriel, the man who she'd met at previous networking events—

who'd taken an interest in *Joie*—wore blue slacks and a crisp white shirt with sleeves rolled up. He smiled when their eyes met. Remi raised her glass, hoping they would have a chance to chat before the night was done. Her marketing team, Pinnacle Strategies, mingled with other guests.

When Leo appeared in the doorway wearing white linen and a straw hat, he nearly took her breath away. She couldn't take her eyes off of him as he shook hands with a man he knew. He reached for a glass of rosé and sipped—and his eyes finally landed on her. His grin was wide and beautiful. He gave her a wink. She blushed.

Eventually he eased next to her. "You look so beautiful, Miss Winery Owner."

"You look very nice yourself." She wanted to add that he smelled good too—his cologne was intoxicating—but she didn't.

"Everything is very nice. Very elegant. Not that I expected any less."

"Thank you." She looked around the room at all her guests. "I'm very pleased with the turnout."

"Are you surprised?" he asked. "People were clamoring to get here . . . to see this place. To be a part of this movement."

She laughed nervously. "Stop."

"No," he said. "*Joie* is the talk of the town."

Remi's heart raced. She'd been so deeply involved in planning this event, she hadn't taken the time to put her ear to the street. She didn't know that *Joie* had gained so much momentum that people were actually chattering about it.

"I didn't know that."

"Not only is she beautiful, she's humble." Leo grinned widely and pretended to talk to someone else. "Humility is attractive as hell."

"You are attractive as hell," she flirted with the man who was beginning to tug at her heartstrings.

"I'm going to mingle before you have a grown man blushing," he said. "I'll catch up with you before the night is over."

Remi giggled. "You'd better catch up with me sooner rather than later."

"I promise," he said.

Remi found her way to the center of the two spaces, a mic in her hand.

"Hello, everyone. Welcome to *Joie*."

She paused as light applause rippled through the crowd. Her smile was easy.

"We hope that you're enjoying the music and the rosé," she continued. "I'm truly thrilled to have you all here tonight. It means so much."

Guests were smiling and nodding in agreement.

"This evening we'll be tasting three whites and two reds—all from the Ortiz Vineyard, just across the way." She gestured toward the far side of the vineyard, where the sun was beginning to dip behind the rows of vines. "That land has been in the Ortiz family for generations, and it's an honor to partner with them."

She let a moment pass before adding, "They've been instrumental in helping bring *Joie* to life, and tonight we're literally bringing joy to your glass, and to your palate."

A few soft laughs rippled. Glasses raised in silent agreement.

"So," she said, lifting her own glass, "let us begin."

The tasting moved through *Joie*'s signature whites first—a citrusy Sauvignon Blanc, a buttery Chardonnay, and a crisp Pinot Grigio. Then the reds—an earthy Pinot Noir and a bold Zinfandel. Each wine was paired with one of several small bites—fried goat cheese bites, honeycomb, local chèvre, and crusty bread drizzled with olive oil.

As the night wore on, the sky began to shift. Blue skies became deeper as dusk approached. Inside the mood was light and mellow. It was the kind of gathering where no one cared about the time. Guests were comfortable and lingered long after the tasting was done.

Paloma stood next to her as she said goodbye to a few guests.

"You knocked it out of the park tonight," she said.

"*We* knocked it out of the park." Remi grabbed Paloma by the waist. "Could not have done it without you."

"We make a great team." Paloma rested her head against Remi's. Then she released her waist, started toward the kitchen area. "I'm going to check on the winery staff, make sure they're wrapping things up."

"What a great event," Bianca said, walking up. "I couldn't be prouder."

"Thank you."

"You—as your daughter so eloquently put it—are a badass." Bianca grinned widely.

Remi and Bianca laughed.

"Thank you for your help tonight," she told Bianca.

"It was my pleasure. Seriously."

Remi hugged her for the first time since everything happened. It was easy and genuine, and she held on for an extra moment.

Bianca smiled at Remi. "I'm headed back to Bodega Bay tonight."

"You sure? It's late. You might as well stay and leave in the morning."

"Thanks, but I'd like to sleep in my own bed tonight." Bianca gave a wicked grin. "Someone I know might be coming for a visit," she said with a nod toward the door.

Remi looked up. "Harry?" she whispered.

Bianca laughed. "I didn't think he would actually show up."

Remi grabbed her by the arm. "You have a lot of explaining to do," she said softly.

"I promise. I will tell you everything," Bianca said. "In the meantime, someone is waiting for you also, ma'am." Bianca nodded toward the tasting room.

Leo stood there, leaned against the bar, hands in his pockets. He watched Remi and gave her a wide grin when she looked his way.

"Go handle that," Bianca said and then made long strides toward Harry.

Remi moved across the room with grace and stood close to Leo. He pulled her into an embrace. His cologne penetrated her nose. She relaxed in his arms with ease—naturally, lovingly.

She leaned back and looked up at him. "You wanna take a drive with me?"

"I'm always up for a drive with you." He gently, playfully, touched her nose.

Remi sat in the passenger seat of Leo's car, her body relaxed against the smooth leather seat. She was still in her linen outfit but had swapped out her shoes for a pair of flip-flops. Soulful sounds drifted from the speakers as they talked, replaying the wine tasting—critiquing the night piece by piece.

"Everything was beautiful," he said. "You should be very proud."

"I felt like tonight was perfect. Really introduced *Joie* to the world."

They laughed easily.

Leo slowly pulled into the park and backed into a space.

"Got your permit?"

Remi lifted the folded paper in the air. "Right here."

"You ready?"

She looked out toward the darkness of the coastline. "I need a minute," she said softly. She was honest and transparent. There was no pretending; this would be hard. And she wouldn't reduce it to something smaller than it was.

Leo shut off the engine and stepped out of the car. He gave her the space she needed to breathe. He walked away, hands in his pockets. Remi sat still, her mind a myriad of thoughts. She thought it would be easier, but it wasn't. It was hard. She hadn't anticipated that she would need permission to spread Gerard's ashes along the Sonoma Coast, even though it was what he wanted. But the State of California had their rules—adding an additional layer to this daunting task. She hadn't expected how much it would weigh on her.

He had betrayed her in the worst way, so how did he deserve the grace of having his wishes honored? More than once she'd considered tossing them into the trash can instead. Yet here she was at the edge of the ocean in the middle of the night, the cardboard box resting on the leather seat behind her.

Finally she got out of the car, reached for the box, opened it, and lifted out the urn. She walked toward the shoreline and found a private area along the beach. For a few minutes Remi stood there watching as the waves crashed against the shore. Her hands trembled as she loosened the lid on the urn.

"I guess this is goodbye, Gerard," she whispered. Goodbye to everything that she thought they shared.

She emptied the ashes and watched as they blew away with the wind, as her life, her love, her marriage disappeared into the night. She tossed the urn and the box into the receptacle and returned to Leo's car. Remi stood next to it and waited for him.

When Leo returned to the car he pulled her into his arms and held her tightly. He didn't ask any questions, only provided comfort. She rested her head against his chest. He held her until she was ready to leave. When she had gathered her emotions she nodded, and he released her. Then he opened the passenger door for her and she climbed in. As they pulled away, she gazed into the area where she'd just released the ashes, then looked straight ahead.

The drive back to Napa was quiet. Leo reached for her hand and held it in his, their fingers intertwined for the rest of the drive home.

He walked her to the door and stood there while she unlocked it.

"You want to come in?" she asked.

"If you want me to," he said. "I don't want to intrude. I want you to grieve in this moment . . . alone if you need to."

"I don't want to be alone," she said softly. "I don't want to grieve. I want the night to continue to be celebratory."

He followed her inside. The house was dim, lit only by the glow of the light over the stove and the soft moonlight that spilled in through the windows. Remi slipped off her flip-flops by the door and walked slowly to the kitchen. Leo followed but kept a respectful distance, his eyes on her.

Remi went to the cellar and grabbed a bottle of Merlot. She pulled two glasses from the shelf and poured, handing him one without speaking a word. They stood for a moment in the kitchen, the silence between them thick but comfortable.

"To what are we toasting?" he asked, searching her face, trying to gauge the moment.

She looked up at him, her expression solemn. "To getting through tonight and still finding a way to celebrate the good. To finding joy in the middle of things that aren't joyful."

Their glasses clinked.

Remi took a sip and exhaled slowly, like she'd been holding her breath the whole drive home. She set down her glass and leaned against the counter, her eyes soft and glossing over.

"Do you remember the night we had that moment?" she asked.

Leo nodded. "The kiss?"

"I really wanted to kiss you," she said. "But I didn't want to confuse comfort with something else. I didn't really know what I was feeling at that time."

"And now?" he asked in a quiet voice.

"I'm still unsure. Still hesitant," she admitted. "But . . . I'm so damn attracted to you."

Leo stepped closer, careful not to move too quickly. He set down his glass beside hers on the granite counter. "I'm not here to take advantage of you or this time when you're feeling vulnerable," he said. "But I'm also not going to pretend I don't want to be close to you."

She nodded and then leaned into him—just slightly. He caught her in his arms, and she rested there, as if that was where she belonged. They stayed like that for a long time. There was no urgency to move, no expectations.

His hands gently touched the small of her back and gently pulled her closer into him. She pressed her forehead against his chest, feeling his breath rise and fall. When she looked up his eyes met hers. He cupped her face with his hands—his fingertips brushing against her cheeks. She leaned into his touch, her lips parting slightly.

The kiss was soft, as gentle as the first time but different. It was like a conversation without words—warm and loving. There was a light tingle in the pit of her stomach. He kissed her again, his hands exploring her spine. She wrapped her arms around his neck, drawing him closer. Remi didn't want it to end, but she didn't want it to go any further, either. She wasn't ready for more yet.

"I feel better now," she whispered.

"I'm glad."

The moment wasn't about fixing anything, or deciding what happened next. It was about right now. It was about removing any guilt that lingered from the first kiss. It was about quieting the voices in their heads about whether it was too soon for them. It was about giving each other permission to do whatever came next. Whenever it came.

Chapter Forty

Bianca

Bianca reached for her ringing phone on the nightstand, squinting at the screen. Her fingers fumbled with it. It was seven o'clock in the morning and Dr. Lee was calling. Her stomach clenched. She sat up slowly, careful not to wake Harry, who lay beside her, barely covered by the thin white sheet, his face relaxed, light snores gently escaping from his mouth.

For a moment she just looked at him, more like admired his body. His arms were still chiseled. It looked as if he still hit the gym three times a week as he always had in the past. His torso was still solid as it peeked from beneath the sheet.

The night before they'd talked all night. The conversation had started light, with jokes that had them laughing until they both had tears in their eyes. But somewhere along the way the conversation had shifted. Walls were let down and guards were dropped. Revelations were made.

They started talking about things that hadn't been spoken aloud since the divorce—things buried so deep, neither of them had been sure they would ever resurface. There were thoughts that had gone unsaid, so many regrets and misunderstandings. Matters that had been left unresolved. But last night they made confessions—real ones.

He wasn't blaming her anymore. He was just giving voice to what had lingered in his mind for years, and she spoke her truths too.

She had hurt him in the worst way, and between the shots he'd plainly said it without anger. He told her he'd only gotten involved with Jen in a desperate attempt to stop thinking about her, to move on with his life. But it hadn't worked. Yes, Jen had been easy to be with, listening to him without judgment. She filled a void. But eventually the comparisons crept in. He realized he was measuring Jen against someone she could never be.

"I thought I could replace you with her," he'd said. "But there was no chance of that happening. You really are one of a kind."

Bianca hadn't said anything right away. She let his words, his honesty, press against her chest. She'd never stopped carrying her own guilt, and she told him so. She admitted to him that she still loved him—deeply. That for years she'd secretly held on to hope that they would reconcile.

They'd talked through it all, and then there was nothing more to be said.

Now she slipped from the bed, wrapped her naked body in a robe, and made her way to the kitchen, her bare feet tiptoeing down the hall against the hardwood floors.

She answered the phone quietly, her voice still hoarse from drinking. "Hello."

"Good morning, Bianca. Dr. Lee here." The voice on the other end was cheerful. "I have the results of your imaging test."

Bianca tried to compose herself as much as possible. "And?" she asked.

"Unfortunately, there's really been no change since our

last testing. There has been no further shrinking of the tumors." She paused. "But they haven't expanded either. No new growth."

"Okay," Bianca said softly.

Dr. Lee, sensing her pause, said, "So, I guess that's both good and bad. We'll just continue to monitor them regularly."

"Okay; thank you, Dr. Lee." Bianca stood. "Thank you for calling."

"You're welcome, Bianca. Have a great rest of your day."

"You do the same."

Bianca slipped into the bathroom, stared at her face in the mirror. She brushed her teeth and washed her face. Then she slid her fingers through her soft, dark curls. She opened the medicine cabinet and pulled out a bottle of Tylenol, emptied two pills into her hand to ease the headache she felt coming on.

She tiptoed back to the kitchen and poured herself a small glass of orange juice. She popped the pills into her mouth and let them slide to the back of her throat. She moved to the couch and allowed her body to slowly sink into the cushions—let the Tylenol settle and closed her eyes as the pain started to leave.

Thoughts of last night's intimacy with Harry caused a light smile to creep into the corners of her mouth. He had kissed her aggressively, with urgency. She liked it that way—intense. Back in the day, she'd taught him how to love her. She didn't want him to be gentle with her—she wasn't fragile or breakable. She wanted passion. Life was meant to be lived fully, fiercely, and not half-assed. Lovemaking with them had always been vigorous, energetic. And last night had been no different.

She couldn't believe he'd actually shown up in Napa and

then driven her to Bodega Bay last night. She'd half teased him about coming to California, half hoped he would. Still, his unannounced appearance at Remi's wine tasting had stunned her. And at the same time it made her heart happy. Seeing his face in that moment felt like grace, like God was giving her a second chance at life—to breathe and love again. This time she wouldn't mess it up. She'd cherish each moment, just like Dr. Lee said.

She pulled herself together enough to make it to the kitchen. The hardwood floor felt cold against her bare feet. She laid strips of bacon on a baking sheet and slid them into the oven, then moved to the stove to scramble some eggs. Sliced potatoes sizzled in a skillet with onions, bell peppers, and garlic. The scent of it all was sure to wake up Harry.

She was focused on the eggs when he slid up behind her, his body warm against hers, wrapping his arms around her waist. He gently kissed the back of her neck, nibbled her ear.

"Good morning," she said without turning around.

"Good morning," he whispered in her ear.

He walked over to the window, wearing nothing more than a pair of boxers.

"Last night was . . ." he started, and then turned to face her.

"Amazing?" she asked.

"Yes." He grinned. "I also learned some things I didn't know."

"Like?"

He stepped closer, his expression softer, more serious. "Like . . . you still love me."

She tilted her head, teasing. "That's all you heard?"

"That's what stuck with me," he said. "Because—"

"Because?"

"Because I never stopped loving you, Bianca."

Her heart leapt at his words. They were unexpected. The

truth of them slipped into her chest and warmed her heart. She didn't respond right away, just let herself feel it for a minute. She just wanted to bask in the presence of him. Watching as the light of the morning beamed through the windows.

Then she looked at him fully and said, "I know."

Chapter Forty-one

Remi

End of Summer

Remi sat in her office, resting in the comfort of the leather chair, allowing it to draw her in as she reviewed inventory lists and skimmed through budgets. The quiet rhythm of paperwork balanced by the liveliness just beyond her walls. She smiled at the sound of familiar commotion—the chime of the front door as customers came and went, their voices raised in laughter and conversations.

A private tasting was underway in the tasting room next door—a group of women celebrating someone's birthday. Conversation and light giggles filled that room. From farther back she could hear Paloma's voice carrying through the hallway as she led a small group through the barrel room, giving them a tour, pointing out vintages, offering the history behind the wines and the Ortiz vineyard.

The winery was alive in every room. It had been busy since the day she opened the doors for the first time. Their schedule was booked through December with tastings, tours, and private events. Poetry nights had become a regular thing; on

Thursdays people faithfully gathered in the barrel room, wine in hand, to hear local poets spill their rhymes. The energy on those nights was electric and intimate. And Friday nights belonged to jazz. Couples and strangers alike filled the garden, drawn from as far away as San Francisco and Oakland. Under the strings of white lights, saxophones and bass guitars serenaded guests.

Joie wasn't just a business anymore. It had become home to some, a regular hangout, and a cozy retreat for others.

When her phone rang she glanced at the screen. Zoe's face lit it up, framed in curls—she'd taken down her braids. Remi's heart was warmed as she swiped to answer.

"Hello, sweetheart. What's going on?"

"Mom, how are you?"

"I'm good," Remi said, leaning back into her chair. "Busy but good. We have a full tasting today and the Friday night setup starts in a couple of hours. Jazz tonight."

"Oh, the usual trio?"

"Yes. People love them. And we have a food truck coming in to set up—good food," Remi said. "What about you? How's school?"

"Chaotic. My professor just pushed our project deadline up two days, so I might not get any sleep for the next forty-eight hours."

Remi smiled. "You'll be fine. You always are."

There was a pause, and then Zoe said, "I saw the pictures online—seems *Joie* has a lot going on these days."

"It's been busy," Remi said. "Have you seen Mila on campus?"

"All the time. She's making new friends. Seems to be doing okay."

"That's good to hear."

"How's Aunt B?"

"Good. She comes down at least twice a week to help out

at the winery. She's looking for a new retail space right now. Hoping to bring Chic Threads to California."

"Wow, that's amazing." Zoe smiled. "Mila has been working part-time at the one in the French Quarter. I might apply for a job during Christmas. I could use some extra cash. Take the weight off of you, Mom."

"Don't you worry about me. Whatever you need, you let me know," Remi said. "Though getting a job is not a bad idea. Nothing beats a hard day's work."

"Mostly I just want new clothes at a discount." Zoe laughed.

"Well, there it is. The truth." Remi laughed too.

"How are you and Aunt B getting along, anyway? Are things better?"

"They are better," Remi told her as she gazed out her window and saw Bianca's car backing into a space. "In fact she just pulled up. She's going to help out tonight."

"Good, I'm glad to hear it." Zoe smiled brightly. "Anyway, I have to go, Mom. A few of us are going out for pizza, and they're all waiting for me. I'll talk to you later."

"Have fun, baby. I love you."

"Love you, too, Mom. Take care."

Remi watched as Bianca stepped out of her Mercedes SUV, a pair of Ray-Bans on her face, a bottle of mineral water in her hand. Her hair had grown a bit, her face was full, her signature lipstick was on her lips. She wore a colorful sundress that hugged her curves.

A minute later she was standing in the doorway of Remi's office. "Is Scott working the bar today?" Bianca asked. "There's a gentleman out there looking for two bottles of rosé."

"Can you grab them for him?" Remi asked.

"I'll take care of it." Bianca disappeared down the hall, her sandals click-clacking against the hardwoods.

She was back a few minutes later and seated on the opposite side of Remi's desk. They chatted briefly before preparing for the night's event.

It was a full house at *Joie*. The garden was filled with laughter and pulsed with life—every table taken, every chair filled with conversation. Glasses clinked and laughter drifted in the air. The white lights glowed overhead as darkness fell upon the garden.

The jazz band played, and tonight they'd brought a vocalist—an older man wearing a suit and a bow tie, who moved through the crowd singing in a deep baritone. He wove between the tables as he sang, connecting with the crowd, allowing them to sing along occasionally.

Along the gravel path, the food trucks formed a colorful row, each with its own menu—one selling Cajun dishes, one fried catfish, and one smoked barbecue ribs on a huge pit. One of them handed out warm slices of pound cake in wax paper baskets.

It was one of those nights that felt like summer would never end. Music moved through the garden like it would live there forever. But Remi knew better. Summer was winding down. She could feel it in the shift of the evening breeze, and she hated to see it go. This was *Joie*'s first summer—its first real breath—and it had bloomed into more than she could have imagined. The laughter, the music, the poetry, the people who came from near and far just to be a part of it.

She knew the nostalgia of this summer would live in her long after it was over. There was a certain magic in firsts, and she wasn't sure the summers that followed would match the feeling of this one.

But for now she lived in the moment. And she intended to soak in every second of it.

Chapter Forty-two

Bianca

The smell of sweet potato pies and fresh collard greens drifted in the air. Bill Withers's "Lovely Day" floated from the speakers; its feel-good groove filled the house. In the oven, Abuelita's Cuban stuffing baked slowly—the sweet plantains, chicharrónes, Cuban mojo, and day-old Cuban bread coming together nicely in the dish. Bianca had hunted for every ingredient, scouring several markets, but managed to find them all.

Remi's Creole macaroni and cheese—Grandma Lorraine's recipe—rested on the countertop, the top of it a perfect golden brown. Its spices filled the kitchen. Grandma Lorraine's recipe was unwritten but etched in Remi's memory. She'd helped make that rich and soulful dish plenty of times in Louisiana.

Crema de vie—the Cuban version of eggnog made with sweetened condensed milk, cinnamon, and good rum—chilled in the refrigerator. Those little glasses of tradition would be sipped on throughout the day.

The kitchen was alive, not just with food but with history. With the roots of two families coming together—Bianca's and Remi's. All filled with love passed down from generation to generation. They sang the words to "Lovely Day," loudly, while Mila wrestled with the bird, flipping it over on the cutting board with a grunt, her sleeves already dusted with flour and other seasonings. She rubbed it down with butter, pressing it into every crevice and sprinkling it with Cajun herbs. It was her first Butterball turkey and she was determined to get it right.

She removed the stuffing from the oven, set it on top of the stove, and popped in the bird. She smiled to herself, wiped her hands on a towel, and took a step back, proud of her work.

Leo and Harry sat in the living room, beers in hand, eyes locked on the television. They shouted at every key play, groaning at fumbles, cursing penalties, and high-fiving each other after every touchdown. They laughed and talked like old friends, like they hadn't just met that very day.

When the doorbell rang Zoe hopped down from the kitchen stool, her curls bouncing as she moved. "I'll get it!" she called, already halfway to the door.

She swung it open to find Paloma on the doorstep, smiling and holding a bottle of Sauvignon Blanc in the air.

"I brought the wine," she announced.

Behind her stood Bas, wearing an Oakland Raiders jersey, denim shorts, and black slides. He hugged Zoe tightly, flashing an easy smile before stepping inside.

"Hello, everyone," Paloma said as they entered, her voice bright. "It smells amazing in here."

Everyone greeted them as they passed through the house, laughter and music filling Bianca's home. Bas immediately made a beeline for the living room. He quickly settled in with the other men. Paloma drifted toward the kitchen, slipping the wine bottle into Bianca's hand.

"For the lady of the house."

"Thank you." Bianca embraced Paloma. "Make yourself at home. Can I get you something to drink?"

"What is it that you all are drinking?" Paloma asked.

Bianca smiled. "We were all about to have some crema de vie. It's a Cuban eggnog. Would you like some?"

"I would love some," Paloma said, taking a seat at the kitchen table next to Remi.

"Glad you made it." Remi squeezed Paloma's hand.

"I got it, Aunt B," Zoe said, grabbing glasses from the shelf and pouring crema de vie into each one.

Bianca called to the living room, "Would you like something to drink, Bas?"

"Nothing, thanks."

"This is really a beautiful home, Bianca," Paloma said. "I don't get up to Bodega Bay much, but I really love the area. And your view is absolutely amazing."

"Thank you. I love it here."

The ladics sipped their drinks, gathered in the kitchen, laughing and talking while collards simmered on the stove and the turkey browned in the oven. Dinner would be ready soon, but no one was in a rush. They were all enjoying the moment.

Later, Mila removed the turkey from the oven. It was a beautiful bird—perfectly golden brown. She smiled with pride. "I think we're ready now," she said. "Just need someone to carve it."

"I think your father should do the honors," Bianca told Mila with a smile.

Bianca remembered the holidays when she and Harry were still married. Thanksgiving had been festive, family gathered around Abuelita's table. Harry would carve the turkey, sleeves rolled up, grinning as he played host. Everyone would tease him about how long it took him, because he was so intent on doing it well, carving each piece with such precision, like a surgeon.

Those times had given her so much joy.

Harry stepped into the kitchen, grinning like he always

had, ready to perform surgery on the turkey. Mila handed him the carving knife and fork.

"Here you go, Daddy," Mila said, then teased, "and remember, we'd like to eat tonight, if possible."

Laughter filled the kitchen.

"Oh, you got jokes." He kissed Mila's forehead. "Watch and learn, baby girl. Watch and learn."

Mila hadn't stopped smiling since she learned her parents were on the verge of reconciling. Bianca noticed the quiet joy that her daughter undoubtedly felt. She felt it too.

After Harry carved the turkey the women instinctively worked together to transfer food into serving dishes and place them on the kitchen island. Everyone gathered in the kitchen, shoulder to shoulder. Remi slid her hand into Leo's, their fingers intertwined. Bas stood between his mother and Zoe, arms resting casually around their shoulders. Harry wrapped one arm around Mila's shoulders and held tightly to Bianca's hand with the other.

Then Remi bowed her head. She prayed.

"Lord," she began, her voice strong but tender, "we thank you for this food . . . for this gathering of family. Not family in the biological sense, but family nonetheless. We thank you for everything we've been through—all the trials, the healing, the growing—it all made us stronger. And we thank you for where you're taking us next. Bless this food, and all the hands that prepared it. Amen."

"Amen," echoed around the room.

Plates were soon piled high, overlapping with music and laughter as people settled into chairs, nooks, and corners of the intimate space. Bianca stood near the wall, plate in hand, waiting her turn at the island. She looked around the room, at the people in every corner of the room in her home. At the love that radiated throughout. She smiled to herself. Her heart was full. She'd been through so much in a short time, but somehow life had handed her a second chance. Not that she deserved it, but because grace had shown up unexpectedly. And this time she wouldn't mess it up.

She reached over and turned up the stereo. Frankie Beverly & Maze's "Happy Feelin' " rang out, filling the house with soul. The timeless tune completely echoed her mood.

She glanced over at Remi, who gave her a wide smile—a warm one.

Bianca allowed the music to fill her soul, the music resonating deep within her. Her body responded before her mind could catch up.

And she danced, as if it might be her last time. She didn't know if it would be, but she wasn't taking any chances.

Life was too short not to.

Discussion Questions

1. What is your deal-breaker when it comes to friendships and betrayal?

2. What is your deal-breaker when it comes to a spouse? Would you stay with someone who has been unfaithful?

3. If you were Remi, could you have forgiven Bianca? Why or why not?

4. Do you think the truth would've come out had Remi not uncovered it?

5. Have you had a strained relationship with your child before? What was the reason and how did you address it?

6. Should Mila have pursued justice and reported her sexual assault, or did she do the right thing by trying to forget?

7. How did you feel about Remi's and Leo's friendship? Did you feel shocked by it or were you cheering them on? Was it too soon for them to get involved romantically?

8. Do you think there was a genuine connection between Remi and Leo, or was Remi just grieving?

9. Do you think that Remi should've still honored Gerard's wish of having his ashes scattered along the Sonoma Beach? Why or why not?

10. Who was your favorite character and what made him or her your favorite?

11. What part of the story caused you the most angst? What part did you enjoy the most?

12. Did you identify with any character's journey or path?